Stone Mattress

Stone Mattress

Nine Tales

Margaret Atwood

W F HOWES LTD

This large print edition published in 2015 by
W F Howes Ltd
Unit 4, Rearsby Business Park, Gaddesby Lane,
Rearsby, Leicester LE7 4YH

1 3 5 7 9 10 8 6 4 2

First published in the United Kingdom in 2014
by Bloomsbury Publishing Plc

A CIP catalogue record for this book is available
from the British Library

ISBN 978 1 47128 296 6

Typeset by Palimpsest Book Production Limited,
Falkirk, Stirlingshire

Printed and bound in Great Britain
by TJ International Ltd, Padstow, Cornwall

MIX
Paper from
responsible sources
FSC® C013056

CONTENTS

ALPHINLAND

The freezing rain sifts down, handfuls of shining rice thrown by some unseen celebrant. Wherever it hits, it crystallizes into a granulated coating of ice. Under the streetlights it looks so beautiful: like fairy silver, thinks Constance. But then, she would think that; she's far too prone to enchantment. The beauty is an illusion, and also a warning: there's a dark side to beauty, as with poisonous butterflies. She ought to be considering the dangers, the hazards, the grief this ice storm is going to bring to many; is already bringing, according to the television news.

The TV screen is a flat high-definition one that Ewan bought so he could watch hockey and football games on it. Constance would rather have the old fuzzy one back, with its strangely orange people and its habit of rippling and fading: there are some things that do not fare well in high definition. She resents the pores, the wrinkles, the nose hairs, the impossibly whitened teeth shoved right up in front of your eyes so you can't ignore them the way you would in real life. It's like being forced to act as someone else's

1

bathroom mirror, the magnifying kind: seldom a happy experience, those mirrors.

Luckily, on the weather show the personnel stand well back. They have their maps to attend to, their broad hand gestures, like those of waiters in glamorous films of the '30s or magicians about to reveal the floating lady. Behold! Gigantic swaths of whiteness plume across the continent! Just look at the extent of it!

Now the show moves outside. Two young commentators – a boy, a girl, both of them wearing stylish black parkas with halos of pale fur around their faces – hunch under dripping umbrellas as cars grind slowly past them, windshield wipers labouring. They're excited; they say they've never seen anything like it. Of course they haven't, they're too young. Next there are shots of calamities: a multiple car-crash pileup, a fallen tree that's bashed off part of a house, a snarl of electrical wires dragged down by the weight of the ice and flickering balefully, a row of sleet-covered planes stranded in an airport, a huge truck that's jackknifed and tipped over and is lying on its side with smoke coming out. An ambulance is on the scene, a fire truck, a huddle of raingear-clad operatives: someone's been injured, always a sight to make the heart beat faster. A policeman appears, crystals of ice whitening his moustache; he pleads sternly with people to stay inside. *It's no joke,* he tells the viewers. *Don't think you can brave the elements!* His frowning, frosted eyebrows are noble, like those on the

2

wartime bond-drive posters from the 1940s. Constance remembers those, or believes she does. But she may just be remembering history books or museum displays or documentary films: so hard, sometimes, to tag those memories accurately.

Finally, a minor touch of pathos: a stray dog is displayed, semi-frozen, wrapped in a child's pink nap blanket. A gelid baby would have been better, but for lack of one the dog will do. The two young commentators make *Aw cute* faces; the girl pats the dog, which wags its sodden tail feebly. 'Lucky guy,' says the boy. This could be you, it's implied, if you don't behave yourself, only you wouldn't get rescued. The boy turns to the camera and solemnifies his face, even though it's clear he's having the time of his life. There's more to come, he says, because the main part of the storm hasn't even hit! It's worse in Chicago, as it so often is. Stay tuned!

Constance turns off the TV. She crosses the room, dims the lamp, then sits beside the front window, staring out into the streetlight-illuminated darkness, watching the world turn to diamonds – branches, rooftops, hydro lines, all glittering and sparkling.

'Alphinland,' she says out loud.

'You'll need salt,' says Ewan, right in her ear. The first time he spoke to her it startled and even alarmed her – Ewan having been no longer in a tangibly living condition for at least four days – but now she's more relaxed about him, unpredictable though he is. It's wonderful to hear his voice, even if she can't depend on having any sort of a conversation with him. His interventions tend to be one-sided: if she answers him, he doesn't often answer back. But it was always more or less like that between them.

She hadn't known what to do with his clothes, afterwards. At first she left them hanging in the closet, but it was too upsetting to open the door and see the jackets and suits ranged on their hangers, waiting mutely for Ewan's body to be slipped inside them so they could be taken for a walk. The tweeds, the woollen sweaters, the plaid work shirts . . . She couldn't give them away to the poor, which would have been the sensible thing. She couldn't throw them out: that would have been not only wasteful but too abrupt, like ripping off a bandage. So she'd folded them up and stored them away in a trunk on the third floor, with mothballs.

That's fine in the daytimes. Ewan doesn't seem to mind, and his voice, when it turns up, is firm and cheerful. A striding voice, showing the way. An extended index-finger voice, pointing. *Go here, buy this, do that!* A slightly mocking voice, teasing, making light: that was often his manner towards her before he became ill.

At night, however, things get more complex. There have been bad dreams: sobbing from inside the trunk, mournful complaints, pleas to be let out. Strange men appearing at the front door who hold out promises of being Ewan, but who are not. Instead they're menacing, with black trench

4

coats. They demand some garbled thing that Constance can't make out, or, worse, they insist on seeing Ewan, shouldering their way past her, their intentions clearly murderous. 'Ewan's not home,' she'll plead, despite the muted cries for help coming from the trunk on the third floor. As they begin to tromple up the stairs, she wakes up.

She's considered sleeping pills, though she knows they're addictive and lead to insomnia. Maybe she ought to sell the house and move to a condo. That notion was being pushed at the time of the funeral by the boys, who are not boys any more and who live in cities in New Zealand and France, too conveniently far for them to visit her much. They'd been backed up in spades by their brisk but tactful and professionally accomplished wives, the plastic surgeon and the chartered accountant, so it was four against one. But Constance stood firm. She can't abandon the house, because Ewan is in it. Though she'd been smart enough not to tell them about that. They've always thought she was slightly borderline anyway because of Alphinland, though once such an enterprise makes a lot of money the whiff of nuttiness around it tends to evaporate.

Condo is a euphemism for retirement home. Constance doesn't hold it against them: they want what is best for her, not merely what is simplest for them, and they were understandably perturbed by the disorder they'd witnessed, both in Constance – though they'd made allowances because she was in the throes of mourning – and in, just for example, her refrigerator. There were items in that refrigerator for which there was no sane explanation. *What a swamp*, she could hear them thinking. *Awash in botulism, a wonder she hasn't made herself seriously ill.* But of course she hadn't, because she wasn't eating much in those final days. Soda crackers, cheese slices, peanut butter straight from the jar.

The wives had dealt with the situation in the kindest way. 'Do you want this? What about this?' 'No, no,' Constance had wailed. 'I don't want any of it! Throw it all out!' The three little grandchildren, two girls and a boy, had been sent on a sort of Easter egg hunt, searching for the half-drunk cups of tea and cocoa that Constance had left here and there around the house and that were now covered with grey or pale-green skins in various stages of growth. 'Look, Maman! I found another one!' 'Ew, that's gross!' 'Where is Grandpa?'

A retirement home would provide company for her, at least. And it would take away the burden from her, the responsibility, because a house like hers needs upkeep, it needs attention, and why should she be saddled with all those chores any more? That was the idea set forth in some detail by the daughters-in-law. Constance could take up bridge-playing, or Scrabble, they suggested. Or backgammon, said to be popular again. Nothing too stressful or exciting to the brain. Some mild communal game.

'Not yet,' says Ewan's voice. 'You don't need to do that yet.'

Constance knows this voice isn't real. She knows Ewan is dead. Of course she knows that! Other people – other recently bereaved people – have had the same experience, or close. Aural hallucination, it's called. She's read about it. It's normal. She isn't crazy.

'You're not crazy,' Ewan says comfortingly. He can be so tender when he thinks she's having some anguish.

He's right about the salt. She ought to have stocked up on some form of ice melt earlier in the week but she forgot, and now if she doesn't get some, she'll be a prisoner inside her own house because the street will be a skating rink by tomorrow. What if the layer of ice doesn't melt for days and days? She could run out of food. She could become one of those statistics – old recluse, hypothermia, starvation – because, as Ewan has pointed out before now, she can't live on air.

She'll have to venture out. Even one bag of salt mix will be enough to do the steps and the walk and keep other people from killing themselves, much less herself. The corner store is her best bet: it's only two blocks away. She'll have to take her two-wheeled shopping bag, which is red and also waterproof, because the salt will be heavy. It was only Ewan who drove their car; her own licence lapsed decades ago because once she got so deeply involved in Alphinland she felt she was too distracted to drive. Alphinland requires a lot

7

of thought. It excludes peripheral details, such as stop signs.

It must be quite slippery out there already. If she tries this escapade, she might break her neck. She stands in the kitchen, dithering. 'Ewan, what should I do?' she says.

'Pull yourself together,' Ewan says firmly. Which isn't very instructive, but which was his habitual way of responding to a question when he didn't want to be pinned down. *Where've you been, I was so worried, did you have an accident? Pull yourself together. Do you really love me? Pull yourself together. Are you having an affair?*

After some rummaging, she finds a large zip-lock freezer bag in the kitchen, dumps out the three shrivelled, whiskery carrots inside it, and fills it with ashes from the fireplace, using the little brass fireplace shovel. She hasn't lit a fire since Ewan ceased to be present in visible form, because it didn't seem right. Lighting a fire is an act of renewal, of beginning, and she doesn't want to begin, she wants to continue. No: she wants to go back.

There's still a stack of wood and some kindling; there are still a couple of partially burnt logs in the grate from the last fire they had together. Ewan was lying on the sofa with a glass of that disgusting chocolate nutrient drink beside him; he was bald, due to the chemo and the radiation. She tucked the plaid car rug around him and sat beside him, holding his hand, with the tears running silently

8

down her cheeks and her head turned away so he couldn't see. He didn't need to be distressed by her distress.

'This is nice,' he'd managed to say. It was hard for him to talk: his voice was so thin, like the rest of him. But that isn't the voice he has now. The voice he has now is back to normal: it's his voice of twenty years ago, deep and resonant, especially when he laughs.

She puts on her coat and boots, finds her mittens and one of her woolly hats. Money, she'll need some of that. House keys: it would be stupid to lock herself out and be turned into a frozen lump right on her own doorstep. When she's at the front door with the wheeled shopping bag, Ewan says to her, 'Take the flashlight,' so she trudges upstairs to the bedroom in her boots. The flashlight is on the nightstand on his side of the bed; she adds it to her purse. Ewan is so good at planning ahead. She herself never would have thought of a flashlight.

The front porch steps are sheer ice already. She sprinkles ashes on them from the zip-lock, then stuffs the bag into her pocket and proceeds down crabwise, one step at a time, holding on to the railing and hauling the wheeled shopper behind her with the other hand, bump bump bump. Once on the sidewalk, she opens the umbrella, but that's not going to work – she can't manage those two objects at once – so she closes it again. She'll use it as a cane. She inches out onto the street – it's not as icy as the sidewalk – and teeters along the middle of it, balancing herself with the umbrella. There aren't any cars, so at least she won't get run over.

On the especially sheer parts of the road she sprinkles more of the ashes, leaving a faint black trail. Perhaps she'll be able to follow it home, if push comes to shove. It's the kind of thing that might occur in Alphinland – a trail of black ashes, mysterious, alluring, like glowing white stones in a forest, or bread crumbs – only there would be something extra about those ashes. Something you'd need to know about them, some verse or phrase to pronounce in order to keep their no doubt malevolent power at bay. Nothing about dust to dust, however; nothing involving last rites. More like a sort of runic charm.

'Ashes, bashes, crashes, dashes, gnashes, mashes, splashes,' she says out loud as she picks her way over the ice. Quite a few words rhyme with *ashes*. She'll have to incorporate the ashes into the storyline, or one of the storylines: Alphinland is multiple in that respect. Milzreth of the Red Hand is the most likely provenance for those spellbinding ashes, being a warped and devious bully. He likes to delude travellers with mind-altering visions, lure them off the true path, lock them into iron cages or shackle them to the wall with gold chains, then pester them, using Hairy Hank-Imps and Cyanoreens and Firepiggles and whatnot. He likes to watch as their clothing

– their silken robes, their embroidered vestments, their fur-lined capes, their shining veils – are ripped to shreds, and they plead and writhe attractively. She can work on the intricacies of all that when she gets back to the house.

Milzreth has the face of a former boss of hers when she worked as a waitress. He was a rump-slapper. She wonders if he ever read the series.

Now she's reached the end of the first block. This outing was maybe not such a good idea: her face is streaming wet, her hands are freezing, and melt-water is dribbling down her neck. But she's underway now, she needs to see it through. She breathes in the cold air; pellets of blown ice whip against her face. The wind's getting up, as the TV said it would. Nonetheless there's something brisk about being out in the storm, something energizing: it whisks away the cobwebs, it makes you inhale.

The corner store is open 24/7, a fact that she and Ewan have appreciated ever since they moved to this area twenty years ago. There are no sacks of ice melt stacked outside where they usually are, however. She goes inside, trundling her two-wheeled shopping bag.

'Is there any salt left?' she asks the woman behind the counter. It's someone new. Constance has never seen her before; there's a high turnover here. Ewan used to say the place had to be a money-laundering joint because they couldn't possibly be making a profit, considering the low traffic and the state of their lettuces.

11

'No, dear,' the woman says. 'There was a run on it earlier. Be prepared, I guess is what they had in mind.' The implication is that Constance has failed to be prepared, which in fact is true. It's a lifelong failing: she has never been prepared. But how can you have a sense of wonder if you're prepared for everything? Prepared for the sunset. Prepared for the moonrise. Prepared for the ice storm. What a flat existence that would be.

'Oh,' says Constance. 'No salt. Bad luck for me.'

'You shouldn't be out in this, dear,' the woman says. 'It's treacherous!' Although she has dyed red hair shaved up the back of her neck in an edgy style, she's only about ten years younger than Constance by the look of her, and quite a lot fatter. At least I don't wheeze, thinks Constance. Still, she likes being called *dear*. She was called that when very much younger, then not called it for a long time. Now it's a word she hears frequently.

'It's all right,' she says. 'I only live a couple of blocks away.'

'Couple of blocks is a long way to go in this weather,' says the woman, who despite her age has a tattoo peeking up above her collar. It looks like a dragon, or a version of one. Spikes, horns, bulgy eyes. 'You could freeze your ass off.'

Constance agrees with her, and asks if she can park her shopping bag and umbrella beside the counter. Then she wanders up and down the aisles, pushing a wire store cart. There are no other customers, though in one aisle she encounters a weedy young man transferring cans of tomato juice to a shelf. She picks up one of the barbecued chickens that revolve on spits inside a glass case, day in and day out like a vision from the Inferno, and a package of frozen peas.

'Kitty litter,' says Ewan's voice. Is this a comment on her purchases? He disapproved of those chickens – he said they were probably full of chemicals – though he'd eat one readily enough if she brought it home, back in his eating days.

'What do you mean?' she says. 'We don't have a cat any more.' She's discovered that she has to talk out loud to Ewan because most of the time he can't read her mind. Though sometimes he can. His powers are intermittent.

Ewan doesn't expand – he's such a tease, he often makes her figure out the answers by herself – and then it comes to her: the kitty litter is for the front steps, instead of salt. It won't work as well, it won't melt anything, but at least it will provide some traction. She wrestles a bag of the stuff into the cart and adds two candles and a box of wooden matches. There. She's prepared.

Back at the counter she exchanges pleasantries with the woman about the excellence of the chicken – it's an item the woman likes herself, because who can be bothered with cooking when there's only one, or even only two – and stows her purchases in her wheeled shopper, resisting the temptation to get into a conversation about the dragon tattoo. This topic might swiftly veer into complexities, as she's learned from experience over the years. There are dragons in Alphinland, and they have numerous fans with many bright ideas they are eager to share with Constance. How she ought to have done the dragons differently. How they would do the dragons if it was them. Subspecies of dragons. Errors she has made about the care and feeding of dragons, and so on. It's astonishing how folks can get so worked up over something that doesn't exist.

Has the woman overheard her talking to Ewan? Most likely, and most likely it didn't bother her. Any store that's open 24/7 must get its share of people who talk to invisible companions. In Alphinland, such behaviour would call for a different interpretation: some of its inhabitants have spirit familiars.

'Where exactly do you live, dear?' the woman calls after her when Constance is halfway out the door. 'I could text a friend, get you a walk home.' What sort of friend? Maybe she's a biker's girl, thinks Constance. Maybe she's younger than Constance thought; maybe she's just very weathered.

Constance pretends she didn't hear. It could be a ruse, and next thing you know there will be a gang member bent on home invasion standing outside the door with the duct tape ready in his pocket. They say their car has broken down and can they use your phone, and out of the goodness of your heart you let them in, and before you know it you're duct-taped to the banister and they're inserting push-pins under your fingernails to make

14

you cough up your passwords. Constance is well informed about that sort of thing: she doesn't watch the television news for nothing.

The trail of ashes is no use any more – it's iced over, she can't even see it – and the wind is stronger. Should she open the kitty litter bag right here in mid-journey? No, she'll need a knife, or some scissors; although there's usually a pull string. She peers inside the shopper with the flashlight, but the battery must be low because it's too dim in there to see. She could get chilled to the bone struggling with such a bag; better to make a dash for it. Though *dash* is hardly the word.

The ice seems twice as thick as when she started out. The bushes in the front lawn look like fountains, their luminous foliage cascading gracefully to the ground. Here and there a broken tree branch partially blocks the road. Once she's reached her house, Constance leaves the shopper outside on the walk and hauls herself up the slippery steps by clinging to the railing. Happily the porch light is shining, though she can't remember turning it on. She wrestles with the key and the lock, opens the door, and tramps through to the kitchen, shedding water. Then, kitchen scissors in hand, she retraces her route, descends the steps to the red shopper, cuts open the kitty litter bag, and spreads lavishly.

There. Wheeled shopper up the steps, bump bump bump, and into the house. Door locked behind her. Drenched coat off, soaking wet hat and mitts set to steam on the radiator, boots parked in the hall. 'Mission accomplished,' she says in case Ewan is listening. She wants him to know she got back safely; he might worry otherwise. They'd always left notes for each other, or else messages on the answering machine, back before all the digital gadgets. In her more extreme and lonely moments she's thought of leaving messages on the phone service for Ewan. Maybe he could listen to them through electric particles or magnetic fields, or whatever it is he's using to throw his voice through the airwaves.

But this isn't a lonely moment. It's a better moment: she's feeling pleased with herself for carrying out the salt mission. She's hungry too. She hasn't been this hungry ever since Ewan has failed to be present at meals: eating alone has been too dispiriting. Now, however, she tears off pieces of the broiled chicken with her fingers and wolfs them down. This is what people do in Alphinland when they've been rescued from something – dungeons, moors, iron cages, drifting boats: they eat with their hands. Only the very upper classes have what you'd call cutlery, though just about everyone has a knife, unless they happen to be a talking animal. She licks her fingers, wipes them on the dishtowel. There ought to be paper towels but there aren't.

There's still some milk, so she gulps it down right out of the carton, spilling hardly any. She'll make herself a hot drink later. She's in a hurry to get back to Alphinland because of the trail of ashes. She wants to decipher it, she wants to unravel it, she wants to follow it. She wants to see where it will lead.

Alphinland currently lives on her computer. For many years it unfolded in the attic, which she'd converted to a workspace of sorts for herself once Alphinland had made enough money to pay for the renovation. But even with the new floor and the window they'd punched through, and the air conditioning and the ceiling fan, the attic was small and stuffy, as the top floors of these old brick Victorians are. So after a while – after the boys were in high school – Alphinland had migrated to the kitchen table, where it unscrolled for several years on an electric typewriter – once considered the height of innovation, now obsolete. The computer was its next location, and not without its hazards – things could disappear from it in an infuriating manner – but they've improved the computers over time and she's become used to hers now. She moved it into Ewan's study after he was no longer in there in visible form.

She doesn't say 'after his death,' even to herself. She doesn't use the D-word about him at all. He might overhear it and be hurt or offended, or perhaps confused, or even angry. It's one of her not-fully-formulated beliefs that Ewan doesn't realize that he's dead.

She sits at Ewan's desk, swathed in Ewan's black plush bathrobe. Black plush bathrobes for men were cutting edge, when? The '90s? She'd bought this bathrobe herself, as a Christmas present. Ewan always resisted her attempts to make him cutting edge, not that those attempts had lasted much beyond the bathrobe; she'd run out of interest in how he looked to others.

She wears this bathrobe not for heat but for comfort: it makes her feel that Ewan might still be in the house physically, just around the corner. She hasn't washed it since he died; she doesn't want it to smell of laundry detergent instead of Ewan.

Oh Ewan, she thinks. *We had such good times! All gone now. Why so fast?* She wipes her eyes on the black plush sleeve.

'Pull yourself together,' says Ewan. He never likes it when she sniffles.

'Right,' she says. She squares her shoulders, adjusts the cushion on Ewan's ergonomic desk chair, turns the computer on.

The screensaver comes up: it's a gateway, drawn for her by Ewan, who was a practising architect before he took up the more dependable job of university teaching, though what he taught was not called 'Architecture,' it was called 'Theory of Constructed Space' and 'Human Landscape Creation' and 'The Contained Body.' He'd remained very good at drawing, and he'd found an outlet for it in making funny pictures for the children and then the grandchildren. He'd drawn the screensaver for her as a gift, and to show that he took this thing of hers – this thing that was, let's face it, somewhat embarrassing to him in the more abstract intellectual circles to which he belonged – to show that he took her thing seriously. Or that he took her seriously, both of which she'd had reason to doubt from time to time. Also that he'd pardoned her for Alphinland, for her neglect of him because of it. The way she'd look at him without seeing him.

One of her own ideas is that the screensaver was a repentance gift, making it up to her for something he wouldn't admit he'd done. That period of emotional absence during which Ewan must have been otherwise occupied – if not physically, then emotionally – with another woman. With another face, another body, another voice, another scent. A wardrobe not hers, with its alien belts and buttons and zippers. Who was that woman? She'd suspect, then be wrong. The shadowy presence laughed at her softly from the sleepless darkness of 3 a.m., then slid away. She couldn't pin anything down.

All that time she'd felt like an inconvenient block of wood. She'd felt boring, and only half-alive. She'd felt numb.

She'd never pushed him about that interlude, never confronted him. The subject was like the D-word: it was there, it loomed over them like a huge advertising blimp, but to mention it would

19

have been like breaking a spell. It would have been terminal. *Ewan, are you seeing someone else? Pull yourself together. Use your common sense. Why would I need to do that?* He'd have brushed her off, minimized the question.

Constance could think of a lot of reasons why he would need to do that. But she smiled and hugged him, and asked him what he'd like for dinner, and shut up about it.

The screensaver gateway is made of stone, curved in a Roman arch. It's situated midway in a long, high wall that has several turrets on top of it, with red triangular banners flying from them. There's a heavy barred gate, standing open. Beyond is a sunlit landscape, with more turrets poking up in the distance.

Ewan went to some trouble with this gateway. He cross-hatched, he water-coloured; he even added some horses grazing in a faraway field, though he knew better than to fool around with dragons. The picture is very pretty, very William Morris or perhaps more Edward Burne-Jones, but it misses the point. The gateway and the wall are too clean, too new, too well kept up. Although Alphinland has its corners of luxury, its silks and taffetas, its embroideries, its ornate sconces, for the most part it's ancient and dingy and somewhat decrepit. Also it's frequently laid waste, which makes for a lot of ruins.

Over the screensaver gateway is a legend carved

in the stone, in pseudo-gothic Pre-Raphaelite lettering: ALPHINLAND.

Constance takes a deep breath. Then she goes through.

On the other side of the gateway there's no sunny landscape. Instead there's a narrow road, almost a trail. It winds downhill to a bridge, which is lit – because it's night – by yellowish lights shaped like eggs or water drops. Beyond the bridge is a dark wood.

She'll cross the bridge and move stealthily through the wood, alert for ambushes, and when she comes out on the other side she'll be at a crossroads. Then it will be a matter of which of the roads to follow. All of them are in Alphinland, but each leads to a different version of it. Even though she's its creator, its puppet mistress, its determining Fate, Constance never knows exactly where she might end up.

She began Alphinland a long time ago, years before she met Ewan. She was living with another man then, in a two-room walk-up with a lumpy mattress on the floor and a shared toilet in the hallway, and an electric kettle (hers) and a hotplate (his) they were not officially supposed to have. There was no refrigerator so they put their food containers out on the windowsill, where the food froze in winter and spoiled in summer, though it wasn't too bad in spring and fall, except for the squirrels.

This man she lived with was one of the poets

she used to hang around with under the sweet, youthful belief that she too was a poet. He was called Gavin, an unusual name then, though not unusual now: the Gavins have multiplied. Young Constance felt very lucky to have been taken up by Gavin, who was four years older than she was and knew a lot of other poets, and was lean and ironic and indifferent to the norms of society and grimly satirical, as poets were then. Perhaps they're still like that: Constance is too old to know.

Even to be the object of one of Gavin's ironic or grimly satirical remarks – to the effect that her hypnotic ass was a much more significant part of Constance than her frankly forgettable poetry, for instance – was obscurely thrilling to her. She was also accorded the privilege of appearing in Gavin's poems. Not by name, of course: female objects of desire were addressed in poems as 'Lady' then, or else as 'my truelove,' in a gesture to chivalry and folk songs – but it was enormously seductive for Constance to read Gavin's more erotic poems and know that every time he wrote *Lady* – or, even better, 'my truelove' – it meant her. 'My Lady Reclines on a Pillow,' 'My Lady's First Morning Coffee,' and 'My Lady Licks My Plate' were heart-warming, but 'My Lady Bends Over' was her favourite. Whenever she felt that Gavin was being terse with her, she would get out that poem and reread it.

Along with these literary attractions there was a lot of vigorous and impromptu sex.

22

Once she'd become linked to Ewan, Constance had known better than to reveal the details of her earlier life. Though what was there to worry about? Although Gavin had been intense, he'd also been a shit; so he was clearly no competition for Ewan, a knight in shining armour by comparison. And that particular early life experience had ended badly, with sorrow and mortification for Constance. So why bring Gavin up? It would have served no purpose. Ewan had never asked her about any other men in her life, so Constance had never told. She certainly hopes Ewan has no access to Gavin now, through her unspoken thoughts or in any other way.

One of the good things about Alphinland is that she can move the more disturbing items from her past through its stone gateway and store them in there on the memory palace model much in use in, when was it? The eighteenth century? You associate the things you want to remember with imaginary rooms, and when you want total recall you go into that room.

Thus she keeps a deserted winery in Alphinland, on the grounds of the stronghold currently held by Zymri of the Adamant Fist – an ally of hers – for the sole purpose of Gavin. And since it's one of the rules about Alphinland that Ewan has never been allowed through the stone gateway, he'll never find that winery or discover who she's got stashed inside it.

So Gavin's in an oak cask in the winery. He's

not suffering, although objectively he might deserve to suffer. But Constance has worked at forgiving Gavin, so he's not allowed to be tortured. Instead he's preserved in a state of suspended animation. Every once in a while she stops by the winery and presents Zymri with a gift intended to cement their alliance – an alabaster jar of honeyed Xnamic urchins, a collar of Cyanoreen claws – and says the charm that unlocks the top of the cask and has a look. Gavin is slumbering peacefully. He was always handsome with his eyes closed. He doesn't look a day older than the last time she saw him. It still hurts her to remember that day. Then she replaces the top of the cask and says the charm backwards, sealing Gavin inside until she feels like dropping in for another peek at him.

In real life, Gavin won a few prizes for his poetry and then got a tenured position teaching Creative Writing at a university in Manitoba, though since retiring he's decamped to Victoria, British Columbia, with a lovely view of the Pacific sunset. Constance receives a Christmas card from him every year; actually, from him and his third and much younger wife, Reynolds. Reynolds, what a dumb name! It sounds like a cigarette brand of the '40s, back when cigarettes took themselves seriously.

Reynolds signs the cards for both of them – Gav and Rey, they go by – and encloses chirpy, irritating annual letters about their vacations (Morocco! So lucky they'd packed the Imodium! Though, more recently: Florida! So good to be out of the drizzle!). She also sends an annual account of their local Literary Fiction reading group – only *important* books, only *intelligent* books! Right now they're tackling Bolaño, hard work but so worth it if you persist! The club members prepare themed snacks to go with the books they're reading, so Rey is learning to make tortillas, from scratch. Such fun!

Constance suspects that Reynolds takes an unhealthy interest in Gavin's bohemian youth, and most especially in Constance herself. How could she not? Constance had been Gavin's first live-in, at a time in his life when he'd been so horny he could barely keep his jeans zipped when Constance was within half a mile of him. It was as if she radiated a ring of magic particles; as if she cast an irresistible spell, like Pheromonya of the Sapphire Tresses in Aphinland. There's no way Reynolds can compete with that. She probably has to use a sex aid on Gavin, considering his age. If she bothers at all.

'Who are Gavin and Reynolds?' Ewan would say, every year.

'I knew him at college,' Constance would reply. It was a partial truth: she had in fact quit college in order to be with Gavin, so entranced had she been by him and the combination of aloofness and avidity. But Ewan would not welcome such a piece of information. It could make him sad, or jealous, or even angry. Why unsettle him?

★   ★   ★

Gavin's fellow poets – and the folksingers and jazz musicians and actors who were part of an amorphous, ever-shifting group of artistic risk-takers – spent a lot of their time at a coffee house called the Riverboat, in the Yorkville area of Toronto, morphing then from white-bread quasi-slum to cool pre-hippie hangout. Nothing's left of the Riverboat but one of those depressing historical cast-iron signs marking the spot, out in front of the chi-chi hotel that occupies its former space. *Everything will be swept away*, those signs declare, *and a lot sooner than you think*.

None of the poets and folksingers and jazz musicians and actors had a bean, and Constance didn't have a bean either, but she was young enough to find poverty glamorous. La Bohème, that was her. She started writing the Alphinland stories to make enough money to support Gavin, who viewed that kind of support as part of a truelove's function. She cranked out those early stories on her rickety manual typewriter, improvising as she went; then she managed – to her own surprise, at first – to sell them, though not for very much money, to one of the subcultural magazines in New York that went in for that brand of cheesy fantasy. People with diaphanous wings on the covers, many-headed animals, bronze helmets and leather jerkins, bows and arrows.

She was good at writing those stories, or good enough for the magazines. As a child she'd had fairytale books with pictures by Arthur Rackham

26

and his peers – gnarled trees, trolls, mystic maidens with flowing robes, swords, baldrics, golden apples of the sun. So Alphinland was just a matter of expanding that landscape, altering the costumes, and making up the names.

She was waiting tables at the time as well, at a place called Snuffy's, named after a hillbilly cartoon character and specializing in corn bread and fried chicken; part of the pay was all the fried chicken you could eat, and Constance used to smuggle out extra pieces for Gavin and watch with pleasure while he gobbled them down. The job was exhausting and the manager was a letch, though the tips weren't too bad, and you could up your pay packet if you did overtime, like Constance did.

Girls did that then – knocked themselves out to support some man's notion of his own genius. What was Gavin doing to help pay the rent? Not much, though she suspected him of dealing pot on the side. Once in a while they even smoked some of that, though not often, because it made Constance cough. It was all very romantic.

The poets and folksingers made fun of her Alphinland stories, naturally. Why not? She made fun of them herself. The subliterary fiction she was churning out was many decades away from being in any way respectable. There was a small group that confessed to reading *The Lord of the Rings*, though you had to justify it through an interest in Old Norse. But the poets considered Constance's productions to be far below the

27

Tolkien standard, which – to be fair – they were. They'd tease her by saying she was writing about garden gnomes, and she'd laugh and say yes, but today the gnomes had dug up their crock of golden coins and would buy them all a beer. They liked the free beer part of it, and would make toasts: 'Here's to the gnomes! Long may they roam! A gnome in every home!'

The poets frowned on writing for money, but Constance was granted an exemption because, unlike their poetry, Alphinland was intended to be commercial trash, and anyway she was doing it for Gavin as a Lady should, and in addition she was not so stupid as to take this drivel seriously.

What they didn't understand was that – increasingly – she did take it seriously. Alphinland was hers alone. It was her refuge, it was her stronghold; it was where she could go when things with Gavin weren't working out. She could walk in spirit through the invisible portal and wander through the darkling forests and over the shimmering fields, making alliances and defeating enemies, and no one else could come in unless she said they could because there was a five-dimensional spell guarding the entranceway.

She started spending more and more time in there, especially after it became semi-evident to her that not every 'Lady' in Gavin's new poems referred to her. Unless, that is, he was remarkably confused about the colour of his Lady's eyes, once described as 'blue as witches' and/or 'distant stars,' now said to be of an inky darkness. 'My Lady's Ass Is Nothing Like the Moon' was a tribute to Shakespeare – that's what Gavin said. Had he forgotten that there was an earlier poem – a little coarse, but heartfelt – that claimed his Lady's ass *was* like the moon: white, round, softly shining in the dark, alluring? But this other one was tight and muscular; it was active rather than passive, gripping rather than enticing; more like a boa constrictor, though of course not the same shape. With the aid of a hand-held mirror, Constance examined her back view. No way to rationalize it: there was just no comparison. Could it be that when Constance was working her formerly poeticized ass off waiting tables at Snuffy's – which wore her out so much that she wanted sleep more than she wanted sex – Gavin was rolling around on their lumpy mattress with a fresh and sprightly new truelove? One with a gripping ass?

In the past Gavin had always taken a certain pleasure in humiliating Constance in public, with the sardonic, ironic remarks that were one of his poetic specialties: it was a form of compliment, she felt, since it made her the focus of his attention. He was showing her off in a sense, and since that turned him on, she meekly let the humiliation wash over her. But now he stopped humiliating her. Instead, he was ignoring her, which was much worse. When they were alone in their two rented rooms, he no longer kissed her neck and tore off her clothes and threw her onto their mattress in

29

a flamboyant display of uncontrollable lust. Instead he'd complain of a back spasm, and suggest – more than that, demand – that she compensate for his pain and immobility by giving him a blowjob.

This was not her favourite form of activity. She was unpractised at it, in addition to which there was a long list of other things she would rather put into her mouth.

By contrast, no one in Alphinland ever demanded a blowjob. But then, no one in Alphinland had a toilet either. Toilets weren't necessary. Why waste time on that kind of routine bodily function when there were giant scorpions invading the castle? Alphinland did have bathtubs though, or rather, square pools sunk in jasmine-scented gardens and heated by underground springs. Some of the more depraved Alphinlanders bathed in the blood of their captives, who were chained to stakes around the pool to watch as their life drained slowly away into the scarlet bubbles.

Constance stopped going to the group gatherings at the Riverboat because the others were giving her pitying looks, and also asking leading questions, such as 'Where did Gavin get to? He was here just a minute ago.' They knew more than she did. They could see that things were coming to a head.

The new Lady's name turned out to be Marjorie. A name, thinks Constance now, that has all but disappeared: the Marjories are going extinct, and not a moment too soon for her. Marjorie was the dark-haired, dark-eyed, lanky-legged part-time volunteer bookkeeper at the Riverboat, given to vibrant African textiles wound around her waist, and to dangling handmade bead earrings, and to a braying guffaw that suggested a mule with bronchitis.

Or suggested it to Constance; though obviously not to Gavin. Constance walked in on Gavin and Marjorie while they were in full hump, with no back spasm anywhere on view. Wineglasses littered the table, clothes littered the floor, and Marjorie's hair littered the pillow: the pillow of Constance. Gavin had groaned, either in orgasm or in disgust at Constance's bad timing. Marjorie, on the other hand, had brayed, at Constance or Gavin or else the general situation. It was a derisive bray. It was not kindly, and it rankled.

What was left for Constance to say except, *You owe me half the rent*? She never got it, though; Gavin was nothing if not cheap, a feature of the poets then. Shortly after she'd moved out, taking her electric kettle with her, she'd signed her first Alphinland book contract. Once the rumours of her gnome-generated affluence – her comparative affluence – had spread around the Riverboat, Gavin had appeared at her new three-room apartment – an apartment sporting a genuine bed, shared with one of the folksingers, though that didn't last long either – and had tried to make up with her. Marjorie was a fluke, he said. An accident. Nothing serious. It wouldn't happen again. His real truelove was Constance: surely she too realized that they belonged together!

That move was more than tawdry on the part of Gavin, and Constance told him so. Did he have no sense of shame, no honour? Did he grasp what a leech he was, how lacking in initiative, how selfish? In return for which Gavin, astonished at first by the scrappiness displayed by his erstwhile mild moon-maid, gathered his sarcasm together and told her that she was a flake, that her poems were worthless, that her blowjobs were inept, that her idiotic Alphinland was juvenile pablum, and that he had more talent in his bumhole than she had in her entire tiny powder-puff of a brain.

So much for *true* and *love*.

But Gavin had never grasped the inner significance of Alphinland. It was a dangerous place, and – granted – preposterous in some ways, but it was not sordid. The denizens of it had standards. They understood gallantry, and courage, and also revenge.

Therefore Marjorie is not stored in the deserted winery where Gavin has been parked. Instead she's immobilized by runic spells inside a stone beehive belonging to Frenosia of the Fragrant Antennae. This demigoddess is eight feet tall and covered with tiny golden hairs, and has compound eyes. Luckily she's a close friend of Constance and is thus happy to assist in her plans and devices in return for the insect-related charms that Constance has the ability to bestow. So every day at twelve noon sharp, Marjorie is stung by a hundred emerald and indigo bees. Their stings are like white-hot needles combined with red-hot chili sauce, and the pain is beyond excruciating.

In the world outside Alphinland, Marjorie parted ways both with Gavin and with the Riverboat, and went to business college, and then became something in an advertising company. So said the grapevine. She was last seen by Constance striding along Bloor Street in a beige power suit with big shoulder pads, during the '80s. That suit was amazingly ugly, and so were the clunky shit-kicking shoes that went with it.

Marjorie didn't see Constance, though. Or she pretended not to. Just as well.

There's an alternate version stashed in Constance's inner filing cabinet, in which Constance and Marjorie recognized each other that day with cries of delight, and went for a coffee, and had a big bray over Gavin and his poems and his yen for blowjobs. But that never happened.

Constance descends the path, crosses the bridge with the dim, egg-shaped lamps, and enters the dark wood. Hush! It's important to go quietly. There's the trail of ashes, up ahead. Now for the charm. Constance types:

> *It mashes, it smashes*
> *And sometimes it gnashes;*

The dread tooth of Time
Will turn all to ashes.

But that's a description, she decides; it's not a charm. Something more like an incantation is needed:

Norg, Smithert, Zurpash,
Bright Teldarine,
Let light be seen,
Avaunt the evil in this ash.
By the Mauve Blood of . . .

The phone rings. It's one of the boys, the one who lives in Paris; or rather, it's his wife. They've seen the ice storm on television, they were concerned about Constance, they wanted to make sure she's all right.

What time is it there? she asks them. What are they doing up so late? Of course she's all right! It's only a little ice! Nothing to get into a twist about. Love to the kids, now you get some sleep. Everything's fine.

She hangs up as quickly as she can: she resents the interruption. Now she's forgotten the name of the god whose Mauve Blood is so efficacious. Luckily, on her computer she has a list of all the Alphinland deities and their attributes and oath words, alphabetized for easy reference. There are a lot of deities by now; they've accumulated over the years, and she had to make up some extra

34

ones for the animated series of a decade ago, and then even more of them – bigger, scarier, with enhanced violence – for the video game they're currently putting the final touches on. If she'd foreseen that Alphinland was going to last so long and be so successful, she would have planned it better. It would have had a shape, a more defined structure; it would have had boundaries. As it is, it's grown like urban sprawl.

Not only that, she wouldn't have called it Aphinland. The name sounds too much like Elfinland, when what she'd really had at the back of her mind was Alph the sacred river, out of the Coleridge poem, with its measureless caverns. That, and Alpha, the first letter of the alphabet. A smart-alecky young interviewer had once asked her if her 'constructed world' was called Alphinland because it was so full of alpha males. She'd responded with the slightly fey laugh she'd cultivated for defensive purposes once that smarty-pants kind of journalist had decided she was worth an interview. That was around the time all the books they were now lumping together as genre were getting some attention from the press. Or at least the big sellers were.

'Oh no,' she'd said to him. 'I don't think so. Not alpha males. It just sort of happened that way. Maybe . . . I always loved that breakfast cereal. Alpine?'

She comes across as fatuous in every interview she's ever given, which is why she no longer gives them. Nor does she attend conventions any more: she's seen enough kids dressed up like vampires and bunnies and *Star Trek,* and especially like the nastier villains of Alphinland. She really can't bear one more inept impersonation of Milzreth of the Red Hand – yet another apple-cheeked innocent in quest of his inner wickedness.

She also declines to engage in social media, despite her publisher's constant urging. It does no good for them to tell her she'll increase the sales of Alphinland and extend the reach of its franchise. She doesn't need any more money, because what would she use it for? Money had not saved Ewan. She'll leave it all to the boys, as their wives expect her to. And she has no wish to interact with her devoted readers: she knows too much about them already, them and their body piercings and tattoos and dragon fetishes. Above all, she doesn't wish to disappoint them. They'd be expecting a raven-haired sorceress with a snake bracelet on her upper arm and a stiletto hair ornament, instead of a soft-spoken, paper-thin ex-blonde.

She's just opening up the Alphinland file folder on her screen to consult the list of gods when Ewan's voice says, right in her ear and very loudly, 'Turn it off!'

She jumps. 'What?' she says. 'Turn what off?' Has she left the burner on under the kettle again? But she hasn't made the hot drink!

'Turn it off! Alphinland! Turn it off now!' he says.

He must mean the computer. Shaken, she looks over her shoulder – he was right there! Then she clicks the Shut Down button. Just as the screen darkens, there's a heavy, dull thud, and the lights go off.

All the lights. The streetlights too. How did he know in advance? Does Ewan have prophetic vision? He never used to.

She gropes her way down the stairs and along the hall to the front door, opens it cautiously: to the right, a block along, there's a yellow glow. A tree must have fallen across a hydro line and pulled it down. Heaven only knows when they'll be around to fix it: this outage must be one of thousands.

Where did she leave the flashlight? It's in her purse, which is in the kitchen. She shuffles and gropes her way along the hall, fumbles in her purse. Not much juice left in the flashlight batteries, but enough so she manages to get the two candles lit.

'Turn the water off at the mains,' says Ewan. 'You know where that is, I showed you. Then open the faucet in the kitchen. You need to drain the system, you don't want the pipes to burst.' This is the longest speech he's made for a while. It gives her a warm, fuzzy feeling: he's genuinely worried about her.

Once she's accomplished the faucet quest, she assembles a collection of insulating items – the duvet from the bed, a pillow, some clean wool socks, and the plaid car rug – and makes a nest in front of the fireplace. Then she gets the fire going. As a precaution, she pulls the fire screen across in front of it: she wouldn't want to go up in flames during the night. There isn't enough wood for a whole day, but there's enough to get her through until dawn without freezing to death. It will surely take hours for the house to cool down. In the morning she'll think about alternatives; perhaps by then the storm will have blown past. She snuffs out the candles: no sense in setting herself alight.

She curls up inside the duvet. In the fireplace the flames flicker. It's surprisingly cozy, at least for now.

'Well done,' says Ewan. 'That's my gal!'

'Oh Ewan,' says Constance. 'Am I your gal? Was I always? Were you having an affair, that time?'

No answer.

The trail of ashes leads through the woods, glimmering in the moonlight, the starlight. What has she forgotten? There's something wrong. She comes out from under the trees: she's on an icy street. It's the street where she lives, where she's lived for decades, and there's her house, the house where she lives with Ewan.

It shouldn't be here, in Alphinland. It's in the wrong place. All of it is wrong, but she follows the trail of ashes anyway, up the front steps and in through the door. Sleeves wrap around her, sleeves of black cloth. A trench coat. It isn't Ewan. There's a mouth, pressing against her neck. There's a long-lost taste. She's so tired, she's losing power; she can feel it draining away from her, out through the ends of her fingers. How did Gavin get in here? Why is he dressed like an undertaker? With a sigh she melts into his arms; wordlessly she falls back onto the floor.

Morning light wakes her, streaming in through the window with its extra pane of ice. The fire has gone out. She's stiff from sleeping on the floor.

What a night. Who would have thought she was capable of having such an intense erotic dream, at her age? And with Gavin: how idiotic. She doesn't even respect him. How did he manage to work his way out of the metaphor she's kept him bottled up in for all these years?

She opens the front door, peers outside. The sun is shining, the eaves are growing bright icicles. The kitty litter on her steps is a mess; as things melt, it will turn to damp clay. The street is a shambles: branches everywhere, ice at least two inches thick. It's glorious.

But the inside of the house is cold, and getting colder. She'll have to go out into all that dazzling space to buy more wood, if there is any. Or else she could find a shelter of some sort: a church, a coffee shop, a restaurant. Some place that still has power and heat.

That would mean leaving Ewan. He'd be alone here. That wouldn't be a good thing.

For breakfast she has vanilla yogourt, spooning

39

it straight from the container. While she's eating it, Ewan announces himself. 'Pull yourself together,' he says, quite sternly.

She fails to grasp his point. She doesn't need to pull herself together. She's not dithering, she's only eating yogourt. 'What do you mean, Ewan?' she says.

'Didn't we have good times?' he says, almost pleading. 'Why are you ruining it? Who was that man?' Now his voice sounds hostile.

'Who do you mean?' she says. She has a bad feeling. It can't be possible that Ewan has access to her dreams.

Constance, she tells herself. *You're out of control. Why wouldn't he have access to your dreams? He's only inside your head!*

'You know,' says Ewan. His voice comes from behind her. 'That man!'

'I don't think you have any right to ask,' she says, turning around. No one there.

'Why not?' says Ewan, more faintly. 'Pull yourself together!' Is he fading?

'Ewan, did you have an affair?' she asks. If he really wants to get into it, two can play.

'Don't change the subject,' he says. 'Didn't we have good times?' There's a tinny quality to the voice now: something mechanical.

'You're the one who was always changing the subject,' she says. 'Just tell me the truth! You have nothing to lose any more, you're dead.'

She shouldn't have said that. She's gone about this all wrong, she ought to have reassured him.

She shouldn't have used that word, it slipped out because she was angry. 'I didn't mean it!' she says. 'Ewan, I'm sorry, you're not really . . .'

Too late. There's a tiny, barely audible explosion, like a puff of air. Then silence: Ewan is gone.

She waits: nothing. 'Stop sulking!' she says. 'Just snap out of it!' She's briefly angry.

She goes out for food. On one of the sidewalks, a thoughtful soul has laid down sand. The corner store, miraculously, is open: they have a generator. There are other people in there, bundled and swaddled: they've lost their power too. The woman with the dyed hair and the tattoo has plugged in a crock pot and heated up some soup. She's selling the barbecued chickens, cut up into pieces so there will be enough to go around. 'There you are, dear,' she says to Constance. 'I was worried about you!'

'Thank you,' says Constance.

She warms up, eats chicken and soup, hears ice-storm stories from the others. Narrow escapes, frights, quick thinking. They tell one another how lucky they are, ask one another if there's any way they can help. It's companionable here, it's friendly, but Constance can't stay long. She needs to go back to the house, because Ewan must be waiting.

Once there she creeps from one cold room to another, calling softly as if to a frightened cat: 'Ewan, come back! I love you!' Her own voice echoes in her head. Finally she climbs the stairs to the attic and opens the trunk with the mothballs.

41

It's only clothes. They lie there, flattened, inert. Wherever else Ewan is, he's not here.

She was always afraid to push that question before, the question of the affair. She wasn't an idiot, she knew what he was doing, though not who with: she could smell it on him. But she was terrified that Ewan might leave her the way Gavin had. She couldn't have survived that.

And now he has left her. He's gone silent. He's gone.

But though he's gone from the house, he can't be gone from the universe, not altogether. She won't accept that. He must be somewhere.

She needs to concentrate.

She goes into the study, sits in Ewan's chair, stares at the blank screen of her computer. Ewan must have wanted to save Alphinland; he didn't want it to be fried by an electrical spasm. This was why he ordered her to shut down the computer. But what was his reason for doing that? Alphinland isn't his territory: secretly he hated its fame, he thought it was silly, he was humiliated by its intellectual shallowness. He resented her deep immersion in it, even while indulging her about it. And he's excluded from it, from her private world: invisible bars keep him out. They've always kept him out, ever since they met. He can't go in there.

Or can he? Maybe he can. Maybe the rules of Alphinland no longer hold, because the hexed ashes have done their work and the ancient charms are broken. That's why Gavin was able to pop open the lid of his cask last night and turn up in Constance's house. And if Gavin can get out of Alphinland, it stands to reason that Ewan can get in. Or could get drawn in, if only by the lure of the forbidden.

That must be where he's gone. He's passed through the gateway in the turreted stone wall, he's in there now. He's following the dim, winding road, he's crossing the moonlit bridge, he's entering the hushed, precarious wood. Soon he'll reach the shadowy crossroads, and then which way will he turn? He'll have no idea. He'll get lost.

He's already lost. He's a stranger to Alphinland, he doesn't know its dangers. He's runeless, he's weaponless. He has no allies.

Or he has no allies but her. 'Wait for me, Ewan,' she says. 'Wait right there!' She'll have to go in and find him.

REVENANT

Reynolds bustles into the living room, carrying two pillows. An indeterminate number of years ago, those two pillows billowing upward from Rey's encircling arms like two plump, inflatable breasts, soft but firm, would have suggested to Gavin the real breasts, equally soft but firm, that were hidden underneath. He might have hammered together a clever metaphor incorporating, for example, two sacks of feathers, and, by way of them, two sexually receptive chickens. Or possibly – because of the bounciness, the resilience, the rubberiness – two trampolines.

Now, however, these pillows recall – in addition to the breasts – an overdone avant-garde production of *Richard the Third* they'd seen in a park the previous summer. Reynolds made them go; she said it was good for Gavin to get out of his rut and be in the outdoors and expose himself to new concepts, and Gavin said he would rather just be in the outdoors and expose himself, and Rey nudged him playfully with her elbow and said, 'Bad Gavvy!' It was one of her kittenish tropes to pretend that Gavin was a dysfunctional pet. Not

44

so far from the truth, he thinks bitterly: he hasn't yet taken to crapping on the carpet and destroying the furniture and whining for meals, but close.

On their expedition to the park, Reynolds took a packsack with a plastic sheet to sit on and a couple of car rugs in case Gavin got chilled, and two thermoses, one of hot cocoa and one containing vodka martinis. Her plan was transparent: if Gavin complained too much she would dose him with alcohol and cover him up with the car rugs and hope he'd go to sleep so she could immerse herself in the deathless bard.

The plastic sheet was a good idea, as it had rained in the afternoon and the grass was damp. Secretly hoping for more rain so he could go home, Gavin settled himself onto the car rug and complained that his knees hurt, and also he was hungry. Reynolds had foreseen both of these areas of disgruntlement: out came the RUB A535, with Antiphlogistene – one of Gavin's favourite examples of meaningless words – and a salmon salad sandwich. 'I can't read the fucking program,' said Gavin, not that he wanted to. Rey handed him the flashlight, and also a magnifier. She's up to most of his dodges.

'This is exciting!' she said in her best Miss Sunshine voice. 'You're going to enjoy it!' Gavin had a twinge of remorse: she has such a touching belief in his innate capacity to enjoy himself. He could do it if he tried, she claims: his problem is that he's too negative. They've had this conversation

45

more than once. He'll reply that his problem is that the world reeks, so why doesn't she stop trying to fix him and concentrate on that? And she will reply that reekiness is in the nose of the sniffer, or some other exercise in Kantean subjectivism – not that she'd know Kantean subjectivism if she fell over it – and why doesn't he take up Buddhist meditation?

And Pilates, she's strongly urging Pilates. She's already lined up a girl Pilates instructor who's willing to give him private sessions, contrary to her usual practice, because she admires his work. This idea is dismaying: having some estrogen-plumped babe a quarter of his age contort his stringy, knobbled limbs while comparing the dashing protagonist of his earlier poems, replete with sexual alacrity and sardonic wit, to the atrophied bundle of twine and sticks he has become. *Look on this picture, then on this.* Why is Reynolds so keen to hook him up to the Pilates torture apparatus and stretch him upon it until he snaps like an outworn rubber band? She wants to know he's suffering. She wants to humiliate him and feel virtuous about it at the same time.

'Stop trying to pimp me out to all these groupies,' he tells her. 'Why don't you simply rope me into a chair and charge admission?'

The park was pullulating with activity. Kids played Frisbee in the background, babies yowled, dogs barked. Gavin pored over the program notes. Pretentious crap, as usual. The play was late

46

starting: some spasm in the lighting system, they were told. The mosquitoes were gathering; Gavin swatted at them; Reynolds produced the Deep Woods Off. Some fool in a scarlet unitard and pig's ears blew a trumpet to get them all to shut up, and after a minor explosion and a figure in a ruff sprinting off in the direction of the refreshment kiosk – In search of what? What had they forgotten? – the play began.

There was a prelude showing a film clip of Richard the Third's skeleton being dug up from underneath a parking lot – an event that had in fact taken place, Gavin saw it on the television news. It was Richard all right, complete with DNA evidence and many injuries to the skull. The prelude was projected onto a piece of white fabric that looked like a bedsheet, and probably was one – arts budgets being what they were, as Gavin commented to Reynolds, *sotto voce*. Reynolds dug him with her elbow. 'Your voice is louder than you think,' she whispered.

The soundtrack led them to understand – over a crackling loudspeaker and in lousy iambic pentameter Elizabethan pastiche – that the entire drama they were about to see was unfolding postmortem from inside Richard's battered skull. Zoom to an eyehole in the skull, and then right on through it to the inside of the cranium. And blackout.

Whereupon the bedsheet was whisked away and there was Richard in the floodlights, all set

47

to caper and posture, to flounce and denounce. On his back was a preposterously large hump, decorated in a jester's red and yellow stripes – like Mr Punch, the program notes had explained, who himself was derived from Punchinello; for the director's vision was that Shakespeare's Richard was modelled on *commedia dell'arte*, a troupe of which had been playing in England at the time. The largeness of the hump was deliberate: the inner core of the play ('As opposed to the outer core,' Gavin had snorted to himself) was all about the props. These were symbols of Richard's unconscious, which accounted for their enlargement. The director's thinking must have been that if the audience members were staring at outsized thrones and humps and whatnot and wondering what the fuck they were doing in this play, it wouldn't bother them so much that they couldn't hear the words.

So in addition to his gigantic, varicoloured, metonymous hump, Richard had a kingly robe with a sixteen-foot-long train attached to it, carried by two pageboys wearing outsized boar's heads because Richard's coat of arms had a boar on it. There was a huge butt of malmsey for Clarence to be drowned in and a couple of swords that were as tall as the actors. For the smothering of the princes in the Tower, performed in dumb show like the play within the play in *Hamlet,* two enormous pillows were borne in on stretchers like corpses or roasted suckling pigs, with pillowcases that matched the motley of Richard's hump, just in case the audience missed the point.

Death by hump, thinks Gavin, eyeing the approaching pillows borne towards him by Reynolds. What a fate. And Reynolds as First Murderer. But that would be fitting, all things considered; and Gavin does consider all things. He's got the time for it.

'Are you awake?' says Reynolds brightly as she clacks across the floor. She's wearing a black pullover with a silver and turquoise belt cinched around her waist and tight jeans. She's getting a little flubber on the outsides of her thighs, which otherwise have the heft and contours of a speed skater's. Should he point out those pockets of flubber? No; better to hold them back for a more strategic moment. And maybe it isn't flubber, maybe it's muscle. She works out enough.

'If I wasn't awake before, I would be now,' says Gavin. 'You sound like a wooden railroad.' He dislikes those clogs, and he's told her so. They do nothing for her legs. But she doesn't care what he thinks about her legs as much as she used to. She says the clogs are comfortable, and that comfort trumps fashion as far as she's concerned. Gavin has tried quoting Yeats to the effect that women must labour to be beautiful, but Reynolds – who used to be a passionate Yeats fan – is now of the opinion that Yeats is entitled to his point of view, but that was then and social attitudes were different, and in actual fact Yeats is dead.

Reynolds tucks the pillows in behind Gavin, one behind his head, one at the small of his back. This pillow arrangement, she claims, makes him look taller and therefore more impressive. She straightens the plaid car rug that covers his legs and feet, and which she insists on calling his nap blanket. 'Oh, Mr Grumpy!' she says. 'Where's your smile?'

She's taken to renaming him according to her own analysis of his mood of the day, or his mood of the hour, or his mood of the minute: according to her, he's moody. Each mood is personified and given an honorific, so he's Mr Grumpy, Mr Sleepy, Dr Ironic, Sir Sardonic, and sometimes, when she's being sarcastic or possibly nostalgic, Mr Romantic. A while back she used to call his penis Mr Wiggly, but she's given up on that, and on her attempts to revive his non-existent libido with unguents and sex jellies that taste of strawberry jam and invigorating ginger lemon and toothpaste mint. There was also an adventure with a hair dryer that he would prefer to forget. 'It's quarter to four,' she continues. 'Let's get ready for our company!' Next will come the hairbrush – that's one thing he's managed to hold on to, his hair – and then the lint brush. Dog-like, he sheds.

'Who is it this time?' says Gavin.

'A very nice woman,' says Reynolds. 'A nice girl. A graduate student. She's doing her thesis on your work.' She herself had once been doing her thesis on his work: that had been his downfall. It had been very seductive to him, then, to have an attractive young woman paying such concentrated attention to his every adjective.

Gavin groans. 'Thesis on my fucking work,' he says. 'Christ defend us!'

'Now, Mr Profanity,' says Reynolds. 'Don't be so mean.'

'What the fuck is this learned scholar doing in Florida?' says Gavin. 'She must be a moron.'

'Florida's not the hick town you keep saying it is,' says Reynolds. 'Times have changed; they've got good universities now and a great book festival! *Thousands* of people come to it!'

'Fan-fucking-tastic. I'm impressed,' says Gavin.

'Anyway,' says Reynolds, ignoring him, 'she isn't from Florida. She's flown in from Iowa just to interview you! People all over are doing work on your work, you know.'

'Iowa, fuck,' says Gavin. *Work on your work.* Sometimes she talks like a five-year-old.

Reynolds gets going with the lint brush. She attacks his shoulders, then takes a playful swipe in the direction of his crotch. 'Let's see if there's any lint on Mr Wiggly!' she says.

'Keep your lustful claws off my private parts,' says Gavin. He feels like saying that *of course* there's lint on Mr Wiggly, or dust at any rate, or maybe rust; what does she expect, because as she is well aware Mr Wiggly has been on the shelf for some time. But he refrains.

51

To rust unburnished, not to shine in use, he thinks. Tennyson. Ulysses sets out on his last voyage, lucky him, at least he'll sink with his boots on. Not that Greeks wore boots. One of the first poems Gavin had to memorize in school; he turned out to be good at memorizing. Shameful to admit, but that's what turned him on to poetry: Tennyson, an outmoded Victorian windbag, writing about an old man. Things have a habit of coming full circle: a bad habit, to his mind.

'Mr Wiggly *likes* my lustful claws,' says Reynolds. How gallant of her to put that in the present tense. It used to be a game of theirs – that Reynolds was the seductress, the dominatrix, the femme fatale, and he was her passive victim. She'd seemed to enjoy that scenario, so he went along. Now it's no longer a game; none of the old games work. It would only make both of them sad to attempt to revive them.

This isn't what she signed up for when she married him. She most likely envisioned a fascinating life, filled with glamorous, creative people and stimulating intellectual chit-chat. And that did happen some, when they were first married; that, and the flare-up of his still active hormones. The last kaboom of the firecracker before it fizzled; but now she's stuck with the burnt-out aftermath. In his more lenient moments, he feels sorry for her.

She must be finding consolation elsewhere. He would if he was her. What does she really do when she goes out to her spinning classes or off to her so-called dancing evenings with her so-called girl-friends? He can imagine, and does. Such imaginings once bothered him, but now he contemplates Reynolds's possible transgressions – not only possible, but almost certain – with clinical detachment. She's surely entitled to some of that: she's thirty years younger than him. He probably has more horns on his head – as the bard would say – than a hundred-headed snail.

Serves him right for marrying a youngster. Serves him right for marrying three of them in a row. Serves him right for marrying his graduate students. Serves him right for marrying a bossy, self-appointed custodian of his life and times. Serves him right for marrying.

But at least Reynolds won't leave him, he's fairly certain of that. She's polishing up her widow act; she wouldn't want it to go to waste. She's so competitive that she'll hang in there to make sure neither of the two previous wives can lay claim to any part of him, literary or otherwise. She'll want to control his narrative, she'll want to help write the biography, if any. She'll also want to cut out his two children – one from each ex-wife, and hardly children any longer, since one of them must be fifty-one, or maybe fifty-two. He hadn't paid much attention to them when they were babies. They and their pastel, urine-soaked paraphernalia had taken up so much space, they'd attracted so much attention that ought to have been his, and he'd decamped in each case before they were three; so they don't like him much, nor does he blame them, having hated his own father. Nevertheless there's sure to be some squabbling after the funeral: he's making sure of that by not finalizing his will. If only he could hover around in mid-air to watch!

Reynolds gives him a final stroke with the lint brush, does up his second-from-the-top shirt button, tugs his collar into place. 'There,' she says. 'Much better.'

'Who is this girl?' he says. 'This girl who's so interested in my so-called work. Got a cute butt?'

'Stop that,' says Reynolds. 'Your whole generation was obsessed with sex. Mailer, Updike, Roth – all of those guys.'

'They were older than me,' says Gavin.

'Not much. It was sex, sex, sex with them, all the time! They couldn't keep it zipped!'

'Your point being?' says Gavin coolly. He's relishing this. 'Is that bad, sex? Are you a little prude all of a sudden? What else should we have been obsessed with? Shopping?'

'My point being,' says Reynolds. She has to pause, reconsider, rally her inner battalions. 'Okay, shopping is a poor substitute for sex, granted. But faut de mieux.'

That hurts, thinks Gavin. 'Faut de what?' he says.

'Don't play dumb, you understood me. My point being, not everything is about butts. This woman's name is Naveena. She deserves to be treated with respect. She's already published two papers on the Riverboat years. She happens to be very bright. I believe she's of Indian extraction.'

Of Indian extraction. Where does she pick up these archaic locutions? When she's trying to be properly literary she talks like a comic lady in an Oscar Wilde play. 'Naveena,' he says. 'Sounds like cheese food slices. Or better – like a hair-removal cream.'

'You don't have to disparage people,' says Reynolds, who used to dote on the fact that he disparaged people, or at least some people; she'd thought it meant that he had a superior intellect and an informed taste. Now she thinks it's merely nasty, or else a symptom of a vitamin deficiency. 'It's so knee-jerk with you! Running them down doesn't make you any bigger, you know. Naveena happens to be a serious literary scholar. She has an M.A.'

'And a cute butt, or else I'm not talking to her,' says Gavin. 'Every halfwit has an M.A. They're like popcorn.' He puts Reynolds through this every time – every time she trots out some new aficionado, some new aspirant, some new slave from the salt mines of academe – because he has to put her through something.

'Popcorn?' says Reynolds. Gavin flounders momentarily – now what did he mean by that? He takes a breath. 'Tiny little kernels,' he says. 'Superheated in the academic cooker. The hot air expands. Poof! An M.A.' Not bad, he thinks. Also true. The universities want the cash, so they lure these kids in. Then they turn them into puffballs of inflated starch, with no jobs to match. Better to have a certificate in plumbing.

Rey laughs, a little sourly: she has an M.A. herself. Then she frowns. 'You should be grateful,' she says. Here comes the scolding, the whack with the rolled-up newspaper. Bad Gavvy! 'At least someone's still interested in you! A young person! Some poets would kill for that. The '60s is hot right now, happily for you. So you can't complain of being neglected.'

'Since when have I done that?' he says. 'I never complain!'

'You complain all the time, about everything,' says Reynolds. She's reaching the fed-up moment; he shouldn't take it any further. But he does.

'I should have married Constance,' he says. That's his ace: plonk! Right down on the table. Those five words are usually very effective: he might score a barrage of hostility, and maybe even some tears. Top marks: a slammed door. Or a projectile. She winged him with an ashtray once.

Reynolds smiles. 'Well, you didn't marry Constance,' she said. 'You married me. So suck it up.'

Gavin misses a beat. She's playing impervious. 'Oh, if only I could,' he says, with exaggerated longing.

'Dentures are no impediment,' says Reynolds

56

crisply. She can be a bitch when he pushes her too far. The bitchiness is a thing he admires in her, though reluctantly when it's turned on him. 'Now I'm going to get the tea ready. If you don't behave yourself when Naveena comes, you won't get a cookie.' The cookie ploy is a joke, her attempt to lighten things up, but it's faintly horrifying to him that the threat of being deprived of such a cookie hits home. No cookie! A wave of desolation sweeps through him. Also he's drooling. Christ. Has it come down to this? Sitting up to beg for treats?

Reynolds marches out to the kitchen, leaving Gavin alone on the sofa gazing at the view, such as it is. There's a blue sky, there's a picture window. The window gives onto a fenced enclosure in which there's a palm tree. Also a jacaranda, or is it a frangipani? He wouldn't know, they only rent this house.

There's a swimming pool that he never uses, although it's heated. Reynolds plunges into it occasionally before he wakes up in the morning, or so she says: she likes to flaunt such examples of her physical agility. Leaves fall into the pool from the jacaranda or whatever it is, and also spiky prongs from the palm. They float around on the surface, swirling in the slow eddy caused by the circulation pump. A girl comes by three times a week and skims them out with a net on a long handle. Her name is Maria; she's a high school student; she's included in the rent. She lets herself in through the garden gate with a key and moves over the tiled and slippery patio noiselessly on rubber soles. She has long dark hair and a lovely waist, and may possibly be Mexican; Gavin doesn't know because he's never spoken to her. She always wears shorts, light blue denim or darker blue denim, and she bends over in her denim shorts while skimming out the leaves. Her face, when he's able to see it, is impassive, though verging on the solemn.

Oh Maria, he sighs to himself. Are there troubles in your life? If not, there soon will be. What a trim ass you have. All the better to wig and wag.

Does she ever see him watching her through the picture window? Most likely. Does she think he's a lecherous old man? Very probably. But he isn't exactly that. How to convey the mix of longing, wistfulness, and muted regret that he feels? His regret is that he isn't a lecherous old man, but he wishes he were. He wishes he still could be. How to describe the deliciousness of ice cream when you can no longer taste it?

He's writing a poem that begins, 'Maria skims the dying leaves.' Though technically speaking the leaves are already dead.

The doorbell rings, and Reynolds clatters into the hall. There are female greeting sounds from the entranceway, that cooing and come-inning and pigeon oodle-ooing that women do nowadays. They're going over each other with the woo-woo ooo sounds as if they're best friends, though they've never met. The contact was through email, which Gavin despises. He should not have despised it, however: handing over control of his correspondence to Reynolds has been a mistake, because it's given her the keys to the kingdom: she's now the gatekeeper to the Kingdom of Gavin. Nobody gets in unless she says so.

'He's just been having a nap,' says Reynolds, using that mock-reverential tone she slides into when about to display him to third parties. 'Would you like a peek at his study first? Where he does his writing?'

'Oh, ooodle-oo,' says the voice of Naveena, which must indicate delight. 'If it's all right.' Clickety-click down the corridor go their two pairs of shod feet.

'He can't write on a computer,' Reynolds is saying. 'He has to use a pencil. He says it's a hand-eye thing.'

'Awesome,' says Naveena.

Gavin hates his study with a rancorous hatred. He hates this study – which is only a temporary one – but especially he hates his real study, back in British Columbia. It was designed for him by Reynolds, and has quotations from his most-anthologized poems stencilled on its kidney-coloured walls in white paint; so he has to sit in there surrounded by monuments of his own decaying magnificence while all around him the air is thick with shreds and tatters of the stellar poetic masterpieces he'd once revered: the shards of well-wrought urns, the broken echoes of other men's wit and scope.

Reynolds tends both of his studies as if they're shrines and he their graven image. She makes a production of sharpening his pencils and blocking all phone calls and shutting him in there. Then she tiptoes around outside as if he's on life support, and then he can't write a word. He can't spin straw into gold, not in that mausoleum of a study: Rumpelstiltskin, the malicious dwarf who's the most likely shape of his Muse these days – tardy Rumpelstiltskin never shows up. Then it will be lunchtime, and Reynolds will gaze at him hopefully across the table and say, 'Anything new?' She's so proud of how she protects his privacy, and fosters his communion with his own poetic juices, and enables what she calls his 'creative time.' He doesn't have the heart to tell her he's dry as a bone.

He needs to get out, out of here; at least outside the study, the two studies, with their arid scent of embalmed pages. In the '60s, when he was living with Constance in that cramped, sultry steam bath of a room where they stewed like prunes, back when they had no money and he certainly had no la-de-dah *study*, he could write anywhere – in bars, in fast-food joints, in coffee shops – and the words would flow out of him and through the pencil or the ballpoint onto anything flat and handy. Envelopes, paper napkins; a cliché, granted, but it was true all the same.

How to get back there? How to get that back?

★   ★   ★

Clickety-click, heading in his direction. 'Right through here,' says Reynolds.

Naveena is ushered into the living room. She's a beautiful little creature, practically a child. Big, shy dark eyes. She has earrings in the shape of octopuses, or octopi. You've got seafood on your ears, he might begin if he was intending to pick her up in a bar, but he doesn't try that now. 'Oh, please don't get up,' she says, but Gavin makes a show of hauling himself to his feet so he can shake her hand. He holds it – deliberately – a little too long.

Then the pillows must be rearranged by Reynolds, doing her competent-nurse act. What would happen if Gavin were to grab the black-pullovered tit that's being thrust into his eye and use it as a lever to flip Reynolds over onto her back like a turtle? *A jolly thriving wooer.* Screaming, recriminations, the Saran Wrap ripped off their bowl of marital leftovers, in front of a galvanized audience of one. Would that kind of uproar get him out of this bush-league interview?

But he doesn't want to get out of it, not yet. Sometimes he enjoys these ordeals. He enjoys saying he can't remember writing that piece of word salad, whatever it may be; he enjoys blowing off the poems these sentimental kids produce as their favourites. *Crap, drivel, trash!* He enjoys telling tales on his erstwhile poet buddies, his erstwhile rivals. Most of them are dead, so no harm done. Not that harm done would stop him.

Rey inserts Naveena into the easy chair where she can get a full frontal view of him. 'It's such an honour to meet you,' she says, deferentially enough. 'This is nerdy, but I feel as if I, like . . . as if I kind of actually know you. I guess it's because of studying your work, and everything.' She may be of Indian extraction, but the voice is pure Midwest.

'Then you have the advantage of me,' says Gavin. He leers like a troll: it can throw them off their stride, that leer of his.

'Pardon?' says Naveena.

'He means that although you know a lot about him, he doesn't know anything about you,' says Reynolds, interposing herself as usual. She casts herself as his interpreter; as if he's an oracle, spouting gnomic sayings that only the high priestess can decipher. 'So why don't you tell him what you're working on? What part of his work? I'll go and make us some tea.'

'I'm all ears,' says Gavin, holding his leer.

'Don't bite her,' says Reynolds with a parting twitch of her tight jeans. Good exit line: the possibility of biting, so double-edged, so vague as to location and intent, hovers in the air like an aroma. Where would he begin, if biting was on offer? A gentle nibbling at the nape of the neck?

It's no use. Even this prospect fails to stir him. He stifles a yawn.

Naveena fidgets with a miniature gadget that she then places on the coffee table in front of him.

She's wearing a miniskirt that rides up over her knees – displaying patterned stockings like lace window curtains dyed black – and also painfully high-heeled boots with metal studs. It makes Gavin's feet hurt to look at the boots. Surely her toes must be squashed into wedges, like bound Chinese feet in sepia photos. Those deformed feet were a sexual turn-on, or so Gavin has read. Guys would slide their Mr Wigglies into the moist orifice formed by the recurved, stunted toes. He can't see it himself.

She's wearing her hair in a bun, like a ballerina's. Buns are so sexy. They used to be a treat to take apart: it was like opening a gift. Heads with the hair pulled back into buns are so elegant and confined, so maidenish; then the undoing, the dishevelment, the wildness of the freed hair, spilling down the shoulders, over the breasts, over the pillow. He enumerates in his head: *Buns I have known.*

Constance did not have a bun. She didn't need one. She more or less was a bun: neat and contained, and then so tumultuous when unleashed. His first live-in, Eve to his Adam. Nothing could ever replace that. He remembers the ache of waiting for her in their cramped, stuffy Eden with the hotplate and the electric kettle. She would come in through the door with that supple but luscious body of hers and the remote, contradictory head on top, her face pale as a waning moon, with the floss of her light hair escaping from around it like rays, and he would enfold her in his arms and sink his teeth into her neck.

Not *into*, not in actuality; but he'd feel like doing that. Partly because he was always hungry then, and she'd smell of Snuffy's fried chicken. And because she adored him, she would melt like warm honey. She was so pliable. He could do anything with her, arrange her as he pleased, and she would say yes. Not just yes. *Oh yes!*

Has he ever been adored like that since, purely adored, with no ulterior motives? Because he wasn't famous then, not even famous with the moderate in-group fame accorded to poets. He hadn't won anything, any prizes; he hadn't published any thin, meritorious, envied collections. He had the freedom of a nobody, with a blank future unrolling before him on which anything at all might be written. She'd adored him only for himself. His inner core.

'I could eat you all up,' he'd say to her. Mmm, mmm. Rrrr, rrrr. *Oh yes!*

'Excuse me?' says Naveena.

He snaps back into the present. Was he making a noise? A yum-yummy noise, a growling noise? And if so, so what? He's earned his noises. He'll make all the noises he wants.

But soft you, the fair Naveena. Nymph, in thy glossaries be all my puns remembered. Some more practical remark is called for.

'Are those boots comfortable?' he says cordially. Best to ease into this: let her talk about something she knows, such as boots, because pretty soon she'll be in over her depth.

'What?' says Naveena, startled. 'Boots?' Is that a blush?

'Don't they pinch your toes?' he says. 'They look very fashionable, but how can you walk?' He would like to ask her to get up and prance across the room – it's one of the functions of high heels to tilt the woman's pelvis so that her butt curves out behind and her tits thrust forward, lending her the serpentine curve of beauty – but he won't ask her to do that. She is after all a total stranger.

'Oh,' says Naveena. 'These. Yes, they're comfortable, though maybe I shouldn't wear them when there's ice on the sidewalks.'

'There isn't any ice on the sidewalks,' says Gavin. Not too bright, this nymph.

'Oh no, not here,' she says. 'I mean, it's Florida, right? I meant back home.' She giggles nervously. 'Ice.'

Gavin, watching the television weather, has noted with interest the polar vortex gripping the north, the east, the centre. He's seen the pictures of the blizzards, the ice storms, the overturned cars and broken trees. That's where Constance must be right now: in the eye of the storm. He imagines her holding out her arms to him, clothed in nothing but snow, with an unearthly radiance streaming out from around her. His lady of the moonglow. He's forgotten why they broke up. It was a trivial thing; nothing that should have mattered to her. Some other woman he'd gone to bed with. Melanie, Megan, Marjorie? It wasn't really anything, the woman had practically jumped on him out of a tree. He'd tried to explain that to Constance, but she hadn't understood his predicament.

Why couldn't the two of them have gone on and on forever? Himself and Constance, sun and moon, each one of them shining, though in different ways. Instead of which he's here, forsaken by her, abandoned. In time, which fails to sustain him. In space, which fails to cradle him.

'Florida. Yes? What's your point?' he says, too sharply. What was this Naveena nattering on about?

'There isn't any ice here,' she says in a small voice.

'Right, of course, but you're going back soon,' he says. He must show her that he isn't drifting away, losing the plot. 'Back to – where is it? Indiana? Idaho? Iowa? Lots of ice there! So if you do fall, don't put out your hand,' he says, assuming an instructive and fatherly tone. 'Try to hit with your shoulder. That way you won't break your wrist.'

'Oh,' says Naveena again. 'Thank you.' There's an awkward pause. 'Could we maybe talk about you?' she says. 'And, you know, your, well, your work – when you were doing your early work. I've got my tape recorder; can I turn it on? And I brought some video clips we could maybe watch, and you could tell me about the, about who, about the context. If you wouldn't mind.'

'Fire away,' he says, settling back. Where the crap is Reynolds? Where's his tea? And the cookie: he's earned it.

'Okay, so, what I'm working on is, well, kind of the Riverboat years. The mid-'60s. When you wrote that sequence called *Sonnets for My Lady*.' She's setting up some other technical doodad now: one of those tablets. Reynolds has just bought a green one. Naveena's is red, with a cunning triangular stand.

Gavin puts his hand in front of his eyes in mock embarrassment. 'Don't remind me,' he says. '*Sonnets* – that was apprentice work. Flabby, amateur garbage. I was only twenty-six. Can't we move on to something more substantial?' In point of fact those sonnets were noteworthy, first of all because they were sonnets in name only – how daring of him! – and secondly because they broke new ground and pushed the boundaries of language. Or so it said on the back of the book. In any case, that book snagged his first-ever prize. He'd pretended to view it with indifference, even disdain – what were prizes but one more level of control imposed on Art by the establishment? – but he'd cashed the cheque.

'Keats died when he was twenty-six,' Naveena says severely, 'and look what he accomplished!' A rebuke, a palpable rebuke! How dare she? He was already middle-aged when she was born! He could have been her father! He could have been her child molester!

'Byron called Keats's stuff "Johnny-wet-your-bed poetry,"' he says.

'I know, right?' says Naveena. 'I guess he was jealous. Anyway, those sonnets are great! "My lady's mouth on me" . . . It's so simple, it's so sweet and direct.' She doesn't seem to realize that the subject is a blowjob. Very different from 'My lady's mouth on mine': back then, 'me' in such a context was a disguised reference to 'cock.' The first time Reynolds read that *mouth* line she laughed out loud: no such pure-mindedness in his very own festering lily.

'So you're working on the "Lady" sonnets,' he says. 'Let me know if there are any points you'd like me to elucidate for you. Something from the horse's mouth, to flesh out your thesis. As it were.'

'Well, it's not exactly them I'm working on,' she says. 'They've been done quite a lot.' She looks down at the coffee table; now she's blushing in earnest. 'As a matter of fact, I'm doing my thesis on C. W. Starr. You know, Constance Starr, though I realize that Starr wasn't her real name – on her Alphinland series, and, well, you knew her at that time. At the Riverboat, and all of that.'

Gavin feels as if cold mercury has been poured through his veins. Who let this creature in? This defacer, this violator! Reynolds, that's who. Was treacherous Reynolds aware of the harpy's true mission? If so, he'll pull out her molars.

But he's cornered. He can't pretend this matters to him – to be cast as a mere secondary source in the main action, the main action being Constance. Constance the fluffball, with her idiotic gnome stories. Constance the flake. Constance the bubble-head. To show anger would be to reveal his soft underbelly, to pile more humiliation upon the primary humiliation. 'Oh yes.' He laughs indulgently, as if recalling a joke. '*And all of that* is right! So much *all*, and so much *that*! It was *all* and *that* from morning to night! But I had the stamina for it then.'

'Excuse me?' says Naveena. Her eyes are shining: she's getting some of the blood she came for. But she won't get all of it.

'My dear child,' says Gavin. 'Constance and I *lived* together. We *shacked up*. It was the dawning of the Age of Aquarius. And though that age hadn't fully dawned, we were very busy all the same. We spent a lot more time taking our clothes off than putting them on. She was . . . amazing.' He allows himself a reminiscent smile. 'But don't tell me you're doing serious academic work on Constance! What she wrote wasn't in any way . . .'

'Well, yes, as a matter of fact I am,' says Naveena. 'It's an in-depth examination of the function of symbolism versus neo-representationalism in the process of world-building, which can be studied so much more effectively through the fantasy genres than in its more disguised forms in so-called realistic fiction. Wouldn't you say?'

Reynolds clacks in, carrying a tray. 'Here's our tea!' she announces, in the nick of time. Gavin can feel the blood pounding in his temples. What the fuck was Naveena just saying?

'What kind of cookies?' he says, to put neo-representationalism in its place.

'Chocolate chip,' says Reynolds. 'Did Naveena show you the video clips yet? They're fascinating! She sent them to me in a Dropbox.' She sits down beside him and begins to pour out the tea.

Dropbox. What is it? Nothing comes to mind but an indoor cat-poo station. But he won't ask.

'This is the first one,' says Naveena. 'The Riverboat, around 1965.'

It's an ambush, it's a betrayal. However, Gavin cannot choose but look. It's like being drawn into a time tunnel: the centrifugal force is irresistible.

The film is grainy, black and white; there's no sound. The camera pans around the room: some amateur starfucker, or was this shot for an early documentary? That must be Sonny Terry and Brownie McGhee onstage, and is that Sylvia Tyson? A couple of his fellow poets of those days, hanging out at one of the tables, in their period haircuts, their downy, defiant, optimistic beards. So many of them dead by now.

And there he is himself, with Constance beside him. No beard, but he's got a cigarette dangling out of his mouth and an arm casually draped around Constance. He isn't looking at her, he's looking at the stage. She's looking at him, though.

She was always looking at him. They're so sweet, the two of them; so unscarred, so filled with energy then, and hope; like children. So unaware of the winds of fate that were soon to sweep them apart. He wants to cry.

'She must be tired,' says Reynolds, with satisfaction. 'Check out those bags under her eyes. Big dark circles. She must be really whipped.'

'Tired?' says Gavin. He never thought of Constance as being tired.

'Well, I guess she would be tired,' says Naveena. 'Think of all she was writing then! It was epic! She practically created the whole Alphinland ground plan, in such a short time! Plus she had that job, with the fried-chicken place.'

'She never said she was tired,' says Gavin, because the two of them are staring at him with what might possibly be reproach. 'She had a lot of stamina.'

'She wrote to you about it,' says Naveena. 'About being tired. Though she said she was never too tired for you! She said you should always wake her up, no matter how late you came in. She wrote that down! I guess she was really in love with you. It's so endearing.'

Gavin's confused. Wrote to him? He doesn't remember that. 'Why would she write me letters?' he says. 'We were living in the same place.'

'She wrote notes to you in this journal she had,' says Naveena, 'and she'd leave it for you on the table because you always slept in, but she had to go to her job, and then you would read the notes.

71

And then you would write notes back to her that way, underneath hers. It had a black cover, it's the same sort of journal she used for the Alphinland lists and maps. There's a different page for every day. Don't you remember?'

'Oh, that,' says Gavin. He has a dim recollection. Mostly he can remember the radiance of those mornings, after a night with Constance. The first coffee, the first cigarette, the first lines of the first poem, appearing as if by magic. Most of those poems were keepers. 'Yes, vaguely. How did you get hold of that?'

'It was in your papers,' says Naveena. 'The journal. The University of Austin has the papers. You sold them. Remember?'

'I sold my papers?' says Gavin. 'Which papers?' He's drawn a blank, one of those gaps that appears in his memory from time to time like a tear in a spiderweb. He can't recall doing any such thing.

'Well, technically I sold them,' says Reynolds. 'I made the arrangements. You asked me to take care of it for you. It was when you were working on the *Odyssey* translation. He gets so immersed,' she says to Naveena. 'When he's working. He'd even forget to eat if I didn't feed him!'

'I know, right?' says Naveena. The two of them exchange a conspiratorial look: Genius must be humoured. That, thinks Gavin, is the kindlier translation: *Old poops must be lied to* would be the other.

'Now let's see the other clip,' says Rey, leaning

forward. *Mercy,* Gavin pleads with her silently. *I'm on the ropes. This teen princess is wearing me down. I don't know what she's talking about! Bring it to an end!*

'I'm tired,' he says, but not loudly enough, it seems: the two of them have their agenda.

'It's an interview,' says Naveena. 'From a few years ago. It's up on YouTube.' She clicks on the arrow and the video starts to play, this time with colour and sound. 'It's at the World Fantasy Convention in Toronto.'

Gavin watches with mounting horror. A wispy old woman is being interviewed by a man dressed in a *Star Trek* outfit: a purple complexion, a gigantic veined skull. A Klingon, Gavin supposes. Though he doesn't know much about this cluster of memes, his poetry workshop students used to attempt to enlighten him when the subject came up in their poems. There's a woman onscreen too, with a glistening, plasticized face. 'That's the Borg Queen,' Naveena whispers. The wispy oldster is supposed to be Constance, says the YouTube title line, but he can't credit it.

'We're thrilled to have with us today someone who, you could say, is the grandmother of twentieth-century world-building fantasy,' says the Borg Queen. 'C. W. Starr herself, the creator of the world-famous Alphinland series. Should I call you Constance, or Ms Starr? Or how about C. W.?'

'Whatever you like,' says Constance. For it is indeed Constance, though much diminished. She's

73

wearing a silver-threaded cardigan that hangs on her loosely; her hair's like disordered egret plumage, her neck's a Popsicle stick. She peers around her as if dazzled by the noise and lights. 'I don't care about the name or any of that,' she says. 'I only ever cared about what I was doing, with Alphinland.' Her skin is oddly luminous, like a phosphorescent mushroom.

'Didn't you feel brave, writing what you did, back when you started?' says the Klingon. 'That whole genre was a man's world then, yes?'

Constance throws back her head and laughs. This laugh – this airy, feathery laugh – was once charming, but now it strikes Gavin as grotesque. Misplaced friskiness. 'Oh, nobody was paying any attention to me then,' she says. 'So you couldn't really call it brave. Anyway, I used initials. Nobody knew at first that I wasn't a man.'

'Like the Brontë sisters,' says the Klingon.

'Hardly that,' says Constance, with a sideways glance and a self-deprecating giggle. Is she flirting with the purple-skinned, veiny-skulled guy? Gavin winces.

'Now she really does look tired,' says Reynolds. 'I wonder who put that awful makeup on her? They shouldn't have used the mineral powder. How exactly old is she, anyway?'

'So, how do you go about creating an alternate world?' says the Borg Queen. 'Do you make it up out of nothing?'

'Oh, I never make anything up out of nothing,'

says Constance. Now she's being serious, in that ditzy way she had. *This is me being serious.* It had never convinced Gavin at the time: it was like a little girl wearing her mother's high heels. That seriousness, too, he had found charming; now he finds it bogus. What right has she to be serious? 'You see,' she continues, 'everything in Alphinland is based on something in real life. How could it be different?'

'Does that go for the characters too?' says the Klingon.

'Well, yes,' she says, 'but I sometimes take parts of them from here and there and put them together.'

'Like Mr Potato Head,' says the Borg Queen.

'Mr Potato Head?' says Constance. She looks bewildered. 'I don't have anyone of that name in Alphinland!'

'It's a toy for children,' says the Borg Queen. 'You stick different eyes and noses onto a potato.'

'Oh,' says Constance. 'That was after my time. Of being a child,' she adds.

The Klingon fills the pause. 'There's a big bunch of villains in Alphinland! Do you get those from real life too?' He chuckles. 'Lots to choose from!'

'Oh yes,' says Constance. 'Especially the villains.'

'So for instance,' says the Borg Queen, 'Milzreth of the Red Hand is someone we might meet walking along the street?'

Constance does the thrown-back-head laugh again; it sets Gavin's teeth on edge. Someone needs to tell her not to open her mouth so wide; it's no longer becoming; you can see that she has a couple of back teeth missing. 'Oh my goodness, I hope not!' she says. 'Not in that outfit. But I did base Milzreth on a man in real life.' She stares pensively out of the screen, right into the eyes of Gavin.

'Maybe some old boyfriend?' says the Klingon.

'Oh, no,' says Constance. 'More like a politician. Milzreth is very political. But I did put one of my old boyfriends into Alphinland. He's in there right now. Only you can't see him.'

'Go on, tell us,' says the Borg Queen, smiling fit to kill.

Constance turns coy. 'It's a secret,' she says. She looks behind her, fearfully, as if she suspects there's a spy. 'I can't tell you where he is. I wouldn't want to disturb, you know. The balance. That would be very dangerous for us all!'

Is this getting out of hand? Is she, perhaps, a little crazy? The Borg Queen must think so because she's cutting this off right now. 'It's been such a privilege, such an honour, thank you so much!' she says. 'Boys and girls, a big hand for C. W. Starr!' There's applause. Constance looks bewildered. The Klingon takes her arm.

His golden Constance. She's gone astray. She's lost. Lost and wandering.

Blackout.

'Wasn't that great? She's so amazing,' says Naveena. 'So, I thought maybe you could give me

76

some idea . . . I mean, she practically said she wrote you into Alphinland, and it would be really a big thing for me – for my work – if I could figure out which character. I've narrowed it down to six, I've made a list with their different features and their special powers and their symbols and coats of arms. I think you must be the Thomas the Rhymer character because he's the only poet in the series. Though maybe he's more of a prophet – he has the second sight as his special power.'

'Thomas the what?' says Gavin coldly.

'The Rhymer,' says Naveena, faltering. 'He's in a ballad, it's well known. You can find it in Childe. The one that was stolen away by the queen of Fairyland, and rode through red blood to the knee, and wasn't seen on earth for seven years, and then when he came back he was called True Thomas because he could foretell the future. Only that isn't his name in the series, of course: he's Kluvosz of the Crystal Eye.'

'Do I look like someone with a crystal eye?' says Gavin, straight-faced. He's going to make her sweat.

'No, but . . .'

'Definitely not me,' says Gavin. 'Kluvosz of the Crystal Eye is Al Purdy.' This is the most delectable lie he can think of. Big Al with his poems about carpentry and working in a dried blood factory, being stolen away by the queen of Fairyland! If only Naveena will put that into her thesis he will be forever grateful to her. She'll work the dried blood into it, she'll make it all fit. He keeps his mouth still: he must not laugh.

'How do you know it's Al Purdy?' says Reynolds suspiciously. 'Gavvy's a liar, you do realize that,' she says to Naveena. 'He falsifies his own biography. He thinks it's funny.'

Gavin bypasses her. 'Constance told me herself. How else?' he says. 'She often discussed her characters with me.'

'But Kluvosz of the Crystal Eye didn't come into the series until Book Three,' says Naveena. '*The Wraith Returns*. That was way after . . . I mean, there aren't any documents, and you didn't know Constance any more by then.'

'We used to meet secretly,' he says. 'For years and years. In nightclub washrooms. It was a fatal attraction. We couldn't keep our hands off each other.'

'You never told me about that,' says Reynolds.

'Baby,' he says. 'There's so much I never told you.' She doesn't believe a word of this, but she can't prove he's fabricating.

'That would change everything,' says Naveena. 'I'd have to rewrite . . . I'd have to rethink my central premise. This is so . . . so crucial! But if you aren't Kluvosz, who are you?'

'Who, indeed?' he says. 'I often wonder. Maybe I'm not in Alphinland at all. Maybe Constance blotted me out.'

'She told me you were in it,' says Naveena. 'In an email, just a month ago.'

'She's going scatty,' says Reynolds. 'You can tell from that video, and it was shot even before her husband died. She's mixed everything up, she probably can't even . . .'

Naveena bypasses Reynolds, leans forward, widening her eyes at Gavin, dropping her voice to an intimate almost-whisper. 'She said you were *hidden*. Like a treasure, isn't that romantic? Like those pictures where you have to find the faces in the trees – that's how she put it.' She wants to jig and amble, she wants to lisp, she wants to suck the last slurp of essence out of his almost-voided cranium. Avaunt, wanton!

'Sorry,' he says. 'I can't help you. I've never read any of that crap.' False: he has read it. Much of it. It's only confirmed his opinion. Not only was Constance a bad poet, back when she was trying to be one, but she's a terrible prose writer as well. *Alphinland*: the title says it all. *Aphidland* would be even more accurate.

'Excuse me?' says Naveena. 'I don't think that's a very respectful way of . . . that's an elitist . . .'

'Can't you find a better use for your time than trying to decipher that turgid puddle of frog spawn?' he says. 'A fine specimen of womanhood like you going to waste, your cute butt withering on the vine. Getting any?'

'Excuse me?' says Naveena, again. It's evidently her fail-safe: the plea that she be excused.

'Any scratch for your itch. Any humpety-hump. Any sex,' says Gavin. Reynolds digs him in

79

the ribs with her elbow, hard, but he ignores her. 'There must be some jolly thriving wooer who's putting it to you. Much better a good healthy fuck for a beautiful girl like you than wasting your eyesight footnoting that drivel. Don't tell me you're a virgin! That would be preposterous!'

'Gavin!' says Reynolds. 'You can't talk to women like that any more! It isn't . . .'

'I'm not sure my private life is your concern,' says Naveena stiffly. Her lower lip is quivering, so maybe he's hit it right. But he won't let her off.

'You have no scruples about delving into mine,' he says. 'My private life! Reading my journal, rummaging in my papers, sniffing around my . . . my ex-girlfriend. It's indecent! Constance is *my* private life. Private! I don't suppose you ever thought about that!'

'Gavin, you sold those papers,' says Reynolds. 'So now it's public.'

'Bullshit!' says Gavin. 'You sold them, you double-crossing bitch!'

Naveena closes up her red tablet, not without dignity. 'I think I should go,' she says to Reynolds.

'I'm so sorry,' says Reynolds. 'He gets like that sometimes,' and the two of them are up, up, and away, ooing and oodling and so-sorrying their way down the hall. The front door shuts. Reynolds must be walking the girl to the taxi stand in front of the Holiday Inn a couple of blocks away. They'll be talking about him, no doubt. Him and his tetchy outbursts. Maybe Reynolds will be trying to repair the damage. Or maybe not.

It will be a frigid evening. Bets are that Reynolds boils him an egg and then plasters on a glitter face and goes dancing.

He let himself get angry; he shouldn't do that. It's bad for the cardiovascular. He needs to think about something else. His poem, the poem he's writing. Not in the so-called study, he can't write in there. He shuffles into the kitchen, retrieves his notebook from the drawer in the telephone table where he likes to keep it, locates a pencil, then makes his way out the garden door and down the three tiled steps to the patio and carefully across it. The patio is tiled too, and can be slippery around the pool. He achieves the deck chair he's been aiming for, lowers himself down.

The fallen leaves revolve in the eddy; maybe Maria will come in silently in her denim shorts with her skimmer and skim them out.

> *Maria skims the dying leaves.*
> *Are they souls? Is one of them my soul?*
> *Is she the Angel of Death, with her dark hair,*
> *with her darkness, come to gather me in?*
>
> *Faded wandering soul, eddying in this cold*
>   *pool,*
> *So long the accomplice of that fool, my body,*
> *Where will you land? On what bare shore?*
> *Will you be nothing but a dead leaf? Or . . .*

No. Too much like Whitman. And Maria's just a nice, ordinary high school girl making a few extra bucks, dime a dozen, nothing special. Hardly a nymphet, hardly the beckoning sapsucker from 'Death in Venice.' How about 'Death in Miami'? Sounds like a TV cop drama. Dead ends, dead ends.

Still, he likes the idea of Maria as the Angel of Death. He's about due for one of those. He'd rather see an angel at his dying moment than nothing at all.

He closes his eyes.

Now he's back in the park, with Richard the Third. He's had two paper cupfuls out of the martini thermos, he needs to pee. But it's the middle of a scene: Richard, in leather gear and carrying an outsized whip, is accosting Lady Anne, who's escorting the bier of her murdered husband. Lady Anne has been costumed in an SM fetishist outfit; while performing their venomous duet they take turns setting their boots on each other's necks. It's preposterous, but when you come to think of it, it all fits. He skewers her husbuddy, she spits at him, he offers to let her stab him, and so forth. Shakespeare is so kinky. Was ever woman in this fashion won? Check the box for Yes.

'I'm off to take a leak,' he says to Rey when Richard has finished bragging about his conquest of Lady Anne.

'It's back there by the hot dog stand,' says Reynolds. 'Shhh!'

'Real men don't piss in porta-potties,' he says. 'Real men piss in the bushes.'

'I'd better come with you,' Reynolds whispers. 'You'll get lost.'

'Leave me alone,' he says.

'At least take the flashlight.'

But he declined the flashlight as well. To strive, to seek, to find, and not to yield. He ambles off into the darkness, fumbles with his zipper. He can hardly see a thing. At least he's missed his feet: no warm socks this time. Relieved, he zips and turns, ready to navigate back. But where is he? Branches brush his face: he's lost track of the direction. Worse: the foliage may be filled with thugs, waiting to mug such a witless target. Shit! How to summon Reynolds? He refuses to wail for help. He must not panic.

A hand seizes his arm, and he wakes with a start. His heart's pounding, he's breathing quickly. *Calm down*, he tells himself. It was only a dream. It was only a larval poem.

The hand must have belonged to Reynolds. She must have followed him into the shrubbery, with the flashlight. He can't remember, but that's how it has to have been, because otherwise he wouldn't be here in this deck chair, would he? He would never have made it back.

How long was he asleep? It's twilight. *Between the dark and the daylight, When the night is beginning to lower. Just a song at twilight.* What a Victorian word; nobody says *twilight* any more. *Still to us at twilight comes Love's sweet something or other.*

Time for a drink.

'Reynolds,' he calls. No answer. She's abandoned him. Serves him right. He didn't behave very well this afternoon. But it was enjoyable, not behaving well. *You can't talk to women like that any more.* Sod that, who says he can't? He's retired, he can't be fired. He chuckles to himself.

He levers himself out of the deck chair, points himself towards the steps up to the house. Slippery on the tiles, and it's so dim out here in the yard. Crepuscular, he thinks: it sounds like a crayfish. A spiky, hard-shelled word, with pincers.

Here are the steps. Lift the right foot. He misses, cascades, impacts, abrades.

Who would have thought the old man to have so much blood in him?

'Oh my God!' says Reynolds when she finds him. 'Gavvy! I can't leave you alone for a minute! Now look what you've done!' She bursts into tears.

She's managed to drag him onto the deck chair and prop him in place with the two pillows; she's wiped off some of the blood and stuck a wet dishtowel onto his head. Now she's on the phone trying to locate an ambulance. 'You *can't* put me on hold!' she's saying. 'He's had a *stroke*, or else . . . This is supposed to be an *emergency* service! Oh *fuck*!'

Gavin lies between the pillows, with something

84

neither cold nor hot trickling down his face. It isn't twilight after all because the sun's just setting, a glorious pinkish red. The palm fronds are waving gently; the circulation pump is throbbing, or is that his pulse? Now the field darkens, and Constance is hovering in the middle of it; the old, withered Constance with the mask-like makeup job, the pale, wrinkled face he saw on the screen. She looks at him with bewilderment.

'Mr Potato Head?' she says.

But he pays no attention to that, because he's moving through the air towards her, very quickly. She doesn't get any nearer: she must be flying away from him at the same speed. *Faster*, he urges himself, and then he closes the gap and zooms right up close, then in through the black pupil of her blue, bewildered eye. Space opens up around him, so bright, and there is his Constance, young again and welcoming, the way she used to be. She smiles happily and opens her arms to him, and he enfolds her.

'You got here,' she says. 'At last. You're awake.'

DARK LADY

Every morning at breakfast Jorrie reads the obituaries in all three of the papers. Some of the write-ups make her laugh, but to the best of Tin's knowledge none of them has ever made her cry. She's not much of a sniveller, Jorrie.

She marks the noteworthy dead people with an X – two Xs if she plans to attend the funeral or the memorial service – and hands the papers across the table to Tin. She gets the real *paper* papers, delivered right to their townhouse doorstep, because according to her they skimp on the obituaries in the digital versions.

'Here's another,' she'll say. ' "Deeply missed by all who knew her," I think not! I worked with her on the Splendida campaign. She was a sick bitch.' Or else: ' "Peacefully, at home, of natural causes." I doubt that very much! I bet it was an overdose.' Or: 'Finally! Creepy Fingers! He groped me at a company dinner in the '80s with his wife sitting right beside him. He was such a lush they won't even have to embalm him.'

Tin himself would never go to the funeral of someone he dislikes, unless it's to comfort some needy survivor. The early days of AIDS were hellish; it was like the Black Death: wall-to-wall funerals, widespread numbness and glazed disbelief, survivors' guilt, a run on handkerchiefs. But for Jorrie, loathing is an incentive. She wants to tap dance on the graves, figuratively speaking; neither of them is up to the actual dancing any more, though he at least was an agile rock 'n' roller in high school.

Jorrie wasn't agile, as such; more like enthusiastic. She was rangy, she was coltish, she flung herself around, and her hair slipped out of restraint. But the gang thought it was neat when the two of them took the floor together, on account of their being twins, and he could make Jorrie look like a better dancer than she was: it was his calling from childhood to defend her when possible from her own impetuousness. Also, dancing with her gave him a short respite from whatever belle of the ball he was supposed to be going out with. He had his pick, he played the field. Best that way.

Astonishing to him how popular he'd been with the teenaged lovelies; but not surprising, when he comes to think of it. He'd had a sympathetic manner, and he'd listened to their plaints, and had not tried to disrobe them violently in parked cars, though he'd done the mandatory spate of post-dance necking so they wouldn't think they had halitosis. When extra favours were offered, including the unhooking of the pointy-titted wired bra and the peeling off of the adhesive panty-girdle, he would considerately decline.

'You'd hate yourself in the morning,' he'd counsel them. And they would have hated themselves, and cried on the telephone, and begged him not to tell; and also they would have feared pregnancy, as kids did in those days before the pill. Or they might even have hoped for it, with a view to trapping him in an early marriage – him, Martin the Magnificent! What a catch!

Nor did he ever tell boastful fibs about his dates, as lesser, pimplier youths were in the habit of doing. When the subject of his previous night's adventures would come up in the chilly, no-frilly, naked-willie boys' locker room, he would smile enigmatically, and the others would grin and nudge one another and wallop him on the arm in a brotherly fashion. It helped that he was tall and nimble, and a star at track and field. The high jump was his specialty.

What a rascal.

What a gent.

Jorrie doesn't want to tap dance on the graves alone because she doesn't want to do anything alone. If she keeps at it she can nag Tin into attending these doleful bun-fests with her, even though he says he has no desire to be bored out of his occiput by a crowd of faux-gloomy old farts gumming the crustless sandwiches and congratulating themselves on still being alive. He finds Jorrie's interest in such terminal rites of passage excessive and even morbid, and has told her so.

'I'm only being respectful,' she says, at which Tin

snorts. It's a joke: neither of them has ever made respectfulness a priority except for outward show.

'You just want to gloat,' he replies; and Jorrie snorts in her turn because this is so accurate.

'Do you think we're brittle?' she's been known to ask him. *Terrific sense of humour* is one thing, but *brittle* is another.

'Of course we're brittle,' he has answered. 'We were born brittle! But seek the bright side: you can't have much taste unless you're brittle.' He doesn't add that Jorrie fails to have much taste anyway; less, as time goes on.

'Maybe we could have been brilliant psycho-pathic murderers,' she said once, perhaps a decade ago, when they were barely in their sixties. 'We could have committed the perfect crime by killing a total stranger at random. Pushed them off a train.'

'Never too late,' Tin replied. 'It's certainly on *my* bucket list. But I'm waiting till we get cancer. If we've got to go, we'll go in style; take a few with us. De-burden the planet. More toast?'

'Don't you dare get cancer without me!'

'I won't. Cross my heart and spit. Unless it's prostate cancer.'

'Don't do that,' said Jorrie. 'I'd feel left out.'

'If I get prostate cancer,' said Tin, 'I pledge to arrange a prostate transplant for you so you can share the experience. I know a lot of guys who wouldn't mind heaving their prostates out the window about now. They could at least get a good night's sleep: dispense with the pee parade.'

Jorrie grinned. 'Thanks a bundle,' she said. 'I've always wanted a prostate. One more thing to whine about in the golden years. Think the donor might like to throw in the whole scrotum?'

'That remark,' said Tin, 'is lacking in fastidiousness. As you intended. More coffee?'

Because they're twins they can be who they really are with each other, a thing they haven't managed very well with anyone else. Even when they're putting on a front, they fool only outside people: to each other they're transparent as guppies, they can see each other's innards. Or that's their story; though, as Tin is well aware – having once had a lover with an aquarium – even guppies have their opacities.

He gazes fondly at Jorrie as she frowns at the obituaries through her crimson-framed reading glasses; or frowns as much as she is able to, given the Botox. In recent years – in recent decades – Jorrie has developed the slightly pop-eyed expression of someone who's had too much work done. There are hair issues as well. At least he's been able to stop her from dyeing it jet black: way too Undead with her present-day skin tone, which is lacking in glow despite the tan-coloured foundation and the sparkly bronze mineral-elements powder she so assiduously applies, the poor deluded wretch.

'You're only as old as you feel,' she says too frequently, while trying to talk Tin into some absurdity – rumba classes, watercolour painting holidays, ruinous fads such as spinning. He cannot picture himself on a stationary bicycle, wearing Spandex tights, whirring away like a sawmill and further destroying his wizened crotch. He cannot picture himself on a bicycle of any sort. Painting was a non-starter: if he were going to do that, why would he want to do it in a group of whinnying amateurs? As for the rumba, you have to be able to swivel your coccyx, a skill he lost around the time he gave up on sex.

'Exactly,' he replies. 'I feel two thousand. I am older than the rocks among which I sit.'

'What rocks? I don't see any rocks. You're sitting on the sofa!'

'It's a quotation,' he says. 'A paraphrase. Walter Pater.'

'Oh, you and your quotations! Not everyone lives in quotation marks, you know.'

Tin sighs. Jorrie is not a wide reader, preferring historical romances about the Tudors and the Borgias to anything more substantial. 'Like the vampire, I have been dead many times,' he cites to himself, though he doesn't wish to alarm her by saying it out loud: an alarmed Jorrie is always a lot of work. She wouldn't be afraid of vampires as such: being rash and curious, she'd be the first into the forbidden crypt. But she wouldn't like the thought of Tin turning into one, or turning into anyone other than her idea of him.

Meanwhile, she's firmly bent on turning into someone else herself. She does not come up to her own standards. Her only superstitions have to do with the labels on expensive cosmetics. Jorrie actually believes the deceitful come-hither labels – the plumpings, the firmings, the unwrinklings, the returning of youthful dews, the hints of immortality – despite having been in advertising herself, a vocation guaranteed to take the bloom off ornamental adjectives. There are so many things in life about which she ought to know better but does not, the art of makeup being one of them. He has to keep reminding her not to halt the sparkly bronze procedure halfway down her neck: otherwise her head will look sewed on.

The hair compromise he finally agreed to is a white strip on the left side – geriatric punk, he'd whispered to himself – with, recently, the addition of an arresting scarlet patch. The total image is that of an alarmed skunk trapped in the floodlights after an encounter with a ketchup bottle. He crosses his fingers about that blood-coloured blotch, and hopes he will not be accused of elder bashing.

Gone are the days when Jorrie – once known for her sultry gypsy image and her vivid African prints and clanky ethnic jewellery – could pull off any fashion whim that caught her eye. She's lost the knack, though she's kept her flamboyant habits. *Mutton dressed as Spam*, he's longed to say to her from time to time, though he hasn't said it. Instead he's clamped himself together and held himself back, and said it about other women to make her laugh.

He does usually manage to steer her away from the steeper and more lethal precipices. There was the interlude with the nose ring, back in the '90s: she'd sprung the tacky doodad on him without prior warning, and asked him point-blank what he thought. He'd had to sew his mouth shut, though he'd done some hypocritical nodding and murmuring. She'd jettisoned the tawdry accessory once she'd caught a cold and practically torn her nostril off when her handkerchief got snagged on the ring.

After that came the threat of a tongue stud, but luckily she'd consulted him first. What had he said? 'You want the inside of your mouth to look like a biker's jacket?' Maybe not: too much risk of the answer being yes. Certainly he wouldn't have informed her that some men view such baubles as blowjob advertisements: that might have been an incentive. A health warning: 'You could die of septicemia of the tongue?' Health warnings don't work with her, as she considers them a challenge: her superior immune system will surely crush any microbe the invisible world may toss her way.

More likely he'd said, 'You'd sound like Daffy Duck and you'd spit all over everyone. Not attractive, in my books. Anyway, the stud wave has passed. Only stockbrokers get them any more.' That at least made her giggle.

It's best not to overreact to her. Push, and she pushes back. He hasn't forgotten her childhood tantrums and the fights she used to get into, flailing her long arms ineffectually as the other children laughed and jeered her on. He'd watch, almost in tears himself: he couldn't extricate her, confined to the boys' side of the schoolyard as he was.

So he avoids confrontation. Languor is a more efficient method of control.

The twins were christened Marjorie and Martin, at a time when parents thought alliterative names for children were snappy, and were costumed alike in miniature overalls. Even their mother – not the sharpest knife in the drawer – realized that it would not do to stick Martin into a dress because he might turn into a pansy, her term. So there they are, aged two, in their matching sailor suits and their tiny sailor hats, holding hands and squinting into the sun with their elvish, lopsided smiles: his skewed up at the left, hers at the right. You can't tell whether they're boys or girls, but you have to admit they're delicious. Behind them is a man's body in a uniform, it being the war: their father with the top part of his head cut off, which was shortly to happen to him in reality. Their mother used to weep buckets over that photo when she'd been drinking. She viewed it as a premonition: if only she'd held the camera straight, Weston's head would not have been cropped like that and the fatal explosion would never have happened.

Gazing at their past selves, Jorrie and Tin feel a tenderness they seldom display to anyone in the present. They'd like to hug those scrumptious little scamps, those yellowing, fading echoes. They'd like to assure the pint-sized seafarers that, though their voyage through time is about to take a turn for the worse and will remain worse for a while, it will all work out in the end. Or near the end; which is, let's face it, where they are now.

Because, voilà, here they are together again, full circle. A few inner wounds, a few scars, a few abrasions, but still standing. Still Jorrie and Tin, who'd rebelled at being nicknamed Marje and Marv, and who'd taken to using their last syllables as their real, secret names, known to them alone. Jorrie and Tin, in revolt against society's plans for them: no white weddings, for instance. Jorrie and Tin, who'd refused to knuckle under.

Again, that's their story. Privately Tin can recall quite a few mortifying though satisfying knucklings-under he has submitted to, in the wild nighttime shrubberies of Cherry Beach and elsewhere, but no need to sully the ears of Jorrie with those. At least he never ran into any of his students while nervously prowling the midnight pathways. At least he never got mugged. At least he never got caught.

'So heavenly,' says Tin, smiling at the photograph, which is framed in fumed oak and resides on the dining room wall above the art deco buffet, a steal when Tin acquired it forty years ago. 'Too bad our hair went dark.'

'Oh, I don't know,' says Jorrie. 'Blond is overrated.'

'It's coming back,' says Tin. 'The '50s are having

a moment again, have you noticed? It's the Marilyn thing.'

He does not believe in the '50s moment as portrayed recently on screens large and small. While they were going on, the '50s seemed like normal life, but now they've become the olden days: fodder for television shows in which the colours are wrong – too clean, too pastel – and the crinolines are too numerous. Hardly anyone had a ponytail in real life, nor did the adult men always wear tailored suits, with fedoras tilted at a jaunty angle and white pocket handkerchiefs starched into triangles.

They did smoke pipes, however, though pipes were fading even then. On the weekends they mooched around in moccasins and jeans – primitive jeans, but jeans. They read their newspapers while sitting in their Naugahyde lounge chairs with matching hassocks, drinking a relaxing Manhattan and smoking fit to kill; they lovingly washed and waxed their sharp-finned and over-chromed gas-guzzler cars; they mowed their lawns with push mowers. Or that's what the fathers of the twins' friends did. Tin has a spot of wistfulness in his heart about the bulbous lounge chairs and the shiny, lethal cars and the cumbersome push lawn mowers. If their own father had lived, would things have been better for Tin himself?

No. Things would not have been better, they would have been horrific. He would have had to go fishing: hoick fish up out of the water and assassinate them while uttering manly grunts. Crawl under cars with wrenches, saying things like 'muffler.' Be slapped on the back and told his dad was proud of him. Fat chance.

'Though Ernest Hemingway's mother did it,' said Jorrie.

'Excuse me? Did what?'

'Put Ernie in a dress.'

'Right.'

The twins often revert to a previous point in their ongoing conversation, though they know better than to do that if anyone else is around. It's annoying; not to them, they can pick up each other's dropped stitches, but it can make other people feel excluded. Or else – nowadays – it can make other people feel they are missing a cog or two.

'And then he blew his head off,' said Tin. 'Which I personally have no intention of doing.'

'Better not,' said Jorrie. 'It would make such a mess. Brain salad all over the walls. Leap off a bridge, if the urge comes over you.'

'Thanks a bundle,' says Tin. 'I'll keep that suggestion in mind.'

'Any time.'

That's how they go on: like a '30s wisecrackers' movie. The Marxes. Hepburn and Tracy. Nick and Nora Charles, minus the chain-drinking of martinis, which Jorrie and Tin can't handle any more. They skate over the surfaces, chilled and thin and shiny; they avoid the depths. It wears Tin out a bit, their doubles act. Possibly Jorrie feels the same, but they both understand that they have to keep up their ends.

Tin turned into a pansy anyway, which the twins purport to regard as a hilarious booby trap sprung on their mother, even though she was dead by the time he stopped concealing his pansyhood. The role betrayal should have gone the other way round – Jorrie having been the child gender-crosser as far as the sailor outfits went – but she could never make the jump to lesbianism because she didn't like other women much.

Why would she, considering their mother? Not only was Mother Maeve dumb as a sack of hammers, but as time went by and her grief over their exploded father failed to abate, she'd morphed into a binge drinker who'd robbed the twins' piggy banks for booze money. She also brought home oafs and thugs, for the purpose – said Tin, when describing these episodes at dinner parties, much later – 'for the purpose of *sexual congress.*' Too funny! When the twins would hear the front door opening, they'd skin out the back. Or they'd hide in the cellar, then creep upstairs once things went quiet to spy on the congressional goings-on; or they'd eavesdrop if the bedroom door was closed.

What had they felt about all that when they were children? They can't really recall, since they've papered over the too-frequently-repeated primal scene with so many layers of hare-brained and possibly mythological narration that the original simple outlines have been obscured. (Did the dog really run outside with a large black brassiere in its mouth and bury it in the backyard? Did they even have a dog? Did Oedipus solve the riddle of the Sphinx? Did Jason make off with the Golden Fleece? It's the same sort of question.)

For Tin, the anecdotal family humour has long ceased to be amusing. Their mother died early, and not in a good way. Not that anyone dies in a good way, Tin footnotes to himself, but there are degrees. Being hit by a truck after closing time while jaywalking blinded with mournful tears was not a good way. Though it was quick. And it meant that their life was free of the oafs and thugs by the time they went to university. *Malum quidem nullum esse sine aliquo bono*, Tin noted in the journal he was sporadically keeping then. Every cloud has a silver lining.

Two of the oafs had the nerve to come to the funeral, which may explain Jorrie's fixation on funerals. She still feels she shouldn't have let those assholes get away with it: turning up at the grave side, pretending to be sad, telling the twins what a fine and kind-hearted woman their mother had been, what a good friend. 'Friend, like shit! All they wanted was an easy lay!' she'd raged. She ought to have called them on it; she ought to have made a scene. Punched them in the nose.

Tin's view is that maybe these men really were sad. Is it so out of the question that they could actually have loved Mother Maeve, in one or two or even three senses of the word? *Amor, voluptas, caritas.* But he's kept that view to himself: to express it would be too irritating to Jorrie, especially if he includes the Latin. Jorrie has scant patience with anything Latin. It's a part of his life she's never been able to grasp. Why waste your life on a bunch of fusty, forgotten scribblers in a dead language? He was so smart, he was so talented, he could have been . . . (A long list of things he could have been would follow, none of them in any way possible.)

So best not to hit that button.

'Oafs and thugs' was a phrase they'd lifted from their eighth-grade principal who'd harangued the whole school about the dangers of turning into oafs and thugs, especially if you threw snowballs with rocks in them or wrote swear words on the blackboard. 'Oafs vs. Thugs' became, briefly, a schoolyard game invented by Tin in his popular, pre-pansy period. It was something like Capture the Flag and was played only on the boys' side of the playground. Girls could not be oafs and thugs, said Tin: only boys, which made Jorrie resentful.

It was she who came up with the idea of calling Mother Maeve's on-again, off-again gentleman callers – 'or you could say, in-again, out-again,' Tin would quip later – the Oafs and Thugs. That ruined the game for Tin; no doubt it contributed to his pansyhood, he decided later. 'Don't blame *me*,' said Jorrie. 'I didn't invite them home.'

'Darling, I'm not blaming you, I'm thanking you,' Tin said. 'I'm deeply grateful.' Which, by that time – after he'd sorted out a few things – he really was.

Their mother wasn't drunk all the time. Her binges took place only on weekends: she had an underpaid secretarial job that she needed to make ends meet, the military widow's pension being so minuscule. And she did love the twins in her own way.

'At least she wasn't too violent,' Jorrie would say. 'Though she got carried away.'

'Everyone spanked their kids then. Everyone got carried away.' Indeed it was a point of honour to compare your slice of corporal punishment with those of other children, and to exaggerate. Slippers, belts, rulers, hairbrushes, ping-pong paddles: those were the parental weapons of choice. It made the young twins sad that they didn't have a father to administer such beatings, only ineffectual Mother Maeve, whom they could reduce to tears by pretending to be mortally injured, whom they could tease with relative impunity, from whom they could run away. There were two of them and only one of her, so they ganged up.

'I suppose we were heartless,' Jorrie would say.

'We were disobedient. We talked back. We were out of control. But adorable, you have to grant that.'

'We were brats. Heartless little brats. We showed no mercy,' Jorrie sometimes adds. Is it regret, or bragging?

On the cusp of adolescence, Jorrie had a painful experience with one of the oafs – a sneak attack from which Tin failed to defend her, being asleep at the time. That has weighed on him. It must have messed up her life in regards to men, though most likely her life would have been messed up anyway. She deals with this incident now by making fun of it – 'I was ravished by a troll!' – but she hasn't always managed that. She was downright sullen on the subject of rape in the early '70s when so many women were going on the rampage, but she seems to have got over that by now.

Molesting isn't everything, in Tin's view. He himself never got molested by the oafs, but his relationships with men were just as scrambled, and if anything more so. Jorrie said he had a problem with love: he conceptualizes it too much. He said Jorrie didn't conceptualize it enough. That was back when love was still a topic of conversation for them.

'We should put all of our lovers in a blender,' Jorrie said once. 'Mix them up, average them out.' Tin said she had a brutalist way of putting things.

The truth is, thinks Tin, that the twins never loved anyone except each other. Or they didn't love anyone unconditionally. Their other loves had many conditions.

'Look who just croaked,' says Jorrie now. 'Big Dick Metaphor!'

'That nickname could apply to a lot of men,' says

Tin. 'Though I assume you mean someone in particular. I can see your ears twitching, so he must be important to you.'

'Three guesses,' says Jorrie. 'Hint: He was at the Riverboat a lot, that summer when I was doing their bookkeeping, volunteer, part-time.'

'Because you wanted to hang out with the bohemians,' said Tin. 'I do have a vague recollection. So who? Blind Sonny Terry?'

'Don't be silly,' says Jorrie. 'He was decrepit even then.'

'I give up. I never went there much, it was too fetid for me. Those folksingers made a fetish of not bathing.'

'That's untrue,' says Jorrie. 'Not all of them. I know it for a fact. No fair giving up!'

'Who ever said I was fair? Not you.'

'You should be able to read my mind.'

'Oh, a challenge. All right: Gavin Putnam. That self-styled poet you were so nuts about.'

'You knew all along!'

Tin sighs. 'He was so derivative, him and his poetry both. Sentimental trash. Quite gruesomely putrid.'

'The early ones were very good,' says Jorrie defensively. 'The sonnets, except they weren't sonnets. The Dark Lady ones.'

Tin has slipped up, he's been maladroit. How could he have forgotten that some of Gavin Putnam's early poems had been about Jorrie? Or so she'd claimed. She'd been thrilled by that. 'I'm a Muse,'

103

she'd announced when the Dark Lady suite first appeared in print, or in what passed for print among the poets: a stapled-together mimeo magazine they put out themselves and sold to one another for a dollar. *The Dirt*, they'd called it, in a bid for grittiness.

Tin found it touching that Jorrie was so excited by these poems. He hadn't seen much of her that season. She had, to put it mildly, a hyperactive social life, due no doubt to the alacrity with which she flung herself into bed, whereas he'd been living in a two-roomer over a barbershop on Dundas and having a quiet sexual identity crisis while toiling away at his doctoral thesis.

This was a solid enough but not honestly very inspired re-examination of the cleaner and more presentable epigrams of Martial, though what really drew him to Martial was his no-nonsense attitude towards sex, so much less complicated than that of Tin's own era. For Martial, there was no romantic pussy-footing, no idealization of Woman as having a higher spiritual calling: Martial would have laughed his head off at that! And no taboos: everyone did everything with everyone: slaves, boys, girls, whores, gay, straight, pornography, scatology, wives, young, middle-aged, old, front, back, mouth, hand, cock, beautiful, ugly, and downright repulsive. Sex was a given, like food, and as such was to be relished when excellent and derided when substandard; it was an entertainment, like the

theatre, and could thus be reviewed like a performance. Chastity was not the primary virtue, for
men or for women either, but certain forms of
friendship and generosity and tenderness did get
top marks. His contemporaries labelled Martial as
unusually sunny and good-natured, nor did his
scathing, acerbic wit do anything to diminish that
perception. His criticisms were not directed at indi-
viduals, he claimed, but at types; though Tin had
his doubts about that.

But a thesis was not about why you appreciated
your subject: in academia, he'd come to understand, that kind of thing should be reserved for
social chit-chat. You had to cook up something
more focused. Tin's central hypothesis revolved
around the difficulties of satire in an age lacking
in shared moral standards, which Martial's age did,
in spades: he'd moved to Rome when Nero was in
power. Indeed, was Martial a true satirist or just
a smutty gossip, as some commentators had
claimed? Tin intended to defend his hero against
this charge: there was so much more to Martial,
he would say, than cocks and boy-fucking and sluts
and fart jokes! Though he would not of course use
those crude vernacular terms in his thesis. And
he'd do his own translations, updating the diction
to fit Martial's well-crafted slang, though the filth-
iest of the epigrams were prudently to be avoided:
their time had not yet come.

'You imitate youth, Laetinus, by dyeing your hair.
Presto! Yesterday a swan, you're now a raven. But

105

you can't fool everyone: Proserpina spots your grey hair. And she'll yank your stupid disguise right off your head!' This was the tone he sought in his translations – contemporary, punchy, not stilted. He used to spend a week over one or two lines. But he doesn't do that any more, because who cares?

He'd received a grant for his doctoral studies, though it wasn't large. Jorrie told him Classics was surely going to disappear very soon, and then how would he earn his living? He should have gone into Design, because he would have made a killing. But, said Tin, a killing was exactly what he didn't want to make because to make a killing you had to kill, and he lacked the killer instinct.

'Money talks,' said Jorrie, who despite her bohemian leanings wanted to have lots of it. She had no intention of toiling away in some tedious, soul-grinding factotum job, overworked and underpaid and a prey to oafs and thugs, the way their mother had. Her nascent vision involved flashy cars and vacations in the Caribbean and a closetful of figure-hugging fabrics. She hadn't articulated that vision yet, not out loud, but Tin could see it coming.

'Yes,' said Tin. 'Money does talk, but it has a limited vocabulary.' Martial could have said that. Possibly Martial did say it. He would have to check. *Aureo hamo piscari.* To fish with a golden hook.

The barbers on the ground floor of Tin's building were three elderly misanthropic Italian brothers who did not know what the world was coming to except that it was bad. The shop had a rack of girlie magazines featuring police stories and pictures of hookers with enormous bosoms, which was what men were supposed to like. These magazines made Tin feel queasy – the spectre of Mother Maeve hovered rakishly above anything to do with black brassieres – but he got his hair cut there anyway as a goodwill gesture and leafed through the magazines while he waited. It didn't do to be too openly gay then, and anyway he was still deciding; and the Italian barbers were his landlords and needed to be buttered up.

He'd had to make it clear to them, however, that Jorrie was his twin sister, not a girlfriend of loose character. Despite their stash of lurid magazines, which they probably viewed as professional equipment, they were puritanical about any unsanctioned goings-on in their rental accommodations. They thought Tin was a fine, upstanding scholarly youth, called him The Professor, and kept asking him when he was going to get married. 'I'm too poor,' Tin would say. Or 'I'm waiting for the right girl.' Sage nods from the barbershop trio: both excuses were acceptable to them.

So when Jorrie would arrive on her infrequent visits, the Italian barbers would wave to her through the window and smile in their triste way. How nice that The Professor had such an exemplary sister. It was what a family should be like.

★   ★   ★

When the Dark Lady issue of *The Dirt* came out, Jorrie could hardly wait to share her Musehood with Tin. She'd galloped up the stairs, waving her hot-off-the-mimeo *Dirt*, and plumped herself down in his wicker basket chair.

'Look at this!' she'd said, thrusting the stapled pages at him while sweeping back her long dark hair with one hand. She had a swatch of red-and-ochre block-printed cloth wound around her trim waist, and a necklace of – What were those? Cow's teeth? – dangling over her scoop-necked peasant blouse. Her eyes were shining, her bangles were jangling. 'Seven poems! About *me*!'

She was so guileless. She was so avid. If Tin hadn't been her brother, if he'd been straight, he would have run a mile; but away from her or towards her? She was faintly terrifying. She wanted it all. She wanted them all. She wanted experiences. In Tin's already jaded view, experiences were what you got when you couldn't get what you wanted, but Jorrie had always been more optimistic than him.

'You can't be *in* a poem,' he'd said, crossly, because this infatuation of hers was worrying him. She was bound to cut herself on it: she was a clumsy girl, not skilful with edged tools. 'Poems are made of words. They aren't boxes. They aren't houses. Nobody is *in* them, really.'

'Nitpicker. You know what I mean.'

Tin sighed, and at her insistence he sat down at his rickety third-hand pedestal table with the mug of tea he'd just made for himself and read the poems. 'Jorrie,' he said. 'These poems are not about you.'

Her face fell. 'Yes, they are! They have to be! It's definitely my . . .'

'They're only about part of you.' The lower part, he did not say.

'What?'

He sighed again. 'You're more than this. You're better than this.' How could he put it? *You're not just a piece of cheap tail?* No, too hurtful. 'He's left out your, your . . . your mind.'

'It's you who keeps on about *mens sana in corpore sano*,' she said. 'Sane mind in a sound body, both together. I know what you're thinking: that this is just about the sex. But that's the *point*! I represent – I mean, she, the Dark Lady, she represents a healthy, down-to-earth rejection of the false, wispy, sentimental . . . It's like D. H. Lawrence, that's what he says. That's what Gav *loves* about me!' And on she went.

'So, *in Venus veritas?*' said Tin.

'What?'

Oh, Jorrie, he thought. You don't understand. Men like that get tired of you once they've had you. You're in for a fall. Martial, VII: 76: *It's only pleasure, it isn't love.*

He was right about the fall. It was fast, and it was hard. Jorrie didn't go into the details – she was too stunned – but what he pieced together at the time was that there was a live-in girlfriend, and she'd walked in on Jorrie and the Earthy Poet while they were disporting themselves on the sacrosanct domestic mattress.

'I shouldn't have laughed,' said Jorrie. 'That was rude. But it was such a farce! And she looked so shocked! It must have seemed really mean to her, me laughing. I just couldn't help it.'

The girlfriend, whose name was Constance ('How prissy!' Jorrie snorted) and who was the embodiment of that very same wispiness and sentimentality so despised by the Poetaster – this Constance had gone white as a sheet, even whiter than she already was, and had said something about the rent money. Then she'd turned and walked out. Not even stomped: scuttled, like a mouse. Which just went to show how wispy she was. Jorrie herself would have done some hair-pulling and slapping at the very least, she claimed.

She had felt the departure of Constance ought to be a cause for celebration – the forces of vitality and life and the truths of the flesh had triumphed over those of abstractness and stagnation – but that had not been the outcome. No sooner had the Half-Rhymer been barred from the moon-maiden's chamber than he began caterwauling to get back in: he yowled for his vaporous Truelove like an infant deprived of its nipple.

Jorrie was less than tactful about this excess of whimpering and regret – the words *pussy-whipped* and *limp prick* were thrown about by her with perhaps too much abandon – so her expulsion was inevitable. According to Mr Poetaster, the imbroglio was suddenly all her fault. She'd tempted him. She'd seduced him. She was the viper in the orchard.

There was something to that, Tin supposed; Jorrie had been the huntress, not the hunted. But still, it takes two to tango. The Minor Minnesinger could have said no.

Short form, Jorrie had told him to shut up about Constance, and they'd had a fight about it, and Jorrie had been flung down onto the sewer grating of life like a used condom. No one had ever treated her like that before! His own heart wrenched with pity, Tin had tried to distract her – a movie, a drink, not that he could afford many of either – but she was not to be placated. There were no hysterics, no visible tears, but moping set in, followed by an ill-concealed, smouldering rage.

Would she step over the edge? Would she confront the poet in public, scream, hit? She was angry enough for that. A cruel joke had been played on her, since her Musehood, once a source of pride and joy, had become a torment: the Dark Lady non-sonnets were now enshrined in Gavin's first thin collection, *Heavy Moonlight,* and they sneered at Jorrie from its pages, mockingly, reproachfully.

Worse, these poems accumulated gravitas as Gavin clambered up the ladder of acclaim, collecting the first in what was to be a string of minor but nonetheless career-enhancing prizes. Those early poems had been augmented by others,

111

different in tenor: the lover recognized the mere fleshliness, indeed the grossness and fickleness of the Dark Lady, and returned to the pursuit of his pallidly glowing Truelove. But that ice-eyed paragon had declined to forgive the heartbroken lover, despite his overcrafted and bathos-heavy and subsequently published pleas.

These later poems did not reflect well on Jorrie. She'd had to look up the word *trull* in Tin's *Dictionary of Slang and Unconventional English*. It was wounding.

Jorrie went on a retaliatory stud-gathering riff, plucking lovers like daisies from every wayside ditch and parking lot, then casting them carelessly aside. Not that such behaviour ever has any effect on the one who's spurned you, as Tin knows from his own experience: if it's gone as far as that, they don't care how much you debase yourself to get back at them. You could fuck a headless goat and it would make no earthly difference.

But then the wheels of the seasons turned, and tender-fingered Dawn chalked up three hundred and sixty-two pink morning entrances, and then another year's worth of them, and another; and the moon of desire rose and set and rose again, and so on and so forth; and the Poet of the Sprightly Prick receded into the dim and misty distance. Or so Tin hoped, for Jorrie's sake.

Though it seems he has not receded. All you have to do is kick the bucket and you're right back in the memory spotlight, thinks Tin. He hopes the lingering shade of Gavin Putnam will prove a friendly one, supposing it is indeed lingering.

Now he says, 'Right, the Dark Lady sonnets. I remember them. Absinthe makes the tart grow fonder, but verse is cheaper: it certainly hooked *you*. You used to stagger into my barbershop enclave reeking of gutter sex, you stank like a week-old whitefish. You were cross-eyed over that dickhead the whole summer. I never could see it, myself.'

'Because he never would show it to you,' says Jorrie. She laughs at her own joke. 'It was well worth the sight. You'd have been jealous!'

'Just don't claim you were in love with him,' says Tin. 'It was low, sordid lust. You were out of your mind on hormones.' He understands that kind of thing, he's gone through similar infatuations. They're always comic in the eyes of others.

Jorrie sighs. 'He had a great body,' she says. 'While it lasted.'

'Never mind,' says Tin. 'It can't be much of a great body any more, since it's a corpse.' The two of them snicker.

'Will you come with me?' says Jorrie. 'To the memorial service? Have a gawk?' She's putting on a jaunty air, but she fools neither of them.

'I don't think you should go. It would be bad for you,' says Tin.

'Why? I'm curious. Maybe a few of his wives will be there.'

113

'You're too competitive,' says Tin. 'You still can't believe some other woman elbowed you out and you didn't win the prize pig. Face it, you two were never meant for each other.'

'Oh, I know *that*,' says Jorrie. 'We burnt out. Too hot to last. I just want to see the double chins on the wives. And maybe What's-her-name will be there. Wouldn't that be a hoot?'

Oh please, thinks Tin. Not What's-her-name! Jorrie's still so knotted up over Constance, the live-in girlfriend whose mattress she'd defiled, that she won't even pronounce her name.

Unfortunately Constance W. Starr has not faded into obscurity as her wispiness ought to have dictated. Instead she's become obscenely famous, though for a ludicrous reason: as C. W. Starr, she's the author of a brain-damaged fantasy series called Alphinland. Alphinland has made such a vast shit-load of money that Gavin the Relatively Penurious Poet must have been revolving in his grave decades before he actually died. He must have cursed the day he allowed himself to be led astray by Jorrie's overheated estrogens.

As the Starr star has risen, so has Jorrie's own star faded: she no longer twinkles, she no longer monkey-shines. The C. W. Starr feeding frenzy generates long and clamorous lineups in book-stores on the publication days of new books, with children and adults both male and female dressed up like the villainous Milzreth of the Red Hand, or the blank-faced Skinkrot the Time-Swallower, or Frenosia of the Fragrant Antennae, the insect-eyed goddess with her entourage of indigo and emerald magic bees. All of this hoopla must get right up Jorrie's nose, though she's never confessed to having noticed.

From the few times he'd accompanied Jorrie to the Riverboat, Tin has a vague memory of Alphinland's unlikely genesis. The saga began as a clutch of ersatz fairy tales of the sword-and-sorcery variety, published in two-bit magazines of the kind featuring semi-naked girls on the covers being leered at by Lizard Men. The Riverboat hangers-on – especially the poets – used to make fun of Constance, but he guesses they don't do that much any more. Money fishes with a golden hook.

Of course he's read the Alphinland series, or parts of it: he felt he owed it to Jorrie. In case she ever asks for his critical opinion, he can loyally tell her how bad it is. And of course Jorrie has read it too. She'd have been overcome by jealous curiosity, she wouldn't have been able to restrain herself. But neither of them has admitted to having so much as cracked a spine.

Happily, thinks Tin, Constance W. Starr is said to be somewhat of a recluse; more so since her husband died, a newspaper obituary Jorrie had passed over in silence. In a perfect world, C. W. Starr won't turn up at the funeral.

Odds of a perfect world? One in a million.

★   ★   ★

'If this Putnam funeral is going to be all about Constance W. Starr,' says Tin, 'I am definitely vetoing it. Because it will not be, as you say, a hoot. It will be very destructive for you.' What he doesn't say: *You'll lose, Jorrie. The same way you lost the last time. She's got the high ground.*

'It isn't about her, I promise!' says Jorrie. 'That was more than fifty years ago! How could it be about her when I can't even remember her *name*? Anyway, she was so wispy! She was such a *pipsqueak*! I could have blown her over with a *sneeze*!' She gasps with laughter.

Tin considers. Such bluster, in Jorrie, is a sign of vulnerability; therefore, she needs his support. 'Very well. I'll go,' he says, with unfeigned reluctance. 'But I'm not having a happy feeling about this.'

'Shake on it like a man,' says Jorrie. The phrase is from a Western matinee movie routine they used to do when they were kids.

'Where is the dreaded affair?' Tin asks on the morning of the memorial service. It's a Sunday, the one day Jorrie is permitted to cook. Mostly her cooking is a matter of opening takeout containers, but when she gets ambitious there will be smashed crockery, swearing, and incinerations. Today is a bagel day, praise the lord. And the coffee's perfect because Tin made it himself.

'The Enoch Turner Schoolhouse,' says Jorrie. 'It offers a gracious atmosphere reminiscent of a bygone era.'

116

'Who wrote that?' says Tin. 'Charles Dickens?'

'I did,' says Jorrie. 'Years ago. Right after I went freelance. They wanted an archaic tone.' She hadn't exactly gone freelance, as Tin recalls: there had been a civil war at the advertising company and she'd been on the defeated side, having unfortunately told her antagonists what she really thought of them. However, she'd collected a reasonable parachute, which had enabled her to go into real-estate speculation. That had kept her in designer foot-fetish objects and vulgar, overpriced winter vacations until one of her menopause-era lovers made off with her savings. Then she was overleveraged, had to sell in a down market, and lost a crock of gold, so what could Tin do but offer her a refuge? His house is big enough for the two of them, just barely: Jorrie takes up a lot of space.

'I hope this schoolhouse venue isn't a hotbed of kitsch,' says Tin.

'Do we have a choice?'

After ferreting through her closet, Jorrie holds up three of her outfits on hangers so Tin can evaluate them. It's one of his demands – one of his requests – on the days when he agrees to attend events with her. 'What's the verdict?' she says.

'Not the shocking pink.'

'But it's Chanel – an original!' Both of them frequent vintage clothing stores, though only the upmarket end. They've kept their figures, at least: Tin can still wear the elegant three-piece '30s ensembles he's sported for some decades. He even has a lacquer cane.

'That doesn't matter,' he says. 'No one's going to read the label, and you are not Jackie Kennedy. Shocking pink would draw undue attention.'

Jorrie wants to draw undue attention: that's the whole idea! If any of Gavin's wives are there, and especially if What's-her-name shows up, she longs to have them notice her the moment she walks in. But she backs down, because if she doesn't, she knows Tin won't come with her.

'And not the faux-leopard stole either.'

'But they're in fashion again!'

'Exactly. They're far too in fashion. Don't pout, you look like a camel.'

'So you're voting for the grey. May I say *yawn*?'

'You may say it, but that won't change reality. The grey has a beautiful cut. Understated. Maybe with a scarf?'

'To cover up my scraggy neck?'

'You said it, not me.'

'I can always depend on you,' says Jorrie. She means it: Tin saves her from herself, on those occasions when she takes his advice. By the time she walks out the door she'll be confident in the knowledge that she's presentable. The scarf he chooses for her is muted Chinese red: it will perk up the complexion.

'How do I look?' says Jorrie, turning before him.

'Stupendous,' says Tin.

'I love it when you lie for me.'

'I'm not lying,' says Tin. *Stupendous: causing astonishment or wonder. From the gerund of stupere, to be astounded.* That about covers it. After a certain moment, there is only so much a beautifully cut grey outfit can redeem.

At last they are ready to set forth. 'You'll have to wear your warmest coat,' says Tin. 'It's frore out there.'

'What?'

'It's very cold. Twenty below, that's the predicted high. Glasses?' He wants her to be able to read the program for herself, without pestering him to do it for her.

'Yes, yes. Two pairs.'

'Handkerchief?'

'Don't worry,' says Jorrie. 'I don't intend to cry. Not over that bastard!'

'If you do, you can't use my sleeve,' says Tin.

She sticks out her chin, the flag of battle. 'I won't need it.'

Tin insists on driving: being in a car with Jorrie at the wheel is too much like Russian roulette for him. Sometimes she's fine, but last week she ran over a raccoon. She claimed it was dead already, though Tin doubts that. 'It shouldn't have been out anyway,' she said, 'in all that weather.'

They proceed cautiously through the icy streets in Tin's carefully preserved 1995 Peugeot, tires squeaking on the snow. The accumulation from the day before still hasn't been cleared away, though

119

at least it was only a blizzard, not an ice storm like the one that hit over Christmas. Three days in the Cabbagetown house without heat or light had been trying, since Jorrie viewed the storm as a personal insult and complained about its unfairness. How could the weather be doing this to her?

There's a parking lot north of King – Tin has taken care to identify it online, since the last thing he needs is Jorrie issuing false directions – but it's a surprisingly tight squeeze: several cars behind them are turned away. Tin extracts Jorrie from the front seat and steadies her as she slides on the ice. Why didn't he nix those spike-heeled boots? She could have a serious fall and fracture something – a hip, a leg – and if that happens she'll be propped up in bed for months while he carries trays and empties bedpans. Grasping her firmly by the arm, he propels her along King Street, then south on Trinity.

'Look at all the people,' she says. 'Who the hell are they?' It's true, there's quite a crowd heading to the Enoch Turner Schoolhouse. Many of them are what you'd expect – the geezer generation, like Tin and Jorrie – but oddly enough there are quite a few young ones. Could it be that Gavin Putnam is now a youth cult? What an unpleasant notion, thinks Tin.

Jorrie presses closer to his side, her head swivelling like a periscope. 'I don't see her,' she whispers. 'She's not here!'

'She won't come,' says Tin. 'She's afraid you'll

call her What's-her-name.' Jorrie laughs, but not very heartily. She doesn't have a plan, thinks Tin: she's charging in blindly the way she always does. It's a good thing he's here with her.

Inside, the room is crowded and overly warm, though it does have a gracious atmosphere reminiscent of a bygone era. There's a subdued gabble, as of distant waterfowl. Tin helps Jorrie out of her coat, struggles out of his own, and settles back for the duration.

Jorrie elbows him, emits a sizzling whisper: 'That must be the widow, in the blue. Crap, she looks about twelve. Gav was such a perv.' Tin tries to see but fails to spot the likely candidate. How can she tell, from the back?

Now there's a hush: a master of ceremonies has taken the podium – a younger man in a turtleneck and a tweed jacket, a professorial getup – and is welcoming them all to this commemoration of the life and work of one of our most celebrated and best-loved and, if he can put it this way, most essential poets.

Speak for yourself, thinks Tin: not essential to *me*. He tunes out the audio and turns his mind to the honing of a phrase or two from Martial. He doesn't publish his efforts any more because why bother to try, but the impromptu translation process is a private mental exercise that passes the time agreeably on occasions when the time has to be passed.

121

Unlike you, who court our view,
They shun an audience, those whores;
They fuck in secret behind closed doors.
In curtained, sealed chambers;
Even the dirtiest, cheapest ones
Sneak off to ply their trade behind the tombs.
Act more modestly, like them!
Lesbia, you think I'm being mean?
Shag your head off! Only – don't be seen!

Too much like Mother Goose, the rhyme, the rhythm? Then, perhaps, even more succinctly:

Why not emulate the strumpet?
Bump it, pump it, multi-hump it,
Lesbia! Just don't blow your trumpet!

No, that won't do: it's sillier than Martial at his silliest, and with too much detail sacrificed. The tombs in the original deserve to be preserved: there's much to be said for a graveyard assignation. He'll have another run at it later. Maybe he should take a crack at the one about the cherry versus the prune . . .

Jorrie elbows him sharply. 'You're falling asleep!' she hisses. Tin comes to with a start. Hastily he consults the pamphlet that outlines the order of events, with Gavin's photo glowering magisterially from its black border. Where are they in the timeline? Have the grandchildren sung? Apparently so: not even some lugubrious hymn, but, oh horrors

– 'My Way.' Whoever proposed that should be flogged, but luckily Tin himself was zoned out during it.

The grown-up son is now reading, not from the Bible, but from the oeuvre of the deceased troubadour himself: a late poem about leaves in a pool.

> *Maria skims the dying leaves.*
> *Are they souls? Is one of them my soul?*
> *Is she the Angel of Death, with her dark hair,*
> *with her darkness, come to gather me in?*
>
> *Faded wandering soul, eddying in this cold*
>   *pool,*
> *So long the accomplice of that fool, my body,*
> *Where will you land? On what bare shore?*
> *Will you be nothing but a dead leaf? Or . . .*

Ah. The poem's unfinished: Gavin had died while writing it. The pathos of it all, thinks Tin. No wonder there are repressed weeping noises rising around him like spring frog-song. Still, when further refined, the poem could have yielded a passable result, apart from its ill-concealed rip-off of the dying Emperor Hadrian's address to his own wandering soul. Though possibly not *rip-off*: *allusion* is how a well-disposed critic would frame it. That Gavin Putnam knew Hadrian well enough to steal from him has improved Tin's view of the expired versifier considerably. As a poet, that is; not as a person.

'*Animula, vagula, blandula,*' he recites under his breath. '*Hospes comesque corporis/Quae nunc abibis in loca/Pallidula, rigida, nudula/Nec, ut soles. Dabis iocos . . .*' Hard to put it better. Though many have tried.

There's an interlude of silent meditation, during which they're all invited to close their eyes and reflect on their rich and rewarding friendship with their no longer present colleague and companion, and on what that friendship meant to them person-ally. Jorrie digs Tin with her elbow again. *What fun this will be to recall afterwards!* that dig is saying.

The next funeral baked meat treat is not long in coming. One of the less successful Riverboat-era folksingers, much bewrinkled and with a straggling goatee that looks like the underside of a centipede, arises to favour them with a song from the period: 'Mister Tambourine Man.' A curious choice, as the folkie himself admits before singing it. *But this isn't about being, like, mournful, right? It's about celebration! And I know Gav's probably listening in right now, and he's tapping his foot in joy! Hey up there, buddy! We're waving at you!*

Choking sounds from here and there in the room. Spare us, Tin sighs. Beside him, Jorrie is shaking. Is it grief or mirth? He can't look at her: if it's mirth they will both giggle, and that could prove embarrassing because Jorrie might not be able to stop.

Next there's a eulogy, spoken by a criminally pretty coffee-skinned young woman in high boots

124

and a bright shawl. She introduces herself – Naveena something – as a scholar of the poet's work. Then she says she wants to share the fact that, although she met Mr Putnam only on the last day of his life, the experience of his compassionate personality and his contagious love of life had been deeply moving for her, and she is so grateful to Mrs Putnam – Reynolds – for making this possible, and though she has lost Mr Putnam, she has made a new friend in Reynolds through this terrible ordeal they have gone through together, and she is just glad she hadn't left Florida on the day it happened, and was able to be there for Reynolds, and she is sure everyone in the room will join her in sending warm wishes to Reynolds at this tragic and difficult time, and . . . tremulous breakdown of the voice. 'I'm sorry,' she says, 'I wanted to say more, about, you know, the poetry, but I . . .' She hurries from the stage in tears.

Touching little creature.

Tin consults his watch.

At last, the final musical number. It's 'Fare Thee Well,' a traditional folk song said to have been inspirational to Gavin Putnam when he was writing his now-famous first collection, *Heavy Moonlight*. A copper-haired young man who can't be more than eighteen stands on the stage to sing it for them, backed up by two lads with guitars.

> *Fare thee well, my own true love,*
> *And farewell for a while;*

125

I'm going away, but I'll be back
If I go ten thousand miles.

That will do it every time: the promise to return, coupled with the certain knowledge that no return is possible. The singer's quavering tenor fades away, followed by a fusillade of sobbing and coughs. Tin feels a nuzzling against his jacket sleeve. 'Oh, Tin,' says Jorrie.

He told her to bring a handkerchief, but of course she didn't. He digs out his own handkerchief and hands it to her.

Now there's a murmuring, a rustling, a rising, a mingling. There will be an open bar in the Salon and refreshments in the West Hall, they are informed. There's a discreet stampede of footsteps.

'Where's the washroom?' says Jorrie. She's blotted her face, inexpertly: there's mascara running down her cheeks. Tin recovers his handkerchief and dabs away the black smudges as best he can. 'Will you wait outside for me?' she asks plaintively.

'I'm heading there myself,' says Tin. 'I'll meet you at the bar.'

'Just don't take all day,' says Jorrie. 'I need to get out of this henhouse.' She's waxing querulous: her blood sugar must be down. In the fracas of preparation, they forgot to have lunch. He'll funnel some alcohol into her for a quick lift and steer her over to the crustless sandwiches. Then, after a lemon square or two, for what is a funerary

126

occasion without a lemon square, they'll skedaddle out the door.

In the Men's he runs into Seth MacDonald, Emeritus Professor of Ancient Languages at Princeton and the celebrated translator of the Orphic Hymns and, as it turns out, an old acquaintance of Gavin Putnam. Not professionally, no, but they'd been on a Mediterranean cruise together – 'Hotspots of the Ancient World' – where they'd got on well and had followed up with a correspondence over the past few years. Commiserations are exchanged; Tin does some routine prevarication and invents a reason for his own presence.

'We were both interested in Hadrian,' he says.

'Ah, yes,' says Seth. 'Yes. I noticed the allusion. Skilfully done.'

The unexpected delay means that Jorrie makes it out of the washroom before Tin does. He should never have let her out of his sight! She's gone to town with the sparkly metallic bronzer, and on top of that she's applied something else: a coating of large, glittering, golden flakes. She looks like a sequined leather handbag. She must have smuggled these supplies in her purse: payback for his redaction of the shocking-pink Chanel. Of course she hasn't been able to take in the full effect of her applications in the washroom mirror: she wouldn't have been wearing her reading glasses.

'What have you . . .' he begins. She shoots him a glare: *Don't you dare!* She's right: it's too late now.

He grasps her elbow. 'Forward the Light Brigade,' he says.

'What?'

'Let's get a drink.'

Inexpensive but passable white wines in hand, they head for the refreshments table. As they near the crowd surrounding it, Jorrie stiffens. 'With the third wife, look! There she is!' she says. She's quivering all over.

'Who?' says Tin, knowing all too well. It's the gorgon What's-her-name – C. W. Starr in person, recognizable from her newspaper photos. A short, white-haired old lady in a frumpy quilted coat. No glitter powder on her; in fact, no hint of makeup at all.

'She doesn't recognize me!' Jorrie whispers. Now she's bubbling with merriment. Who *would* recognize you, thinks Tin, with that layer of stucco and dragon scales on your face? 'She looked right at me! Come on, let's eavesdrop!' Shades of their childhood snooping. She tugs him forward.

'No, Jorrie,' he says, as if to a poorly trained terrier. But it's no use; onward she plunges, straining at the invisible leash he's failing to tighten around her neck.

Constance W. Starr is clutching an egg salad sandwich in one hand and a glass of water in the other. She looks beleaguered and wary. To her right must be the bereaved widow, Reynolds Putnam, in chaste blue and pearls. She is indeed quite young. She doesn't look overly afflicted, but then, time has passed since the actual death. To the right of Mrs Putnam is Naveena, the fetching young devotee who'd broken down while delivering her funeral oration. She appears to have recovered completely, and is holding forth.

But not on the subject of Gavin Putnam and his deathless verbiage. As Tin attunes himself to her flattish Midwestern speech, he realizes that she's effusing over the Alphinland series. Constance W. Starr takes a bite of her sandwich: she's probably heard this kind of thing before.

'The Curse of Frenosia,' Naveena is saying. 'Book Four. That was so . . . with the bees, and the Scarlet Sorceress of Ruptous walled up in the stone beehive! It's such a . . .'

There's a space to the left of the renowned authoress, and Jorrie slides herself into it. Her hand locks on to Tin's arm. Her head pokes forward, in an attitude of rapt listening. Is she going to pose as a fan? Tin wonders. What's she up to?

'Book Three,' says Constance W. Starr. 'Frenosia first appears in Book Three. Not Book Four.' She takes another bite and chews imperturbably.

'Oh, of course, Book Three,' says Naveena. She gives a nervous titter. 'And Mr Putnam said, he said you'd put him into the series. When you were out of the room, getting the tea,' she says to Reynolds. 'He told me that.'

Reynolds's face has hardened: this is poaching

129

on her territory. 'Are you sure?' she says. 'He always denied specifically . . .'

'He said there were a lot of things he never told you,' says Naveena. 'To spare your feelings. He didn't want you to feel left out because you weren't in Alphinland yourself.'

'You're lying!' says Reynolds. 'He always told me everything! He thought Alphinland was drivel!'

'Actually,' says Constance, 'I did put Gavin into Alphinland.' So far she hasn't acknowledged the presence of Jorrie, but now she turns and looks at her directly. 'To keep him safe.'

'This is inappropriate,' says Reynolds. 'I think you should . . .'

'And it did keep him safe,' says Constance. 'He was in a wine cask. He slept for fifty years.'

'Oh, I knew it!' says Naveena. 'I always knew he was in the series! Which book is that?'

Constance doesn't answer her. She's still talking to Jorrie. 'But now I've let him out. So he can come and go whenever he likes. He's not at risk from you any more.'

What's the matter with Constance Starr? Tin wonders. Gavin Putnam, at risk from Jorrie? But he'd been the rejecting one, the harmful one. Is there vodka in that water glass?

'What?' says Jorrie. 'Are you talking to me?' She's squeezing Tin's arm, but not to keep from laughing. Instead she looks frightened.

'Gavin is not in that fucking *book*! Gavin is *dead*,' says Reynolds. She's beginning to cry. Naveena takes a small step towards her, but then moves back.

'He was at risk from your ill will, Marjorie,' says Constance, her voice level. 'Coupled with your anger. It's a very potent spell, you know. As long as his spirit still had a flesh container on this side, he was at risk.' She knows exactly who Jorrie is: despite the gold flakes and the bronze powder, she must have known from the first minute.

'Of course I was angry, because of what he did to me!' says Jorrie. 'He threw me over, he kicked me out, like, like an old . . .'

'Oh,' says Constance. There's a frozen moment. 'I didn't realize that,' she says at last. 'I thought it was the other way around. I thought you'd wounded him.' Is this a face-off? thinks Tin. Is this matter and anti-matter? Are the two of them going to explode each other?

'Is that what he said?' says Jorrie. 'Shit, it figures! *Of course* he'd say it was my fault!'

'Oh my God,' Naveena says to Jorrie, *sotto voce*. 'You're the Dark Lady! Of the *Sonnets*! Could we maybe talk . . .'

'This is supposed to be a *funeral*,' says Reynolds. 'Not a *conference*! Gavin would *hate* this!' None of the other women shows any sign of having heard her. She blows her nose, gives a furious, red-eyed glare, then walks away towards the bar.

Constance W. Starr sticks the remains of her sandwich into her water glass; Jorrie stares at her as if she's mixing a potion. 'In that case, I'm honour-bound to release you,' Constance says finally. 'I've been under a serious misapprehension.'

'What?' Jorrie almost screams. 'Release me from what? What are you talking about?'

'From the stone beehive,' says Constance. 'Where you've been imprisoned for such a long time, and stung by indigo bees. As a punishment. And to keep you from hurting Gavin.'

'She's the Scarlet Sorceress of Ruptous!' says Naveena. 'This is so wicked! Could you tell me . . .' Constance continues to ignore her.

'I'm sorry about the bees,' she says to Jorrie. 'That must have been very painful.'

Tin grips Jorrie's elbow and attempts to pull her back. It wouldn't be out of the question for her to jump into tantrum mode and kick the old authoress on the shins, or at the very least start yelling. He needs to extract her. They'll go home and he'll pour them each a stiff drink and he'll calm her down, and then they can make fun of this whole thing.

But Jorrie doesn't move, though she lets go of Tin's arm. 'It was very painful,' she whispers. 'It's been so painful. Everything has been so painful, all my life.' Is she crying? Yes: real, metallic tears, sparkling with bronze and gold.

'It was painful for me too,' says Constance.

'I know,' says Jorrie. The two of them are gazing into each other's eyes, locked in some kind of impenetrable mind-meld.

'We live in two places,' says Constance. 'There isn't any past in Alphinland. There isn't any time. But there's time here, where we are now. We still have a little time left.'

'Yes,' says Jorrie. 'It's time. I'm sorry too. And I release you as well.'

She steps forward. Is this a hug? thinks Tin. Are they embracing, or wrestling? Is there a crisis? How can he help? What sort of female weirdness is going on?

He feels stupid. Has he understood nothing about Jorrie, all these decades? Does she have other layers, other powers? Dimensions he never suspected?

Constance has pulled back. 'Bless you,' she says to Jorrie. The white parchment skin of her face is glittering now with golden scales.

Young Naveena can scarcely believe her luck. Her mouth's half open, she's biting the tips of her fingers, she's holding her breath. She's embedding us in amber, thinks Tin. Like ancient insects. Preserving us forever. In amber beads, in amber words. Right before our eyes.

LUSUS NATURAE

What could be done with me, what should be done with me? These were the same question. The possibilities were limited. The family discussed them all, lugubriously, endlessly, as they sat around the kitchen table at night, with the shutters closed, eating their dry, whiskery sausages and their potato soup. If I was in one of my lucid phases I would sit with them, entering into the conversation as best I could while searching out the chunks of potato in my bowl. If not, I'd be off in the darkest corner, mewing to myself and listening to the twittering voices nobody else could hear.

'She was such a lovely baby,' my mother would say. 'There was nothing wrong with her.' It saddened her to have given birth to an item such as myself: it was like a reproach, a judgment. What had she done wrong?

'Maybe it's a curse,' said my grandmother. She was as dry and whiskery as the sausages, but in her it was natural because of her age.

'She was fine for years,' said my father. 'It was after that case of measles, when she was seven. After that.'

'Who would curse us?' said my mother.

My grandmother scowled. She had a long list of candidates. Even so, there was no one she could single out. Our family had always been respected, and even liked, more or less. It still was. It still would be, if something could be done about me. Before I leaked out, so to say.

'The doctor says it's a disease,' said my father. He liked to claim he was a rational man. He took the newspapers. It was he who insisted that I learn to read, and he'd persisted in his encouragement, despite everything. I no longer nestled into the crook of his arm, however. He sat me on the other side of the table. Though this enforced distance pained me, I could see his point.

'Then why didn't he give us some medicine?' said my mother. My grandmother snorted. She had her own ideas, which involved puffballs and stump water. Once she'd held my head under the water in which the dirty clothes were soaking, praying while she did it. That was to eject the demon she was convinced had flown in through my mouth and was lodged near my breastbone. My mother said she had the best of intentions, at heart.

Feed her bread, the doctor had said. *She'll want a lot of bread. That, and potatoes. She'll want to drink blood. Chicken blood will do, or the blood of a cow. Don't let her have too much.* He told us the name of the disease, which had some Ps and Rs in it and meant nothing to us. He'd only seen a case

135

like me once before, he'd said, looking at my yellow eyes, my pink teeth, my red fingernails, the long dark hair that was sprouting on my chest and arms. He wanted to take me away to the city, so other doctors could look at me, but my family refused. 'She's a lusus naturae,' he'd said.

'What does that mean?' said my grandmother. 'Freak of nature,' the doctor said. He was from far away: we'd summoned him. Our own doctor would have spread rumours. 'It's Latin. Like a monster.' He thought I couldn't hear, because I was mewing. 'It's nobody's fault.'

'She's a human being,' said my father. He paid the doctor a lot of money to go away to his foreign parts and never come back.

'Why did God do this to us?' said my mother.

'Curse or disease, it doesn't matter,' said my older sister. 'Either way, no one will marry me if they find out.' I nodded my head: true enough. She was a pretty girl, and we weren't poor, we were almost gentry. Without me, her coast would be clear.

In the daytimes I stayed shut up in my darkened room: I was getting beyond a joke. That was fine with me, because I couldn't stand sunlight. At night, sleepless, I would roam the house, listening to the snores of the others, their yelps of nightmare. The cat kept me company. He was the only living creature who wanted to be close to me. I smelled of blood, old dried-up blood: perhaps that was why he shadowed me, why he would climb up onto me and start licking.

They'd told the neighbours I had a wasting illness, a fever, a delirium. The neighbours sent eggs and cabbages; from time to time they visited, to scrounge for news, but they weren't eager to see me: whatever it was might be catching.

It was decided that I should die. That way I would not stand in the way of my sister, I would not loom over her like a fate. 'Better one happy than both miserable,' said my grandmother, who had taken to sticking garlic cloves around my door frame. I agreed to this plan, I wanted to be helpful.

The priest was bribed; in addition to that, we appealed to his sense of compassion. Everyone likes to think they are doing good while at the same time pocketing a bag of cash, and our priest was no exception. He told me God had chosen me as a special girl, a sort of bride, you might say. He said I was called on to make sacrifices. He said my sufferings would purify my soul. He said I was lucky, because I would stay innocent all my life, no man would want to pollute me, and then I would go straight to Heaven.

He told the neighbours I had died in a saintly manner. I was put on display in a very deep coffin in a very dark room, in a white dress with a lot of white veiling over me, fitting for a virgin and useful in concealing my whiskers. I lay there for two days, though of course I could walk around at night. I held my breath when anyone entered. They tiptoed, they spoke in whispers, they didn't come close, they were still afraid of my disease. To my mother they said I looked just like an angel.

My mother sat in the kitchen and cried as if I really had died; even my sister managed to look glum. My father wore his black suit. My grandmother baked. Everyone stuffed themselves. On the third day they filled the coffin with damp straw and carted it off to the cemetery and buried it, with prayers and a modest headstone, and three months later my sister got married. She was driven to the church in a coach, a first in our family. My coffin was a rung on her ladder.

Now that I was dead, I was freer. No one but my mother was allowed into my room, my former room as they called it. They told the neighbours they were keeping it as a shrine to my memory. They hung a picture of me on the door, a picture made when I still looked human. I didn't know what I looked like now. I avoided mirrors.

In the dimness I read Pushkin, and Lord Byron, and the poetry of John Keats. I learned about blighted love, and defiance, and the sweetness of death. I found these thoughts comforting. My mother would bring me my potatoes and bread, and my cup of blood, and take away the chamber pot. Once she used to brush my hair, before it came out in handfuls; she'd been in the habit of hugging me and weeping; but she was past that now. She came and went as quickly as she could.

However she tried to hide it, she resented me, of course. There's only so long you can feel sorry for a person before you come to feel that their affliction is an act of malice committed by them against you.

At night I had the run of the house, and then the run of the yard, and after that the run of the forest. I no longer had to worry about getting in the way of other people and their futures. As for me, I had no future. I had only a present, a present that changed – it seemed to me – along with the moon. If it weren't for the fits, and the hours of pain, and the twittering of the voices I couldn't understand, I might have said I was happy.

My grandmother died, then my father. The cat became elderly. My mother sank further into despair. 'My poor girl,' she would say, though I was no longer exactly a girl. 'Who will take care of you when I'm gone?'

There was only one answer to that: it would have to be me. I began to explore the limits of my power. I found I had a great deal more of it when unseen than when seen, and most of all when partly seen. I frightened two children in the woods, on purpose: I showed them my pink teeth, my hairy face, my red fingernails, I mewed at them, and they ran away screaming. Soon people avoided our end of the forest. I peered into a window at night and caused hysterics in a young woman. 'A thing! I saw a thing!' she sobbed. I was a thing, then. I considered this. In what way is a thing not a person?

A stranger made an offer to buy our farm. My mother wanted to sell and move in with my sister and her gentry husband and her healthy, growing family, whose portraits had just been painted; she could no longer manage; but how could she leave me?

'Do it,' I told her. By now my voice was a sort of growl. 'I'll vacate my room. There's a place I can stay.' She was grateful, poor soul. She had an attachment to me, as if to a hangnail, a wart: I was hers. But she was glad to be rid of me. She'd done enough duty for a lifetime.

During the packing up and the sale of our furniture I spent the days inside a hayrick. It was sufficient, but it would not do for winter. Once the new people had moved in, it was no trouble to get rid of them. I knew the house better than they did, its entrances, its exits. I could make my way around it in the dark. I became an apparition, then another one; I was a red-nailed hand touching a face in the moonlight; I was the sound of a rusted hinge that I made despite myself. They took to their heels, and branded our place as haunted. Then I had it to myself.

I lived on stolen potatoes dug by moonlight, on eggs filched from henhouses. Once in a while I'd purloin a hen – I'd drink the blood first. There were guard dogs, but though they howled at me, they never attacked: they didn't know what I was.

Inside our house, I tried a mirror. They say dead people can't see their own reflections, and it was true; I could not see myself. I saw something, but that something was not myself: it looked nothing like the kind and pretty girl I knew myself to be, at heart.

But now things are coming to an end. I've become too visible.

This is how it happened.

I was picking blackberries in the dusk, at the verge where the meadow meets the trees, and I saw two people approaching, from opposite sides. One was a young man, the other a girl. His clothing was better than hers. He had shoes.

The two of them looked furtive. I knew that look – the glances over the shoulder, the stops and starts – as I was unusually furtive myself. I crouched in the brambles to watch. They clutched each other, they twined together, they fell to the ground. Mewing noises came from them, growls, little screams. Perhaps they were having fits, both of them at once. Perhaps they were – oh, at last! – beings like myself. I crept closer to see better. They did not look like me – they were not hairy, for instance, except on their heads, and I could tell this because they had shed most of their clothing – but then, it had taken me some time to grow into what I was. They must be in the preliminary stages, I thought. They know they are changing, they have sought out each other for the company, and to share their fits.

They appeared to derive pleasure from their flailings about, even if they occasionally bit each other. I knew how that could happen. What a consolation it would be to me if I, too, could join in! Through the years I had hardened myself to loneliness; now I found that hardness dissolving. Still, I was too timorous to approach them.

One evening the young man fell asleep. The girl covered him with his cast-off shirt and kissed him on the forehead. Then she walked carefully away.

I detached myself from the brambles and came softly towards him. There he was, asleep in an oval of crushed grass, as if laid out on a platter. I'm sorry to say I lost control. I laid my red-nailed hands on him. I bit him on the neck. Was it lust or hunger? How could I tell the difference? He woke up, he saw my pink teeth, my yellow eyes; he saw my black dress fluttering; he saw me running away. He saw where.

He told the others in the village, and they began to speculate. They dug up my coffin and found it empty, and feared the worst. Now they're marching towards this house, in the dusk, with long stakes, with torches. My sister is among them, and her husband, and the young man I kissed. I meant it to be a kiss.

What can I say to them, how can I explain myself? When demons are required someone will always be found to supply the part, and whether you step forward or are pushed is all the same in the end. 'I am a human being,' I could say. But what proof do I have of that? 'I am a lusus naturae! Take me to the city! I should be studied!' No hope there. I'm afraid it's bad news for the cat. Whatever they do to me, they'll do to him as well.

I am of a forgiving temperament, I know they have the best of intentions at heart. I've put on my white burial dress, my white veil, as befits a virgin. One must have a sense of occasion. The twittering voices are very loud: it's time for me to take flight. I'll fall from the burning rooftop like a comet, I'll blaze like a bonfire. They'll have to say many charms over my ashes, to make sure I'm really dead this time. After a while I'll become an upside-down saint; my finger bones will be sold as dark relics. I'll be a legend, by then.

Perhaps in Heaven I'll look like an angel. Or perhaps the angels will look like me. What a surprise that will be, for everyone else! It's something to look forward to.

THE FREEZE–DRIED GROOM

The next thing is that his car won't start. It's the fault of the freak cold snap, caused by the polar vortex – a term that's already spawned a bunch of online jokes by stand-up comics about their wives' vaginas.

Sam can relate to that. Before she finally cut him off, Gwyneth was in the habit of changing the bottom sheet to signal that at long last she was about to dole him out some thin-lipped, watery, begrudging sex on a pristine surface. Then she'd change the sheet again right afterwards to reinforce the message that he, Sam, was a germ-ridden, stain-creating, flea-bitten waste of her washing machine. She'd given up faking it – no more cardboard moaning – so the act would take place in eerie silence, enclosed in a pink, sickly sweet aura of fabric softener. It seeped into his pores, that smell. Under the circumstances he's amazed that he was able to function at all, much less with alacrity. But he never ceases to surprise himself. Who knows what he'll get up to next? Not him.

★　★　★

This is how the day begins. At breakfast, a disaster in itself, Gwyneth tells Sam their marriage is over. Sam drops his fork, then lifts it again to push aside the remains of his scrambled eggs. Gwyneth used to make the most delicate scrambled eggs, so he can only conclude that the scrambled eggs of this morning, tough as boots, are part of the eviction package. She no longer wishes to please him: quite the reverse. She could have waited until he'd had some coffee: she knows he can't focus without his caffeine hit.

'Whoa, hold it a minute,' he says, but then he stops. It's no use. This isn't the opening move in a fracas, a plea for more attention, or an offer in a negotiation: Sam has undergone all three of these before and is familiar with the accessorized facial expressions. Gwyneth isn't snarling or pouting or frowning: her gaze is glacial, her voice level. This is a proclamation.

Sam considers protesting: what's he done that's so major, so stinky, so rotten, so cancerously terminal? Nothing in the way of mislaid cash and illicit lipstick besmearing that he hasn't done before. He could criticize her tone: why is she so crabby all of a sudden? He could attack her skewed values: what's happened to her sense of fun, her love of life, her moral balance? Or he could preach: forgiveness is virtuous! Or he could wheedle: how can a kind, patient, warm-hearted woman like her whack a vulnerable, wounded guy like him with such a crude psychic bludgeon? Or he could promise reformation:

145

What do I have to do, just tell me! He could beg for a second chance, but she'd surely reply that he's used up all his second chances. He could tell her he loves her, but she'd say – as she's been saying recently, with tedious predictability – that love isn't just words, it's actions.

She sits across the table from him girded for the combat she no doubt expects, her hair scraped severely off her forehead and twisted at the back of her neck like a tourniquet, her rectilinear gold earrings and clanky necklace reinforcing the metallic harshness of her decree. Her face has been made up in preparation for this scene – lips the colour of dried blood, eyebrows a storm cloud black – and her arms are folded across her once-inviting breasts: no way in here, buddy. The worst is that, underneath the shell she's enclosed herself in, she's indifferent to him. Now that every kind of melodrama has been used up by both of them, he finally bores her. She's counting the minutes, waiting for him to leave.

He gets up from the table. She could have had the decency to postpone the dropping of her writ until he'd dressed and shaved: a man in his five-day-old PJs is at a pitiful disadvantage.

'Where are you going?' she says. 'We need to discuss the details.' He's tempted to come out with something hurt and petulant: 'Onto the street.' 'As if you care!' 'No longer any of your fucking business, is it?' But that would be a tactical error.

'We can do that later,' he says. 'The legal crap.

146

I need to pack.' If her thing is a bluff, this would be the moment; but no, she doesn't stop him. She doesn't even say, 'Don't be silly, Sam! I didn't mean you had to leave right this minute! Sit down and have a coffee! We're still friends!'

But they are not still friends, it appears. 'Suit yourself,' she says with a level glare. So he's forced to shamble ignominiously out of the kitchen in his sleeping gear printed with sheep jumping over a fence – her birthday gift of two years ago when she still thought he was cute and funny – and his downtrodden woolly slippers.

He knew this was coming, just not so soon. He should have been more alert and dumped her first. Kept the high ground. Or would that have been the low ground? As it is, the role of aggrieved party can be his by rights. He climbs into his jeans and a sweatshirt, throws a bunch of stuff into a duffle bag he's had for a while, part of a seafaring project he'd never carried out. He can come back for the rest of his junk later. Their bedroom, soon to be hers alone – once so charged with sexual electricity, then the scene of their drawn-out push-me pull-you tug-of-war – already looks like a hotel room he's about to abandon. Had he helped to choose their graceless imitation-Victorian bed? He had; or at least he'd stood by while the crime was being committed. Not the curtain material, though, not with those dumb roses on them. He's guiltless of that, at any rate.

Razor, socks, Y-fronts, T-shirts, and so forth. He

segues into the spare room he's been using as an office and whisks his laptop, phone, notebook, and snarl of charging cords into his computer bag. A few stray documents, not that he trusts paper. Wallet, credit cards, passport: he slots them into various pockets.

How can he get out of the house without having her see him – him and his abject retreat? Twist a sheet, climb out the window, shinny down the wall? He's not thinking clearly, he's slightly cross-eyed with anger. To keep himself under control he slides back into the mind-game he often plays with himself: suppose he was a murder victim, would his toothpaste be a clue? *I judge that this tube was last squeezed twenty-four hours ago. The victim was therefore still alive then.* How about his iPod? *Let's see what he was listening to just before the carving knife went into his ear. His playlist may be a code!* Or his awful cufflinks with lion heads and his initials on them, a Christmas gift from Gwyneth two years ago? *These can't be his, a man of taste such as himself. They must be the murderer's!*

But they were his. They were Gwyneth's image of him just after they started dating: the king of beasts, the forceful predator who'd fling her around a bit, do some toothwork on her. Hold her down, writhing with desire, one paw on her neck.

Why does he find it soothing to imagine himself lying on a mortuary slab while a forensic analyst – invariably a hot blonde, though wearing a lab coat over her firm, no-nonsense lady-doctor breasts

148

– probes his corpse with delicate but practised fingers? *So young, so hung!* she's thinking. *What a waste!* Then, nosy, pert little detective that she is, she attempts to re-create his sorrowful snuffed-out life, retrace the wayward footsteps that mixed him up with a sinister crowd and led to his tragic end. *Good luck, honey,* he beams at her silently out of his cold, white head: *I'm an enigma, you'll never get my number, you'll never pin me down. But do that thing with the rubber glove just one more time! Oh yes!*

In some of these fantasies he sits up because he isn't dead after all. Screams! Then: kisses! In other versions he sits up even though he is dead. Eyeballs rolled right up into his head, but avid hands reaching for her lab coat buttons. That's a different scenario.

One more sweatshirt stuffed into the top of his duffle: there, that should do it. He closes the bag, hoists it, picks up his computer case in the other hand, and canters down the stairs, two at a time, as he has done before. Replacing the worn carpet on those stairs is no longer his concern: that's one plus for him, anyway.

In the hall he grabs his winter parka out of the closet, checks the pockets for gloves, his warm scarf, his lambskin hat. He can see Gwyneth, still in the kitchen, elbows on the upmarket glass-topped table sourced from his end of things but that would now be hers, as he has zero intention of squabbling over it. He didn't exactly pay for it in the first place, anyway: he acquired it.

She's studiously ignoring him. She's made herself some coffee; the scent is delicious. And a piece of toast, from the looks of it. She's certainly not too upset to eat. He resents that. How can she chew at a moment like this? Doesn't he mean anything to her?

'When will I see you?' she calls as he heads out the door.

'I'll text,' he says. 'Enjoy your life.' Was that too bitter? Yes: rancour is an error. Don't be a dickhead, Sam, he tells himself. You're losing your cool.

That's the moment when the car decides not to start. Fucking Audi. He should never have accepted this hunk of luxury-car junk in lieu of settlement from a guy who owed him, though it looked like a great deal at the time.

Talk about a definitive exit spoiled. He doesn't even get to roar off around the corner, va-voom and good riddance, the sailor hitting the high seas, and who needs the ladies dragging you down like cement blocks tied to your ankles? A wave of the hand and away he'd go, cruising to ever-new adventures.

He tries the ignition again. Click click, dead as November. His breath turning to smoke in the freezing air, the tips of his fingers whitening, his earlobes numbing, he phones his usual service outfit to come and jump the battery. All he gets is a recording: a representative will be with him shortly, but he should be advised that due to

150

adverse weather conditions the average wait is two hours, please stay on the line because we truly value your business. Then on comes the upbeat music. *Freeze your nuts off,* go the unsung words, *because all praise to the polar vortex, we're making a bundle here. Wise up. Get a block heater. Kiss my ass.*

So back into the house he slouches. Good thing he still has a key, though *Change the locks* is no doubt top of Gwyneth's list. She is a list-making woman.

'What are you doing back here?' she says. Hangdog winsome smile: maybe she would be kind enough to see if her own car would start, and then maybe she could give him a jump? So to speak, he adds to himself silently. He wouldn't mind taking a crack at jumping her to see if he could win her back, at least long enough to cash in on the reconciliation passion, but this is not the time.

'Otherwise I'll have to wait here until they send the truck,' he says with what he hopes is an insouciant grin. 'It could be hours. It could be . . . I could be here all day. You wouldn't want that.'

She doesn't want that. She heaves a long-suffering sigh – a car that won't start is one more item on the endlessly unfurling scroll of his fecklessness – and begins to insulate herself in winter coat, mittens, scarves, and boots. He can hear her rolling up her invisible sleeves: *Let's get this done.* Hauling him out of scrapes, dusting him off, polishing him so he shone like new – that kind of thing was once her cherished avocation. If anyone could fix him, she could.

But she's failed.

When they first hooked up, after she'd walked into his store looking for a match to an ugly antique Staffordshire china spaniel she'd recently inherited, Gwyneth found him next to irresistible: edgy, thrilling, but entertaining, like a supporting character in a '50s musical. Some loveable comic gangster, naughty but trustworthy at heart. Possibly no man had ever paid the kind of attention to her that he had – that in-detail tactile scrutiny, as if she was a valuable teacup. Or possibly she hadn't noticed the come-on lines of males past because she'd been too occupied with her sickly parents to put much time in on men, or to allow them to put much time in on her. So to speak. Not that she wasn't beautiful – she was, in a cameo kind of way – but she didn't seem aware of what she could do with it. She'd had a few boyfriends, true, but as far as he could tell they'd been pathetic wusses.

But by the day of the china spaniel she was ready for action. She shouldn't have been so open with strange men, namely him. She shouldn't have volunteered so much information. The dead parents, the inheritance: enough so she'd been able to quit her school-teaching job, begin to enjoy life. But how?

Enter Sam, on cue, knowledgeable about Staffordshire and smiling at her with polite, appreciative lechery. He was good at enjoyment, a talent few possessed. He was happy to share.

He'd been relatively upfront with her; or rather he hadn't outright lied. He'd told her his income came from the antiques shop, which was partly true. He didn't mention where the rest of it came from. He'd told her he was in business for himself – accurate – though he had a partner, also accurate. What she saw in him was an exciting man of action, a sexual magician; what he saw in her was a respectable facade behind which he could hunker down for a while. It would be nice to stop living in motels or camping out in the back of the shop, so it was handy that she already owned a house, one with room in it for him when he was there. Which, as things eased up, he increasingly wasn't. His work involved a lot of travel, he told her. Checking out antiques.

He can't say he didn't enjoy the convenience of being married to her, at first. The pampering. The comfort.

He wasn't a total asshole: he'd talked himself into the marriage, he'd even believed it could work. He wasn't getting any younger, maybe he should settle down. So what if she wasn't, to outward appearances, a hot babe? Hot babes could be stuck on themselves; they were demanding and fickle. Gwyneth wasn't so alluring that she didn't appreciate what she was getting. One time he'd laid her out naked on the bed and covered her in hundred-dollar bills: heady stuff for a good girl like her, and what an aphrodisiac! But the periodic and increasingly serious lack of hundred-dollar bills, once she found out about that lack – the first time he'd had crap luck and hit her up for a loan – that had the opposite effect. Narrowed her eyes, caused her nipples to shrink like raisins, dried her up like a prune. Just when he could have used a dollop of sympathy and comfort, bang! He was locked into the virtual refrigerator, despite his big blue eyes.

He's relied on them all his life, those big blue eyes of his. Round, candid eyes. Con-man's eyes. 'You look like a baby doll,' one woman had said about his eyes. 'And I'm so breakable,' he'd replied, winningly. Gazing into those eyes, what woman could find it in her heart to disbelieve whatever excuse he was laying out before her like a street peddler's designer-label silk scarf?

Though his big blue eyes are shrinking, he's convinced of it; or is that that his face is growing? Whatever the cause, the ratio between his eyes and his face is changing, as is that between his shoulders and his belly. He can still do the blue-eyed thing; it still works, most of the time; though not of course with men. Men are better at telling when other men are bullshitting. The trick with women is to stare at their mouths. One of the tricks.

He and Gwyneth don't have kids, so the wait in the divorce queue shouldn't be too long. Once they've gone through the formalities, Sam will be at loose ends, yet again. He'll be wandering the world

like a snail, house on his back, which is possibly
how he feels most comfortable. He'll whistle a
merry tune. He'll ramble. He'll smell like himself
again.

Gwyneth's car starts without a problem. She cuts
the engine, stares cow-like out her window at him,
a smug witness to his frozen-fingered manoeuvres
with the jumper cables, hoping perhaps that he'll
electrocute himself. No such luck: he signals to
her to switch on, and juice flows from her car to
his, and he's mobile again. Strained smiles are
exchanged. He eases onto the icy street, gives her
a wave. But she's already turned away.

His parking spot behind the building is unoccu-
pied for once. The store is west on Queen, just
where the advancing wave of grooviness hits the
barren shore of down-at-heels. On one side, trendy
coffee purveyors and boutique nighteries; on the
other, pawnshops and cheap dress stores, their
merchandise yellowing on cracked mannequins.
Metrazzle, proclaims the lettering on his sign. In
the display window is a teak dining room set from
the '50s, complemented with a stereo in blond
wood. Vinyl is back: some kid with rich parents is
going to find that cabinet irresistible.

Metrazzle isn't open yet. Sam jingles his way in
through the multiple locks. His partner is already
there, in the back, engaged in his usual occupation,
which is furniture forgery. No: furniture *enhance-
ment.* Ned is his name, or the one he goes by;

155

distressing is his game, or one of them. He's the Botox doctor of wood, except that he makes it looks older rather than younger. The air is flecked with fine sawdust, and reeks of stain.

Sam heaves his duffle bag into a vintage steel Eames chair. 'Bitch out there,' he says. Ned looks up from his hammer and chisel; he's adding a few faux cracks.

'More on the way,' he says. 'It's dumping on Chicago right now. They shut the airport.'

'When's it due here?' says Sam.

'Later,' says Ned. Tap tap, goes his chisel.

'Guess it's the climate change,' says Sam. That's what people say, the way they used to say, *We've angered God*. And like that, not a fucking thing anyone can do about it, so why even mention it? Party while it lasts. Party if you can. Not that he feels much like partying today. What Gwyneth has done to him is sinking in, sinking down. There's a cold spot right in the middle of him somewhere. 'Fucking snow, I've had enough of it,' he says.

Tap tap tap. Pause. 'Wife kick you out?'

'I left,' says Sam, as indifferently as he can manage. 'Been working up to it.'

'Matter of time,' says Ned. 'Bound to happen.'

Sam appreciates Ned's seamless acceptance of what he must suspect is a fairly major alteration of the truth. 'Yeah,' he says. 'Sad. She's taking it hard. But she'll be okay. It's not like she's out on the street, she's hardly starving.'

'Right, right,' says Ned. He has so many tattoos

up his forearms he looks upholstered. He never says much, having done time and concluded, rightly, that a zipped lip attracts no stilettos. He likes this job and is grateful for it, which is good for Sam because he won't jeopardize it by asking questions. On the other hand, he stores incoming information like a data miner and disgorges it accurately when required.

Sam extracts from him the news that a client dropped by late yesterday, no one Ned has seen before, guy in an expensive leather jacket. He'd examined all the desks. Funny he was out in the snowstorm, but some guys like the challenge. Nobody else in the store, which was no surprise. The handsome reproduction Directoire was the guy's object of interest: he asked for a price, said he'd think about it. Wanted a reserve of two days, put down a deposit of a hundred dollars. Cash not credit. In the sealed envelope beside the register. Name's inside it.

Ned goes back to his chiselling. Sam strolls over to the counter, casually opens the envelope. In with the cash – in twenties – there's slip of paper, which he extracts. There's nothing written on it but an address and a number. He's not fooling Ned, but they operate on a principle of maximum deniability: just assume everything's bugged, is Sam's motto. He looks at the pencilled number, which is 56, files it in his brain, scrunches the paper, sticks it in a pocket. First toilet he encounters, down it will go.

'Guess I'll hit the auction,' he says. 'See what I can pick up.'

'Good luck with it,' says Ned.

The auction is a storage-unit auction. Sam attends two or three of these a week, as many folks in the antiques business do – making the rounds of the storage emporia that ring the city and the neighbouring towns, located in this strip-mall wasteland or that. Sam's on an email list-serv that automatically mails him all upcoming auctions in the province, tagged by postal code. He attends only the ones within reach: nothing farther away than a two-hour drive. Any longer and the returns wouldn't justify the investment, or not on average. Though fortunes have been made by lucky bidders: who knows when a genuine old master may turn up, obscured by dust and varnish, or a boxful of love letters by a dead celebrity to his secret mistress, or a stash of paste jewels that turn out to be genuine? There's been a recent vogue for reality shows that claim to catch people at the moment when they open up the space, then Bingo!, some spectacular life-changing find, with Ohs and Ahs all round.

That's never happened to Sam. Still, there's something exciting about winning an auction, gaining the key to the locked unit, opening the door. Expecting treasures, since whatever junk is inside must have been treasures once or the people wouldn't have bothered to store them.

'Should be back by four,' says Sam. He always

tells Ned his ETA: it's part of that little plot-thread he can't help spinning. *He said he'd be back by four. No, he didn't seem upset about anything. Though maybe he was anxious. Asked me about some strange guy who'd been in the store. Leather jacket. Interested in desks.*

'Text me when to send the van,' says Ned.

'Let's hope there's something worth sending it for,' says Sam. The units have to be cleared out within twenty-four hours, you can't just leave crap there if you don't want it: you win it, you own it. The storage guys don't crave the expense of carting your freshly bought trash to the dump.

The story Sam and Ned wordlessly agree on is that Sam is angling for some decent furniture for Ned to enhance. And he is angling for that, because why not? Sam hopes he may score more in the furniture vein than the assortment of scraps he came back with last time: a busted guitar, a folding bridge table with only three legs, a giant stuffed teddy bear from a fun-fair rifle range, a wooden crokinole game. The game was the only thing with any value: some people collect ancient games.

'Drive safe,' says Ned. *He texted me to send the van. That was at 2:36, I know 'cause I looked at the clock, the art deco one right over there, see? Keeps perfect time. Then, I dunno, he just vanished.*

Did he have any enemies?

I just work here.

Though he did say . . . yeah, told me there'd been a

fight with his wife. That would be Gwyneth. Don't know her that well myself. At breakfast, walked out on her. You could see it coming. Cramped his style, never gave him enough space. Yeah, jealous, possessive, he told me that. She thought the sun shone out his ass, couldn't get enough of him. Would she, did she ever . . . Violent? Naw, he never said that. Except for the time she threw a wine bottle at him, empty one. But sometimes they just snap, women like that. Lose it. Go nuts.

He entertains himself with the discovery of his own body. Naked or clothed? Inside or out? Knife or gun? Alone?

The car starts this time, which Sam takes as a good omen. He zigzags down towards the Gardiner, which maybe won't have fallen down yet – no, it hasn't, maybe there's a God – then heads west. The address in the envelope was that of a storage emporium in Mississauga, not too far away. The traffic is putrid. What is it about winter that causes people to drive as if their hands are feet?

He gets to the site early, parks the car, goes to the main office, registers. Everything just as usual. Now he'll have to hang around till the auction starts. He hates these blocks of dead space-time. He checks his phone for messages. This and that, this and that. And Gwyneth, texting: *Meet tomorrow? Let's get this finalized.* He doesn't reply, but he doesn't delete. Let her wait. He'd like to nip outside for a smoke, but he resists the temptation, having officially quit five months ago for the fourth time.

A couple more folks trickle in, hardly a crowd. Low attendance is good, it thins out the competition, keeps the bids decent. Too cold for the tourists: there's no atmosphere of summer antiquing, no glamorous TV reality-show buzz. Just a bunch of middle-range impatient bundled-up people standing around with their hands in their pockets or looking at their watches or phones.

Couple of other dealers now, ones he knows: he nods at them, they nod back. He's done business with both of them: stuff he's won that didn't fit his niche but did fit theirs. He doesn't do much Victorian: it's too big for condos. Or much wartime, too bulbous and maroon. He likes the pieces with cleaner lines. Lighter. Less ponderous.

The auctioneer bustles in five minutes' late with a takeout coffee and a bag of doughnut holes, casts an annoyed look at the scant turnout, and turns on his handheld mic – which he hardly needs, it's not a football game, but most likely it makes him feel important. There are seven storage units on the block today, seven don't-care no-show owners. Sam bids on five, wins four, lets the fifth one go because it's more plausible that way. The one he really wants is the second, number 56 – that was the number in the envelope, that's where the secret cargo will have been stashed – but he always tries for a cluster of units.

After the event proper is over he settles up with the auctioneer, who hands him the keys to the four spaces. 'Stuff has to be out in twenty-four hours,' the man says. 'Sweep it clean, those are the rules.' Sam nods; he knows the rules, but there's no point in saying that. Guy's an asshole, in training for a prison guard or a politician or some other self-proclaimed dictator job. A non-asshole might offer Sam a doughnut hole – surely the guy isn't going to eat the whole bag, he could benefit from some weight loss – but that philanthropic act does not take place.

Sam walks across to the nearby mall, collar up against the rising wind, scarf over his chin, gets himself a Timmy's double-double and his own sack of doughnut holes – chocolate-glazed – and walks back to inspect his unit purchases at leisure. He likes to wait until the other bidders have cleared off: he doesn't want people looking over his shoulder. He'll leave number 56 till the last; everyone else will have gone by then.

The first unit is stacked high with cardboard boxes. Sam looks inside a few: shit, it's mostly books. He's got no idea how to value books, so he'll make a deal with a guy he knows, a book specialist; if there's anything really noteworthy, Sam will get a cut. Author signatures in them are sometimes good, the guy says; on the other hand, sometimes not, if no one knows them. Dead authors are sometimes good, but not that often; they have to be famous as well as dead. Art books are usually good, depending on the condition. A lot of the time they're rare.

The next unit has nothing in it but an old scooter,

one of those lightweight Italian quasi-tricycles. Sam has no use for it, but someone will. It can be stripped for parts if nothing else. He doesn't linger. No sense freezing his balls off: these units aren't heated, and the temperature's dropping.

He finds his next unit, slips the key into the lock. Third time lucky: what if it's a treasure trove? He can still get excited over the possibility, even though he knows it's like believing in the tooth fairy. He rolls up the door, switches the light on.

Right at the front there's a white wedding dress with a skirt like an enormous bell and big puffed sleeves. It's swathed in a clear plastic zip bag, as if it just came from the store. It doesn't even look worn. There's a pair of new-looking white satin shoes tucked into the bottom of the bag. There are white elbow-length buttoned gloves pinned to the sleeves. They look creepy: they underscore the absence of a head; though there's a white veil, he sees now, wrapped around the shoulders of the dress like a stole, with a chaplet of white artificial flowers and seed pearls attached to it.

Who'd put their wedding dress into a storage unit? Sam wonders. That isn't what women do. Maybe they'd stash it in a closet, or in a trunk or something, but not a storage unit. Where does Gwyneth keep her own wedding dress, come to think of it? He doesn't know. Not that it was as elaborate as this one. They hadn't done the whole hog, not the big church wedding: Gwyneth said those were really for the parents, and hers were dead, as were Sam's, or so he'd told her. No sense in letting his mother yap on to Gwyneth about the amusing ups and downs and the not so amusing ins and outs of his earlier life, it only would have confused her. She would have had to choose between two realities, his reality and his mother's, and that kind of situation was toxic to a romantic atmosphere.

So they'd just done the city hall routine, and then Sam had swept Gwyneth off to a dream honeymoon on the Cayman Islands. Into the sea, out of the sea, roll around in the sand, watch the moon. Flowers on the breakfast table. Sunset again, holding hands at the bar, filling her up with frozen daiquiris, that's what she liked to drink. Sex in the morning, kissing his way up her like a slug on a lettuce, beginning with the toes.

Oh Sam! This is so . . . I never thought . . .

Just relax. That's it. Put your hand here.

It wasn't hard to take. He could afford all of that then, the beaches, the daiquiris, he was flush. The cash wave ebbs and flows, such is its nature, but he's a believer in spending it while you have it. Was that when he'd covered Gwyneth with hundred-dollar bills – on their honeymoon? No, he pulled that one later.

He moves the wedding-dress skirt to the side. It's stiff, it rustles, it crackles. There's more wedding stuff in here: a little night table, and on it a huge bouquet, tied with pink satin ribbon. It's mostly roses, but it's dry as a bone. On the other side, in behind the white skirt, there's the matching night table, holding a giant cake, underneath one of those domed covers they have in bakeries. It's got white icing, pink and white roses made of sugar, and a tiny bride and groom on the top. It hasn't been cut.

He's getting a very odd feeling. He squeezes in past the dress. If what he's thinking is right, there ought to be some champagne: there's always champagne for weddings. Sure enough, here it is, three crates of it, unopened. It's a miracle it hasn't frozen and burst. Beside it are several boxes of champagne flutes, also unopened: glass ones, not plastic, good quality. And some boxes of white china plates, and a big box of white napkins, cloth, not paper. Someone has stored their entire wedding in here. A big-ticket wedding.

Behind the cardboard boxes there's some luggage – brand-new luggage, a matched set, cherry red in colour.

And behind that, in the farthest, darkest corner, is the groom.

'Crap,' says Sam out loud. His breath unfurls in a white plume because of the cold; maybe it's the cold that accounts for the lack of smell. Now that he notices, there is in fact a faint odour, a little sweet – though that could be the cake – and a little like dirty socks, with an undertone of dog food that's been around too long.

Sam wraps his scarf across his nose. He's feeling slightly nauseous. This is crazy. Whoever parked the groom in here must be a dangerous loony,

165

some kind of sick fetishist. He should leave right now. He should call the cops. No, he shouldn't. He wouldn't want them looking into his final unit, number 56 – the one he hasn't opened yet.

The groom's wearing the full uniform: the black formal suit, the white shirt, the cravat, a withered carnation in the buttonhole. Is there a top hat? Not that Sam can see, but he guesses it must be somewhere – in the luggage, he bets – because whoever did this went for the complete set.

Except the bride: there isn't any bride.

The man's face looks desiccated, as if the guy has dried out like a mummy. He's enclosed in several layers of clear plastic; garment bags, maybe, like the one containing the dress. Yes, there are the zippers: packing tape has been applied carefully along the seams. Inside the clear layers the groom has a wavery look, as if he's underwater. The eyes are shut, for which Sam is grateful. How was that done? Aren't corpse eyes always open? Krazy Glue? Scotch tape? He has the odd sense that this man is familiar, like someone he knows, but that can't possibly be true.

Sam backs carefully out of the storage unit, slides the door down, locks it. Then he stands in front of it holding the key. What the shit is he supposed to do now? With the dried-out bridegroom. He can't leave him here, locked inside the unit. He bought this wedding, it's his, he's responsible for removing it. He can't have Ned send the van for it, not unless Ned himself drives – he could be trusted not to say anything. But Ned never drives the van, they use a service.

And suppose he asks Ned to rent a van from a different outfit and drive here, and suppose he waits until Ned arrives, standing outside the unit because he wouldn't want anyone else messing around with this; suppose he stays right here, freezing in what will soon become the dark, and then suppose they load the whole wedding into the van and take it back to the shop – suppose all that, what then? They take the poor shrivelled-up sucker out to a field somewhere and bury him? Throw him into Lake Ontario, making their way over the shore ice, which won't crack and sink them, fat chance? Even if they could manage that, he'd be sure to float. *Mummified groom mystifies crime unit. Suspicious circumstances surrounding freak member of the wedding. Nuptial shocker: she married a zombie.*

Failure to report a dead body: isn't that a felony? Worse: the guy must have been murdered. You don't find yourself encased in several layers of plastic with tape on the zippers, wearing formal wedding fancy dress, without getting murdered first.

As Sam's reviewing his options, a tall woman rounds the corner. She's wearing one of those sheepskin coats with the wool side in, its hood up over her blond hair. She's almost running. Now she's right up to him. She looks anxious, though trying to conceal it.

So, he thinks. The missing bride.

★   ★   ★

167

She touches his arm. 'Excuse me,' she says. 'Did you just buy the contents of this unit? At the auction?'

He smiles at her, opens wide his big blue eyes. Drops his gaze to her mouth, flicks it up again. She's about his height. Strong enough to have lugged the groom into the unit by herself, even if he wasn't yet dried out. 'That's me,' he says. 'I plead guilty.'

'But you haven't unlocked it yet?'

Here's the moment of decision. He could hand her the key, say, *I've seen the mess you made, clean it up yourself.* He could say, *Yes I have, and I'm calling the cops.* He could say, *I took a quick look, it seems to be a wedding. Yours?*

'No,' he says. 'Not yet. I bought a couple of other units too. I was just about to open up this one.'

'Whatever you paid, I'll double it,' she says. 'I didn't want it sold, but there was a mistake, the cheque got lost in the mail, and I was away on business, I didn't get the notification soon enough, and then I took the first plane I could, but then I was stuck in Chicago for six hours because of the storm. It was *so* snowed in! And then the traffic from the airport, it was terrible!' She ends with a nervous giggle. She must have rehearsed this: it comes out of her in one long phrase, like ticker tape.

'I heard about the storm,' he says. 'In Chicago. That's too bad. I'm sorry to hear you were delayed.' He doesn't respond to her financial offer. It hangs in the air between them, like their two breaths.

'That storm's heading here next,' she says. 'It's a serious blizzard. They always travel east. If you don't want to get stuck here, you should hit the road. I'll speed this up for us – I'll pay cash.'

'Thanks,' he says. 'I'm considering. What's in there, anyway? It must be something valuable, to be so important to you.' He's curious to see what she'll say.

'Just family things,' she says. 'Things I inherited. You know, crystal, china, from my grandmother. A few pieces of costume jewellery. Sentimental value. You couldn't sell them for much.'

'Family things?' he says. 'Any furniture?'

'Only a little furniture,' she says. 'Not good quality. Old furniture. Not anything anyone would want.'

'But that's what I deal in,' he says. 'Old furniture. I run an antiques store. Often people don't know the value of what they have. Before accepting your offer, I'd like to take a look.' He glances down at her mouth again.

'I'll triple it,' she says. Now she's shivering. 'It's too cold for you to be going through that unit right now! Why don't we get out of here before the storm hits? We could have a drink, and, I don't know, dinner or something? We can talk it over.' She smiles at him, an insinuating smile. A strand of her hair has come down, it's blowing across her mouth; she tucks it in behind her ear, slowly, then drops her eyes, gazing down in the direction of his belt. She's upping the ante.

'Okay,' he says. 'Sounds good. You can tell me

more about the furniture. But suppose I accept your offer, that unit has to be cleared in twenty-four hours. Or else they'll come in and do it themselves, and they'll keep my cleaning deposit.'

'Oh, I'll make sure it's cleared,' she says. She slips her hand through his arm. 'But I'll need the key.'

'No hurry,' says Sam. 'We haven't set the price.'

She looks at him, no longer smiling. She knows he knows.

He should quit fooling around. He should take the money and run. But he's having too much fun. A real murderess, coming on to him! It's edgy, it's rash, it's erotic. He hasn't felt this alive for some time. Will she try to poison his drink? Get him in a dark corner, whip out a penknife, go for his jugular? Would he be fast enough to grab her hand? He wants to reveal his knowledge to her in a safe place surrounded by other people. He wants to watch her face as she realizes he's got her by the neck, so to speak. He wants to hear the story she'll tell. Or the stories: she must have more than one. He would.

'Out of here, turn right,' he says. 'Next stoplight, go past it. There's a motel – the Silver Knight.' He knows the motel bars near all the storage outfits where he bids at auctions. 'I'll meet you in the bar. Get a booth. I just need to check my other unit.' He almost says, 'Book a room while you're at it, because we both know what this is about,' but that would be rushing things.

'The Silver Knight,' she says. 'Has it got a silver

170

knight on the outside? Riding to the rescue?' She's trying for a light touch. Again the laugh, a little breathless. Sam doesn't play the move back. Instead he opts for a reprimanding frown. *Don't think you can charm me out of it, lady. I'm here to collect.*

'You can't miss it,' he says. Will she skip out on him? Leave him stuck with the fiasco? No one would know how to track her, unless she'd made the mistake of using her real name when she'd rented the unit. It's a risk, letting her out of his sight, but a risk he needs to take. He's 99 per cent certain she'll be sitting in the bar of the Silver Knight when he gets there.

He texts Ned: *Traffic shit. Blizzard crap. We'll PU AM. Nite.* He has a strong impulse to slip the SIM card out of his phone and tuck it into the dried groom's breast pocket, but he resists it. He does go offline, however: not dark, but dark grey.

I dunno, officer, Ned will say. *He texted me from the storage place. Maybe around four. He was fine then. He was supposed to come to the shop in the morning, then we were going to take the van and clear out the units. After that, nothing.*

What dried guy in a monkey suit? Really? No shit! Search me.

One thing at a time. First, he opens up Unit 56. All is as it should be: several pieces of furniture, good-enough quality, the sort of thing they can resell in Metrazzle. Rocking chair, pine, Quebec. Two end tables, '50s, mahogany looks like, spindly ebonized legs. Among them, an Arts and Crafts desk. The sealed white baggies are in the three right-hand drawers.

It's perfect, really. Maximum deniability. There's no traceable line from them to him. *I have no idea how it got in there! I bought the unit at an auction, I won the bid, it could've been anyone. I'm as surprised as you are! No, I didn't open the drawers before I brought it back to the shop, why would I? I sell antiques, not stuff in drawers.*

Then the end destination buys the desk, most likely on Monday, and that's all there is to it. He's just the drop box, he's just the delivery boy.

Ned won't open the drawers either. He has a finely developed sense of which drawers to leave closed.

Sam can leave the shipment safely where it is: no one's going to bother this locked unit before noon the next day. Him and his van will be well on the way before then.

He checks his phone: one new message, from Gwyneth. *I was wrong, please come back, we can talk it through.* He has a tug of nostalgia: the familiar, the snug, the safe; the safe enough. Nice to know it's waiting for him. But he doesn't reply. He needs this oblong of freefall time he's about to enter. Anything at all can happen within it.

When he walks into the bar at the Silver Knight, she's there waiting. She even has a booth. He's cheered by the instant acquiescence. She's minus her coat now, wearing the sort of outfit a woman like her should wear: black, for widow, for spider. It goes well with her ash-blond hair. Her eyes are hazel, her eyelashes long.

She smiles as he slides in opposite her, but she doesn't smile too much: a faint, melancholy smile. In front of her is a glass of white, barely touched. He orders the same. There's a pause. Who'll go first? All the hairs on the back of Sam's neck are alert. On the flat screen over on the wall behind her head, the blizzard is rolling mutely towards them like a huge wave of confetti.

'I think we might be stuck here,' she says.

'Let's drink to that,' says Sam, opening his big blue eyes. He does the direct gaze, raises his glass. What can she do but raise hers?

Yeah, that's him all right, no question. I was tending bar that night, the night of the blizzard. He was with a sizzling blond in a black dress, they seemed on very friendly terms, if you know what I mean. Didn't see them leave. You want to bet they'll find her in a snowbank when it all melts?

'So, you looked inside,' she says.

'Yeah, I did,' says Sam. 'Who was he? What happened?' He hopes she doesn't descend into tears: that would disappoint him. But no, she limits herself to a quivering chin, a biting of the lip.

'It was terrible,' she says. 'It was a mistake. He wasn't supposed to die.'

'But he did,' says Sam in a kindly voice. 'These things happen.'

173

'Oh yes. They do. I don't know how to say this, it sounds so . . .'

'Trust me,' says Sam. She doesn't, but she'll pretend.

'He liked to be . . . Clyde liked to be strangled. It wasn't as if I enjoyed it. But I loved him, I was in love with him, so I wanted to do what he wanted.'

'Of course,' says Sam. He wishes she hadn't given the mummified groom a name: *Clyde* is dorky. He'd have preferred him anonymous. That she's lying is evident to him, but how much is she lying? For his own lies, he likes to stay somewhere within shooting distance of the truth, if at all possible – it means less to fabricate, less to work at remembering – so maybe some of this is true.

'And,' she says, 'then he was.'

'Then he was what?' says Sam.

'Then he was dead. With the spasms, I thought he was just having, you know . . . the way he usually did. But it went too far. Then I didn't know what to do. It was the day before our wedding, I'd been planning the whole thing for months! I told everyone he'd left me a note, he'd vanished, he'd run out on me, he'd jilted me. I was so upset! It was all being delivered, the dress, the cake, all of that, and I, well, this sounds weird, but I dressed him up, with the carnation in the buttonhole and everything, he looked so handsome. And then I packed the whole thing into the storage unit. I wasn't thinking clearly. I'd been so looking forward to the wedding; keeping all the parts of it together was sort of like having it anyway.'

'You put him in there yourself? With the cake and everything?'

'Yes,' she says. 'It wasn't that hard. I used a dolly. You know, for moving heavy boxes, and furniture and things.'

'That was resourceful,' says Sam. 'You're a smart girl.'

'Thank you,' she says.

'That's some story,' says Sam. 'Not many people would believe it.'

She looks down at the table. 'I know,' she says in a small voice. Then she looks up. 'But you believe it, don't you?'

'I'm not good at believing stories,' says Sam. 'Though let's say I believe this one, for now.' Maybe he'll get the truth out of her later. Or maybe not.

'Thank you,' she says again. 'You won't tell?' The tremulous smile, the bitten lip. She's laying it on thick. What did she really do? Whack him over the head with a champagne bottle? Shoot an overdose into him? How much money was involved, and in what form? It had to be money. Was she skimming the poor guy's bank account, did he find out?

'Let's go,' says Sam. 'The elevator's to the left.'

The room's dark, except for the faint light coming in off the street. The traffic's muffled, what there

175

is of it. The snow has arrived in earnest; it's spattering softly against the window like an army of tiny kamikaze mice throwing themselves at the glass, trying to force a way in.

Holding her in his arms – no, holding her down with his arms – is the most electric thing he's ever done. She hums with danger, like a high-tension wire; she's a raw socket; she's the sum of his own ignorance, of everything he doesn't understand and never will. The minute he releases one of her hands, he might be dead. The minute he turns his back. Is he running for his life, right now? Her harsh breath chasing him?

'We should be together,' she's saying. 'We should always be together.' Is that what she said to the other one? To his sad, mummified double? He grips her hair, bites down on her mouth. He's still ahead, he's gaining on her. Faster!

Nobody knows where he is.

I DREAM OF ZENIA WITH
THE BRIGHT RED TEETH

'I had a dream about Zenia last night,' says Charis.

'Who?' says Tony.

'Oh, crap!' says Roz. Charis's black-and-white mystery-mix dog, Ouida, has just smeared her muddy paws down the front of Roz's new coat. The coat is orange, perhaps not the best choice. Charis claims that Ouida has special perceptive powers, and that her paw smearings are messages. What is Ouida trying to say to me? wonders Roz. You look like a pumpkin?

It's autumn. The three of them are shuffling through the dry leaves in the ravine, taking their weekly walk. It's a pact they've made: to get more exercise, to improve their cellular autophagic rates. Roz has read about this in one of the health magazines in the dentist's waiting room: bits of your cells eat other bits that are diseased or dying. This intracellular cannibalism is said to help you live longer.

'What do you mean, "crap"?' says Charis. With her long white crinkly face and her long white

177

crinkly hair, she's more sheep-like than ever. Or more like an angora goat, thinks Tony, who prefers the specific to the general. That inward, ruminative look.

'I didn't mean your dream,' says Roz. 'I meant Ouida. Sit, Ouida!'

'She likes you,' says Charis fondly.

'Sit, Ouida!' says Roz with some annoyance. Ouida bounds away.

'She's so full of energy!' says Charis. She's been a dog owner for just three months, and already every irritating thing that mutt does is beyond adorable. You'd think she'd given birth to it.

'Awesome!' says Tony, who sometimes echoes her students. She's now a professor emeritus, but she still teaches one graduate seminar, 'Early Technologies of War.' They've just done the scorpion bombs, always popular, and have now reached the composite short bows of Attila the Hun, with their bone stiffeners. 'Zenia! Unfuckingbelievable! Did she ooze out of a tomb?'

She peers up at Charis through her round glasses. In her twenties, Tony looked like a pixie. She still does, but a pressed-flower pixie. More papery.

'When was it she died?' says Roz. 'I've lost track. Isn't that awful?'

'Shortly after 1989,' says Tony. 'Or 1990. When the Berlin Wall was coming down. I've got a piece of it.'

'You think it's real?' says Roz. 'People were chipping cement off anything then! It's like the True

Cross, or saints' finger bones, or . . . or fake Rolex watches.'

'It's a memento,' says Tony. 'They don't have to be real.'

'Time isn't the same in dreams,' says Charis, who likes reading about what's going on in her head when she isn't awake, though sometimes, thinks Roz, it's hard to tell the difference. 'In dreams, nobody's dead, really. That's what the man who . . . he says, in dreams the time is always Now.'

'That's not too comforting,' says Tony. She likes things to stay in their categories. Pens in this jar, pencils in that. Vegetables on the right side of the plate, meat on the left. The living here, the dead over there. Too much osmosis, too much wavering – it can be dizzying.

'What was she wearing?' Roz asks. Zenia had dressed stunningly, back when she was alive. She'd favoured luscious colours like sepia and plum. She'd had glamour, whereas Roz has only ever had class.

'Leather,' says Tony. 'With a silver-handled whip.'

'Just a sort of shroud thing,' says Charis. 'It was white.'

'I can't see her in white,' says Roz.

'We didn't use a shroud,' says Tony. 'For the cremation. We chose one of her own dresses, remember? Sort of a cocktail dress. Dark.' Zenia spelled backwards is Ainez, a Spanish-sounding name. There was definitely a Spanish element to Zenia: as a singer, she'd have been a contralto.

179

'The two of you made that decision,' says Roz. 'I'd have put her in a sack.' She had proposed the sack idea, but Charis had argued for proper vestments: otherwise, Zenia might be resentful and hang around.

'Okay, maybe not a shroud,' says Charis. 'More like a nightgown. Sort of floaty.'

'Did it glow?' says Tony with interest. 'Like ectoplasm?'

'What about the shoes?' says Roz. Shoes once played a major part in Roz's life – expensive shoes with high heels – but toe-gnarling and bunions have put paid to that. Walking shoes can be very nice as well, however. She might get those new every-toe-separate kind. They make you look like a frog, but they're supposed to be very comfortable.

'Of course, it was painted gauze, really,' says Tony. 'They stuffed it up their noses.'

'What in heck are you talking about?' says Roz.

'Her feet were not the point,' says Charis. 'The *point* was . . .'

'I suppose she had fangs dripping blood,' says Tony. That would be the sort of overacting Zenia would go in for. Red contact lenses, hissing, claws, the works.

Charis ought to stop watching vampire films at night. It's bad for her; she's so impressionable. Both Tony and Roz think this, so they go over to Charis's house on vampire nights so at least she won't be watching alone. Charis makes mint tea and popcorn for them, and they sit on her sofa

180

like teenagers, cramming popcorn into their mouths, feeding the occasional handful to Ouida, glued to the screen as the music shifts to eerie, and eyes redden or yellow, and teeth elongate, and blood spurts like pizza sauce over everything in sight. Whenever wolves are audible, Ouida howls.

Why are the three of them indulging in these adolescent pursuits? Is it some kind of grisly substitute for diminishing sex? They seem to have thrown away all the maturity and experience and wisdom they've collected like Air Miles over their middle years; just tossed them out, in favour of irresponsible buttery and salty munching and cheesy, adrenaline-soaked time wasting. After these curious orgies, Tony spends days picking white hairs off her cardigans – some from Ouida, some from Charis. 'Have a nice evening?' West would ask, and Tony would say they'd just done a lot of boring girl talk, as usual. She doesn't want West to feel he's missed out.

Things are getting out of hand: Tony catches herself channelling this opinion at least once a day. The crazed weather. The vicious, hate-filled politics. The myriad glass high-rises going up like 3-D mirrors, or siege engines. The municipal garbage collection: Who can keep all those different-coloured bins straight? Where to put the clear plastic food containers, and why isn't the little number on the bottom a reliable guide?

And the vampires. You used to know where you stood with them – smelly, evil, undead – but now

181

there are virtuous vampires and disreputable vampires, and sexy vampires and glittery vampires, and none of the old rules about them are true any more. Once you could depend on garlic, and on the rising sun, and on crucifixes. You could get rid of the vampires once and for all. But not any more.

'Actually, not fangs as such,' says Charis. 'Though her teeth were kind of pointy, come to think of it. And sort of pink. Ouida, stop that!'

Now Ouida is dashing around and barking: being in the ravine and off the leash excites her. She likes to nose under fallen logs and dodge behind bushes, evading the moment of recapture and hiding her – what to call them? Charis disapproves of crass words like *shit*. Roz has offered *poop*, but Charis rejected it as too babyish. Her alimentary canal products? Tony has suggested. No, that sounds too coldly intellectual, said Charis. Her Gifts to the Earth.

Hiding her Gifts to the Earth, then, while Charis dithers along behind, clutching a plastic disposal bag (such bags are almost never used by Charis because she often cannot locate the Gifts) and calling weakly at intervals, as she is doing at present: 'Ouida! Ouida! Come here! Good girl!'

'So there she was,' says Tony. 'Zenia. In your dream. Then what?'

'You think this is stupid,' says Charis. 'But anyway. She wasn't menacing or anything. In fact, she seemed kind of friendly. She had a message for me. What she said was, Billy's coming back.'

182

'News must travel slowly in the afterlife,' says Tony, 'because Billy's already come back, right?'

'Not exactly *back*,' says Charis primly. 'I mean, we're not . . . he's only next door.'

'Which is already too close for comfort,' says Roz. 'Why the heck you ever rented to that deadbeat I just don't get.'

Long ago, when they were all a lot younger, Zenia had stolen a man from each of them. From Tony, she'd stolen West, who did, however, think better of it – or that is Tony's official version to herself – and is safely rooted in Tony's house, fooling with his electronic music system and getting deafer by the minute. From Roz, she'd stolen Mitch, not exactly hard, since he'd never been able to keep it zipped; but then, after emptying not only his pockets but what Charis called his psychic integrity, Zenia had dumped him, and he'd drowned himself in Lake Ontario. He'd worn a life jacket, and he'd made it look like a sailing accident, but Roz had known.

She's over that by now, or as much as a girl can ever be over it, and she has a much nicer husband called Sam, who's in merchant banking and more suitable, with a better sense of humour. But still, it's a scar. And it hurt the children; that's the part she can't forgive, despite the shrink she went to in an effort to wipe the slate. Not that there's any percentage in not forgiving a person who's no longer alive.

From Charis, Zenia had stolen Billy. That was perhaps the cruellest theft, think Tony and Roz, because Charis was so trusting and defenceless, and let Zenia into her life because Zenia was in trouble, and was a battered woman, and had cancer, and needed someone to take care of her, or that was her story – a shameless fabrication in every part. Charis and Billy were living on the Island then, in a little house that was more like a cottage. They kept chickens. Billy built the coop himself; being a draft dodger, he didn't exactly have a steady job.

There wasn't all that much room in the cottage for Zenia, but Charis made room, being hospitable and wanting to share, the way people were on the Island in those days, and in the dodger communities. There was an apple tree; Charis made apple cakes, and other baked items as well, with the eggs. She was so happy, and also pregnant. And the next thing you knew, Billy and Zenia had gone off together and all the chickens were dead. They'd had their throats cut with the bread knife. It was just so mean.

Why had Zenia done it? All of it? Why do cats eat birds? was Roz's unhelpful answer. Tony thought it was an exercise in power. Charis was sure there was a reason, embedded somewhere in the workings of the universe, but she wasn't sure what it could be.

Roz and Tony each ended up with a man in residence, despite Zenia's best ruination efforts, but Charis didn't. That was because she'd never achieved closure, was Roz's theory. She couldn't find anyone ditzy enough, was Tony's. But less than a month ago, who should turn up but that long-lost schmuck of a Billy, and what did Charis do but rent him the other half of her duplex? It's enough to make you tear your hair out by its tiny grey roots, thinks Roz, who still gets hers touched up every two weeks. A nice chestnut colour, not vivid. The complexion can get washed out if you go too bright.

Charis's duplex is a whole other story. Distant cousins should never die, thinks Tony; or if they do, they should never leave their money to kindly fools like Charis.

Because, now that Charis is no longer an ex-flower child and erstwhile dabbler in chicken-raising, living on day-old bread and cat food and God knows what else in a badly insulated summer cottage on the Island, facing an increasingly impoverished and eventually hypothermic old age and fighting off her grown-up Ottawa bureaucrat of a daughter's attempts to move her into a facility; because Charis is no longer an old street bat in training but is worth solid cash, Billy has come back into her life as if teleported.

Not that the distant cousin left a regal fortune, but she'd left enough so that Charis could move off the Island. It was getting too genteel for her anyway, she said, what with the renovations and the snobby people moving in, and she no longer felt really accepted there. Enough to stave off the facility fate and the day-old bread. Enough to buy a house.

Charis could have chosen a detached home, but she was maybe losing track of things sometimes – that was how she put it, causing Tony to say, 'No shit!' privately to Roz over the phone – and the concept was that she would live in one half of the duplex and rent the other half to someone who was, well, better with tools than she was, and she would trade that person lower rent for maintenance and repairs. Skill-trading was so much less mercenary than charging market value rent, didn't Roz and Tony feel that?

They didn't, but Charis had brushed their counsel aside and put an offer up on Craigslist, with (Tony thinks) maybe a little too much description of herself and her tastes, all of which (Roz thinks) amounted to an open invitation to an unscrupulous prick like Billy. And presto, all of a sudden, there he was.

Ouida does not like Billy. She growls at him. Which is some comfort, as Charis pays more attention to Ouida's opinions now than to those of anyone else, including her two oldest friends.

It was Tony and Roz who'd given Ouida to Charis. Now that Charis is living in Parkdale – a location rapidly gentrifying, says Roz, who keeps an eye on real estate prices, and Charis will do well in the long run, but the gentrification is far from complete, and you never know what you might run into on the street, not to mention the drug dealers. Also, says Tony, Charis is such an innocent; she has no instinct for ambushes. And she doesn't like to drive; she prefers to ramble about on foot in the wilder places of the city, ravines and High Park and such, communing with plant spirits. Or whatever the heck she thinks she's doing, says Roz, and let's just hope she doesn't decide the Poison Ivy Fairy is her new best friend.

Neither of them wants to read about Charis in the paper. 'Elderly Woman Mugged Under Bridge.' 'Harmless Eccentric Found Battered.' A dog is a deterrent, and Ouida is a terrier blend, maybe with some border collie, a bright dog at any rate, they'd concluded as they were filling out the rescue dog papers. And with a little training . . .

Well, said Tony, after Ouida had been installed for a month. That was the weak link in the plan: Charis couldn't train a banana. 'But Ouida is very loyal,' said Roz. 'I'd bet on Ouida in a pinch. She's a good growler.'

'She growls at mosquitoes,' said Tony gloomily. As a historian, she has no faith in so-called predictable outcomes.

Ouida is named after a self-dramatizing novelist of the nineteenth century; she'd been a devoted lover of dogs, so what better name for Charis's new pet? said Tony, who'd done the naming. Roz and Tony suspect that Charis sometimes thinks Ouida the dog actually is Ouida the self-dramatizing novelist, since Charis believes in recycling, not only for bottles and plastics but also for psychic entities. She once said defensively that Prime Minister Mackenzie King was convinced his dead mother had reincarnated in his Irish terrier, and nobody found that strange at the time. Tony refrained from commenting that nobody found it strange at the time because nobody knew about it at the time. But they'd found it plenty strange afterwards.

Once Roz gets home from their walk, she calls Tony on her cell. 'What are we going to do?' she asks.

'About Zenia?' says Tony.

'About Billy. The man's a psychopath. He murdered those chickens!'

'Chicken-murdering is a public service,' says Tony. 'Somebody's got to do it or we'd be six feet deep in hens.'

'Tony. Be serious.'

'What can we do?' says Tony. 'She's not underage, we're not her mother. She's already getting that moony woo-woo look.'

'Maybe I'll hire a detective. See what kind of record Billy's got. Before he buries her in the garden.'

'That house hasn't got a garden,' says Tony. 'Only a patio. He'll have to use the cellar. Stake out the hardware store, see if he buys any pickaxes.'

'Charis is our friend!' says Roz. 'Don't make jokes about this!'

'I know,' says Tony. 'I'm sorry. I only make jokes when I don't know what to do.'

'I don't know what to do either,' says Roz.

'Pray to Ouida,' says Tony. 'She's our last line of defence.'

Their regular walks are on Saturdays, but this is a crisis, so Roz fixes lunch for Wednesday.

The three of them used to eat at the Toxique, back in the days of Zenia. Queen Street West was edgier then: more green hair, more black leather, more comic book stores. Now the mid-scale clothing chains have moved in, though there are still some residual tattoo joints and button shops, and the Condom Shack is soldiering on. The Toxique is long gone, however. Roz settles for the Queen Mother Café. A little elderly and battered, but comfy, like the three of them.

Or like the three of them used to be. Today, however, Charis is ill at ease. She fiddles with her vegetarian pad Thai and keeps looking out the window, where Ouida is impatiently waiting, roped to a bicycle stand.

'When's the next vampire night?' says Roz. She's just come from the dentist and is having trouble eating because of the freezing. Her teeth are going the way of her high-heeled shoes, and for the same reasons: crumbling and pain. And the expense! It's like shovelling money into her open mouth. On the bright side, dentistry is far more pleasant than it used to be. Instead of writhing and sweating,

189

Roz puts on dark glasses and earphones and listens to New Age dingle music, borne away on a wave of sedatives and analgesics.

'Well,' says Charis, 'the thing is, vampire night was last night.' She sounds guilty.

'You didn't tell us?' says Tony. 'We would have come over. I bet it gave you bad dreams about Zenia.'

'That was the night before,' says Charis. 'Zenia came and sat at the end of my bed and told me to watch out for this person . . . it was a name I didn't know. It sounded like a woman. A Martian kind of name, you know, it began with a *Y.* This time, she was wearing fur.'

'What sort of fur?' says Tony. She's guessing wolverine.

'I don't know,' says Charis. 'It was black and white.'

'Cripes,' says Roz. 'And then you watched a vampire film by yourself! That was reckless!'

'I didn't,' says Charis – now she's gone pink – 'watch it by myself.'

'Oh, crap,' says Roz. 'Not Billy!'

'Did you have sex?' asks Tony. It's an intrusive question, but she and Roz need to know exactly where the enemy stands.

'No!' says Charis, flustered. 'It was just friendly! We talked! And I feel a lot better now, because how can you really forgive a person if they aren't there?'

'Did he put his arm around you?' says Roz, feeling like her own mother. No: her grandmother.

Charis ducks this. 'Billy thinks we should open an urban B&B,' she says. 'As an investment. They're the coming thing. In one-half of the duplex. He'd do the renovations, and then I'd do the baking.'

'And he'd be in charge of the money, right?' says Roz.

'The name Zenia told you. It wouldn't by any chance be Yllib?' says Tony. Zenia had always been good at codes, and puzzles, and reflections.

'Trust me on this: forget it!' says Roz. 'Billy's a drainpipe. He'll clean you out.'

'What does Ouida have to say about him?' Tony asks.

'Ouida's a little jealous, I have to admit,' says Charis. 'I had to . . . I had to sequester her.' She is definitely blushing now.

'Locked Ouida in the closet, is my guess,' says Tony to Roz on the phone.

'This is dire,' says Roz.

They devise a phone tree: Charis will get two calls a day, one from each of them, to monitor the situation. But Charis stops answering the phone.

Three days pass. Then Tony receives a text message: *Need to talk. Please come. Sorry.* It's from Charis.

Tony collects Roz, or rather Roz collects Tony, in her Prius. When they arrive at the duplex, Charis is sitting at the kitchen table. She's been crying. But at least she's still alive.

'What happened, sweetie?' says Roz. There are no marks of violence; maybe that schmuck Billy has pocketed Charis's life savings.

Tony looks at Ouida. She's sitting beside Charis, ears pricked, tongue out. There's something on her chest fur. Pizza sauce?

'Billy's in the hospital,' says Charis. 'Ouida bit him.' She starts to sniffle. Good dog, Ouida, thinks Tony.

'I'll make us some mint tea,' says Roz. 'Why did Ouida . . .?'

'Well, we were going to, you know . . . in the bedroom. And Ouida was barking, so I had to shut her in the upstairs hall closet. And then, just before . . . I simply had to know. So I said, "Billy, who murdered my chickens?" Because back then, Zenia told me it was Billy who did it, but I never knew what to believe, because Zenia was such a liar, and I just couldn't . . . with someone who'd done that. And Billy said, "It was Zenia, she slit their throats, I tried to stop her." And then Ouida started to bark really loud, as if something was hurting her, and I had to go see what was wrong, and when I opened the closet door she rushed out and jumped up on the bed and bit Billy. He screamed a lot, there was blood on the sheets, it was . . .'

'You can get it out with cold water,' says Roz.

'On the leg?' asks Tony.

'Not exactly,' says Charis. 'He wasn't wearing any clothes, otherwise I'm sure she wouldn't have . . . but they're doing surgery. I feel bad about that. I told them at the hospital, after they'd wheeled him to emerg – I said it was me who bit him, it was a sex thing Billy liked and it went too far, and they were very nice, they said these things happen. I hated to lie, but they might have, you know, put Ouida away. It was very stressful! But at least now I know the answer.'

'What answer?' asks Roz. 'The answer to what?'

Charis says it's all very clear: Zenia has been coming back in dreams to warn her about Billy, who was the chicken-murderer all along. But Charis was too stupid to figure it out – she wanted to believe the best of Billy, and it was so nice at first that he was back in her life, it was like a completion of the circle or something, so Zenia had to take the next step and reincarnate herself in the body of Ouida – that's why she was wearing fur in the second dream – and she was naturally annoyed when she heard Billy sticking the blame onto her for something she hadn't done.

In fact, says Charis, maybe Zenia's intentions were benevolent all along. Maybe she stole Billy to protect Charis from such a bad apple as him. Maybe she stole West to teach Tony a life lesson about, well, music appreciation or something, and maybe she stole Mitch to clear the way for Roz's much better husband, Sam. Maybe Zenia was, like, the secret alter ego of each of them, acting out stuff for them they didn't have the strength to act out by themselves. When you looked at it that way . . .

★　★　★

193

So that is how Tony and Roz have agreed to look at it, at least when they are with Charis, because it makes Charis happier. It takes some doing to pretend that a medium-sized black-and-white dog who wipes her paws on your coat and poops behind logs is in fact Zenia, but they don't have to pretend all the time: Zenia comes and goes, unpredictable as she has always been, and only Charis can tell when Zenia is present inside Ouida and when she is not.

Billy made threatening noises about suing Charis for his injuries, but Roz squashed that: she can out-lawyer him any day of the week, she told him. Thanks to the extensive search done by her hired detective, she has chapter and verse on his career in matron-fleecing, Ponzi schemes, and identity theft, and if he thinks he can use Ouida as his blackmail weapon he should think again, because it's his word against Charis's, and who does he think a jury will believe?

So Billy has gone elsewhere, never to be seen again, and now a jovial retired plumber lives in the other half of Charis's duplex. He's a widower, and Roz and Tony have hopes for him. He's redoing the bathroom, which is a start. Ouida approves of him, and tries to cram herself under the sink when he's down there with his wrench, and licks him wherever possible, and flirts with him shamelessly.

THE DEAD HAND LOVES YOU

The Dead Hand Loves You started as a joke. Or more like a dare. He should have been more careful about it, but the fact was he'd been blowing a fair amount of dope around that time and drinking too much inferior-grade booze, so he hadn't been fully responsible. He shouldn't be held responsible. He shouldn't be held to the terms of the fucking contract. That's what had shackled his ankles: the contract.

And he can never get rid of that contract, because there wasn't any drop-dead date on it. He should have included a good-only-until clause, like milk cartons, like tubs of yogourt, like mayonnaise jars; but what did he know about contracts back then? He'd been twenty-two.

He'd needed the money.

It was so little money. It was such a crappy deal. He was exploited. How could the three of them have taken advantage of him like that? Though they refuse to admit the unfairness of it. They just cite the fucking contract, with those undeniable signatures on it, including his, and then he has to suck it up and fork out. He resisted paying them at first, until Irena got a lawyer; now the three of them have lawyers the way dogs have fleas. Irena should have cut him some slack in view of how close they were once, but no, Irena has a heart of asphalt, harder and drier and more sun-baked every year. Money has ruined her.

His money, since it's because of him that Irena and the other two are rich enough to afford those lawyers of theirs. Top-quality lawyers too, as good as his; not that he wants to get into a snarling, snapping, rending contest among lawyers. It's the client who's always the cracked-bone hyena's breakfast: they take bites out of you, they nibble away at you like a sackful of ferrets, of rats, of piranhas, until you're reduced to a shred, a tendon, a toenail.

So he's had to ante up, decade after decade; since, as they rightfully point out, in a court case he wouldn't stand a chance. He'd signed it, that infernal contract. He'd signed it in red-hot blood.

At the time of the contract, the four of them had been students. Not exactly dirt poor or they wouldn't have been getting a so-called higher education, they'd have been patching frost-heave in the roadways or setting fire to hamburgers for minimum wage, or turning tricks in cheap, vomit-scented bars, at least Irena would; but though not paupers, they didn't have a lot of loose change. They were getting by on summer-job earnings and grudging loans from relatives, and in the case of Irena, a mingy scholarship.

196

They'd met initially through a ten-cent-a-draft beer parlour group given to snide quips and whining and boasting – not Irena, of course, who never did such things. She was more like a den mother, picking up the tab when the rest of them were too pissed to remember where they'd put their dimes and quarters or too slippery to have brought any along, not that she didn't get her cash back later. The four of them had discovered a common need to spend less on accommodations, so they'd rented a house together, right near the university.

It was in the early '60s, back when you could be a student and rent a house in that area, if only a narrow, pointy-roofed, three-storey, stifling in summer, freezing in winter, run-down, pee-flavoured, peeling-wallpapered, warped-floored, clanking-radiatored, rodent-plagued, cockroach-riddled, red-brick Victorian row house. That was before those houses turned into restored Heritage Buildings worth an arm and a bladder, with historical plaques on them affixed by halfwits with nothing better to do than dodder around sticking plaques on overpriced, snootied-up real estate.

His own building – the building in which the ill-advised contract had been signed – has a plaque on it too, saying – surprise! – that he himself once lived there. He knows he once lived there, he doesn't need to be reminded. He doesn't need to read his name, *Jack Dace, 1963–64*, as if he'd only been alive for one fucking year, with underneath it the tiny print that says, 'In this building was written the International Horror Classic, THE DEAD HAND LOVES YOU.'

I'm not a moron! I know all that! he wants to shout at the oval, enamelled blue-and-white plaque. He should forget about it, he should forget the whole episode as much as possible, but he can't because it's chained to his leg. He can't resist peeking at the thing every time he's in town for some filmfest or litfest or comicfest or monsterfest or other. On the one hand, it's a reminder to him of his idiocy in signing the contract; on the other hand, it's pathetically satisfying to read those three words: *International Horror Classic.* He obsesses over it too much, that plaque. Still, it's a tribute to his major life accomplishment. Such as it is.

Maybe that's what it will say on his tombstone: THE DEAD HAND LOVES YOU, INTERNATIONAL HORROR CLASSSIC. Maybe nubile teeny girl fans with Goth eye makeup, and stitch marks tattooed on their necks like the Frankenstein creature, and dotted lines around their wrists with CUT HERE instructions, will visit his grave and leave him tributes composed of withered roses and whitened chicken bones. They send stuff like that to him already, and he's not even dead.

Sometimes they lurk around events he's attending – panel discussions at which he's expected to drone on about the inherent worthiness of 'genres,' or retrospectives of the various movies spawned by his magnum opus – clad in ripped shrouds, with their faces painted a sickly green, bringing envelopes containing photos of themselves naked and/or with black ropes around their necks and their tongues sticking out, and/or baggies containing tufts of their pubic hair and offers of spectacular blowjobs to be performed by themselves while wearing vampire teeth – edgy, that, and he's never accepted one of those jobs. But he hasn't resisted other blandishments. How could he?

It's always a risk though, a risk to his ego. What if he underperforms in the sack, or rather – because these girls like a stimulant of moderate discomfort – on a floor, up against a wall, or on a chair with ropes and knots? What if they say, 'I thought you would be different' while adjusting their leather undergear and slipping back into their spiderweb stockings and repairing their glued-on festering wounds in the bathroom mirror? It's been known to happen, more frequently as age has withered him and custom staled.

'You wrecked my wound' – they've even said things like that. Worse, they've said them straight, without irony. Pouting. Accusing. Dismissive. So it's best to keep such girls at a distance, to let them worship his decadent satanic powers from afar. Anyway, these girls are getting younger and younger, so it's difficult to make conversation with them at those moments when they expect him to talk. Half the time he has no idea what's coming out of their mouths, when it isn't tongues. They have a whole new vocabulary. Some days he thinks he's been buried underground for a hundred years.

Who could have predicted this odd form of success for him? Back when everyone who knew him thought he was a wastrel, including him. *The Dead Hand Loves You* must have been pure inspiration, from some tacky, pulp-hearted, flea-bitten muse; because he'd written that book straight off, with none of the usual stops and starts and dawdlings, the crumpling of the pages, the tossings into the wastebasket, the fits of lethargy and despair that had usually kept him from finishing anything. He'd sat down and typed it out, eight or nine or ten pages a day, on the old Remington he'd scored at a pawn shop. How strange to remember typewriters, with their jammed keys and snarled ribbons and the smudgy carbon paper for copies. It had taken him maybe three weeks. A month, at the max.

Of course he hadn't known it was going to be an International Horror Classic. He hadn't run down two flights of stairs in his underwear and yelled in the kitchen, 'I've just written an International Horror Classic!' And if he had, the other three would only have laughed at him as they sat at the Formica table drinking their instant coffee and eating the pallid casseroles Irena used to cook up for them, using a lot of rice and noodles and onions and cans of mushroom soup and tuna because those ingredients were cheap though nourishing. Irena was big on *nourishing*. Value for the dollar, that was her thing.

The four of them would deposit their weekly food money in the dinner kitty, a cookie jar in the shape of a pig, but Irena contributed less cash because she did the actual cooking. The cooking, the shopping, the paying of the household bills such as light and heat – Irena liked doing all that. Women once did like performing such roles, and men liked that part too. He himself had enjoyed being clucked over and told he should eat more, no denying it. The deal was that the other three, including him, were supposed to do the dishes, though he can't say that happened with any regularity, or not in his case.

To do the cooking, Irena put on an apron. It had a pie appliquéd onto it, and he has to admit she looked good in that apron, partly because it tied around her waist so you could actually see that she had a waist. Her waist was usually concealed under the layers of thick knitted or woven clothing she wore to keep warm. Dark grey clothing, black clothing, like a secular nun.

Having a waist meant she also had a visible bum and some tits, and Jack could not keep himself from picturing what she'd look like without any of her sturdy, nubbly garments on, not even the apron. And with her hair falling down, her blond hair she wore rolled up in the back. She'd look delectable and nourishing, plump and yielding; passively welcoming, like a flesh hot water bottle covered in pink velvet. She could have fooled him, she did fool him: he'd thought she had a soft heart, a heart like a down-filled pillow. He'd idealized her. What a sucker.

Anyway, if he'd come into the noodle-and-tuna-scented kitchen and said he'd just written an International Horror Classic, the three of them would only have laughed at him, because they didn't take him seriously then and they don't take him seriously now.

Jack had the top floor. The attic. It was the worst location. Boiling in summer, freezing in winter. The fumes went up there: cooking fumes, dirty sock fumes from the floors below, toilet stenches – they all wafted upward. There was nothing he could do in retaliation for the heat and the cold and the smells except stomp around on the floor; but that would bother only Irena, who was directly below him, and he didn't want to annoy her because he wanted to get into her underthings.

These were black in colour, as he'd shortly had an opportunity to discover. He'd thought black underwear was sexy at the time, sexy in a sleazy way, as in grotty five-and-dime police magazines. He'd been unacquainted with real-life panty colours other than white and pink, which was what his dates in high school had worn, not that he'd ever managed a good look at those panties in the frustrating darkness of parked cars. He's realized in hindsight that Irena's choice of black was not provocative but pragmatic: her black was a penny-pinching black, devoid of lace or any crisscross or peek-a-boo features, and had been selected not to display flesh but merely to hide the dirt and save on washings.

Having sex with Irena was like having sex with a waffle iron, he used to joke to himself later, but that was after the sequel had distorted his retrospective glance and sheathed her in metal.

Irena was not alone on the second floor. Jaffrey lived there too, a cause of jealous brooding for Jack: how easy for Jaffrey to slither along the hall in his malodorous wool sock feet, drooling and slavering with unwholesome lust, to Irena's door, unseen, unheard, when Jack himself was dead to the world in his attic cubbyhole. But Jaffrey's room was over the tacked-on, tar-papered, insufficiently insulated and subcutaneously grime-ridden kitchen that jutted out from the back of the house, so there was no ceiling above Jaffrey's head that could be stomped on.

Rod was similarly out of stomping range, and he, too, was suspected by Jack of having designs on Irena. His room was on the ground floor, in what would originally have been the dining room. They'd nailed shut the double doors with frosted glass panels that led to what was once the parlour and was now a kind of opium den, though they didn't have any opium, only some fusty maroon cushions, a carpet in dog-vomit brown with potato chips and nut fragments ground into it, and a broken-down easy chair that stank of sickly sweet Old Sailor Port, the winos' tipple of choice, drunk ironically by visiting philosophy students because it cost nearly nothing.

That parlour was where they lounged around and had parties, not that it was large enough for that, so the parties spilled out into the narrow hall and up the stairs and back into the kitchen, the party-goers self-segregating into pot-smokers and drinkers – the pot-smokers not being hippies as such because those hadn't happened yet, but a whiff of things to come, a mangy, self-conscious, quasi-beatnik group who hung out with jazz players and took up with their marginally trans-gressive ways; and at such times he – Jack Dace, the now be-plaqued one, revered author of an International Horror Classic – at such times he was glad his room was at the very top of the house, apart from the milling throng and the stench of alcohol and cigarette smoke and weed, and some-times of upchuck because people didn't know when to stop.

With a room of his own, a room at the top, he could proffer a temporary refuge to some lovely, fatigued, world-weary, sophisticated, black-turtlenecked, heavily-eyelinered girl he might lure up the stairs into his newspaper-strewn boudoir and onto his Indian-bedspreaded bed with the promise of artistic talk about the craft of writing, and the throes and torments of creation, and the need for integrity, and the temptations of selling out, and the nobility of resisting such temptations, and so forth. A promise offered with a hint of self-mockery in case such a girl might think he was pompous and cocksure and full of himself. Which he was, because at that age you have to be that way in order to crawl out of bed in the morning and sustain your faith in your own illusory potential for the next twelve hours of being awake.

But a successful luring of such a girl never actually took place, and if it had, it might have ruined his chances with Irena, who was giving tiny signs of maybe coming across. Irena did not drink or smoke weed herself, though she went around wiping up after those who did, and took mental notes of who was doing what to whom, and remembered everything in the morning. She never said that in so many words, she was discreet, but you could tell by what she avoided saying.

After *The Dead Hand Loves You* was published to such acclaim – no, not acclaim, because that kind of book didn't gather anything you could call acclaim, not then; only much later, once pulp and genre had established a toehold and then a beach-head on the shores of writerly legitimacy – after the book had been made into a film, then – that kind of luring became much easier for him. Once he had a reputation, at least as a commercial writer, a commercial writer with large paperback sales and book covers with raised gold lettering. He couldn't get away with the Art gambit any more; but, in compensation, quite a few girls liked the macabre, or said they did. They liked it even then, before the Goth wave hit. Maybe it reminded them of their inner lives. Though maybe they were just hoping he'd help get them into the movies.

Oh Jack, Jack, he tells himself, eyeing his baggy eyes in the mirror, fingering the thin patch at the back of his head, sucking in his belly, though he can't hold it in for long. You're such a wreck. You're such a dupe. You're so alone. Oh Jack be nimble, Jack be quick, with your once-dependable candlestick and your knack for impromptu bullshit. You used to be so full of beans. You used to be so trusting. You used to be so young.

The contract thing had started off in an aggravating way. It was a day in late March, the lawns heaped with grey and porous melting snow, the air chilly and damp, the tempers peevish. It was lunchtime. Jack's three roomies were sitting at the Formica kitchen table – red, with pearly swirls and chrome legs – chewing their way through the leftovers Irena typically dished up for lunch because she didn't like to waste food. He himself had slept in, and no wonder: there had been a party the night before, an unusually foul and tedious party at which, thanks to Jaffrey – who liked to hold forth at length on the subject of foreign, impenetrable authors – Nietzsche and Camus had been under discussion, which was worse luck for him,

Jack Dace, since what he knew about either of them could fit in a salt shaker. Though he could do a fair-enough riff on Kafka, who'd written the side-splitter in which the guy turns into a beetle, which was what he himself felt like on most mornings anyway. Some sadist had brought a flask of lab alcohol to the night-before party and mixed it with grape juice and vodka, and, crazed by the droning of competitive literary display, he, Jack Dace, had drunk too much of it and puked up his kneecaps. That, in addition to whatever he'd been smoking, which was most likely cut with crotch-itch powder.

So he'd been in no mood to discuss the topic that was produced by Irena over the noodle-and-tuna leftovers, mercilessly, right off the bat.

'You're three months behind on the rent money,' she said. Before he even had a chance to drink his instant coffee.

'Christ,' he said. 'Look at that, my hands are shaking. I really tied one on last night!' Why couldn't she be more understanding and nurturing, for fuck's sake? Even a perceptive comment would have been assuaging. 'You look like hell,' for instance.

'Don't change the subject,' said Irena. 'As you're aware, the rest of us have been forced to pay your share of the rent for you; otherwise we'll all get evicted. But this has to stop. Either you find some way of paying or you'll have to leave. We'll need to rent out your room to someone who actually does pay.'

Jack slumped down at the table. 'I know, I know,' he said. 'Geez. I'm sorry. I'll make it good, I just need a little more time.'

'Time for what?' said Jaffrey with a disbelieving smirk. 'Absolute time, or relative time? Internal or measurable? Euclidean or Kantean?' It was way too early in the day for him to be starting up with the hair-splitting Philosophy 101 wordplay. He was such an asshole that way.

'Anyone have an aspirin?' said Jack. It was a weak move, but the only one he could lay his hands on. He did in truth have a fearsome head-ache. Irena stood up to get him a painkiller. She couldn't resist the urge to play nursie.

'How much more time?' said Rod. He had out his little greenish-brown notebook, the one in which he made his mathematical calculations: he was the bookkeeper for their joint enterprise.

'You've been needing more time for weeks,' said Irena. 'Months, actually.' She set down two aspi-rins and a glass of water. 'There's Alka-Seltzer too,' she added.

'My novel,' said Jack, not that he hadn't waved this excuse around before. 'I need the time, I really . . . I'm almost finished.' This was untrue. In fact, he was stuck on the third chapter. He'd outlined the characters: four people – four attractive, hormone-sodden students – living in a three-storey pointy brick Victorian row house near the univer-sity, uttering cryptic sentences about their psyches and fornicating a lot, but he couldn't move beyond that because he didn't know what else they could possibly do. 'I'll get a job,' he said feebly.

'Such as what?' said obsidian-hearted Irena. 'There's ginger-ale, if you want some.'

'Maybe you could sell encyclopedias,' said Rod, and the three of them laughed. Encyclopedia-selling was known to be the last resort of the feckless, the inept, and the desperate; in addition to which the idea of him, Jack Dace, actually selling anything to anyone struck them as funny. Their view of him was that he was a fuck-up and a jinx from whom stray dogs fled because they could smell failure on him like catshit. Of late the three of them wouldn't even let him dry the dishes because he'd dropped too many of them on the floor. He'd done that on purpose, since it was useful to be considered inept when it came to chore division, but it was working against him now.

'Why don't you sell shares in your novel?' said Rod. He was in Economics; he played the stock market with his spare change and wasn't too bad at it, which was how he paid his own fucking rent. It made him smug and insufferable on the subject of money, characteristics he has retained ever since.

'Okay, I'm game,' Jack said. It was make-believe at that point. The three of them were humouring him – giving him a break, pretending to acknowledge his claim to talent, opening up a pathway to fiscal rectitude for him, if only a theoretical one. That was their story later: that they'd colluded in order to give him a boost up, lead him to believe that they believed in him, toss him some validation. Then he might actually get off his ass and do something, not that they expected this to actually happen. It wasn't their fault that it had worked, and so spectacularly.

Rod was the one who drew up the contract. Rent for three months plus one – the three Jack hadn't paid in the past, and the one that was about to happen. In return, the shares of the proceeds from his yet-to-be-completed novel were divided into four, with a quarter going to each of them, including Jack. It would be negatively motivating if there was no upside built in for Jack himself. With nothing to gain he might not feel energized about finishing the thing, said Rod, who was a believer in Economic Man. He sniggered at this last point, since he didn't think Jack would finish it anyway.

Would Jack have signed such a contract if he hadn't been so hung over? Probably. He didn't want to be evicted. He didn't want to land on the street, or, worse, back in his parents' rec room in Don Mills, besieged by hand-wringing and pot roasts from his mother and tut-tutting lectures from his dad. So he'd agreed to every term, and signed, and breathed a sigh of relief, and, at Irena's urging, had eaten a couple of forkfuls of noodle casserole because it was best to get something into his stomach, and had gone upstairs to take a nap.

★　　★　　★

But then he had to write the fucker.

No hope with the four student characters living in the Victorian row house. It was clear they'd refuse to get their paralyzed buttocks off the third-hand kitchen chairs onto which their anuses were at present stuck like the suckers of a collective octopus, even if he lit their feet on fire. He'd have to try something else, something very different; and fast, because writing the novel – any novel – had become a matter of pride. He couldn't allow Jaffrey and Rod to continue jeering at him; he could no longer endure the pitying, dismissive look in Irena's lovely blue eyes.

Please, please, he prayed to the gelid, fume-filled air. Help me out here! Anything, whatever! Anything that will sell!

In such ways are devil's bargains made.

And there, suddenly, shimmering before him like a phosphorescent toadstool, was the vision of *The Hand*, fully formed: all he needed to do was more or less write it down, or so he said later on talk shows. Where did it come from, *The Dead Hand Loves You*? Who knows? Out of desperation. Out from under the bed. Out of his childhood nightmares. More possibly, out from the gruesome black-and-white comic books he used to filch from the corner drugstore when he was twelve: detached, dried-up, self-propelling body parts were a regular feature of those.

The plot was simple. Violet, a beautiful but cold-hearted girl who bore a resemblance to Irena, but an Irena even thinner of waist and plumper of boob, threw over her lovelorn fiancé, William, a handsome, sensitive young man at least six inches taller than Jack but with the same hair colour. She did this for crass motives: her other suitor, Alf, a dead ringer for Jaffrey as far as appearance went, was rich as stink.

Violet did her act of jilting in the most humiliating way possible. Straight-arrow William had a date with Violet and had arrived at her moderately substantial house to pick her up. But Alf was there before him, and William caught Violet and Alf locked in a hot and immodest clinch on the porch swing. Worse, Alf had his hand up Violet's skirt, a liberty William had never even attempted, the fool.

Outraged and shocked, William angrily challenged the two of them, but this got him nowhere. After scornfully flinging William's hand-gathered bouquet of meadow daisies and wild roses down on the sidewalk along with the plain gold engagement band that had cost him two months' earnings from his job at the encyclopedia company, Violet marched emphatically away on her audacious, red, high-heeled shoes, and she and Alf drove off in Alf's silver Alfa Romeo convertible, a vehicle he had bought on a whim because it fitted with his name: he could afford flamboyant gestures like that. Their mocking laughter echoed in poor William's ears; and to cap it off, the engagement band rolled along the street and clinked down through a sewer grating.

William was mortally wounded. His dreams were shattered, his image of perfect womanhood destroyed. He moped along to his cheap but clean rooming house, where he wrote down his will: he wanted his right hand cut off and buried separately from him, beside the park bench where he and Violet had spent so many idyllic evenings ~~necking~~ ~~smooching~~ tenderly embracing. Then he shot himself in the head with a service revolver inherited from his dead father – for William was an orphan – and used by the father, heroically, during the Second World War. That detail added a note of symbolic nobility, Jack felt.

William's landlady, a kindly widow with a European accent and gypsy intuition, saw to it that his wish about the cut-off hand was honoured. In fact, she crept into the funeral parlour at night and severed the appendage herself with a fretsaw from her departed husband's woodworking bench, a scene that, in the film – both films, the original and the remake – allowed for some ominous shadows and an eerie glow coming from the hand. That glow gave the landlady quite a turn, but she carried on. Then she buried the hand beside the park bench, deep enough so that it would not be dug up by skunks. She placed her crucifix on top of it; for, being from the old country, she was superstitious.

Like the hardhearted bitch she was, Violet snubbed the funeral, and she didn't know about the severed hand. Nobody knew about it except the landlady, who shortly thereafter moved far away to Croatia, where she became a nun in order to expunge from her soul the possibly satanic act she had committed.

Time passed. Violet was now engaged to Alf. Their lavish wedding was being planned. Violet felt a little guilty about William and a little sorry for him, but all in all she gave him scarcely a passing thought. She was too busy trying on expensive new clothes and showing off the various diamond and sapphire objects bestowed on her by crass Alf, whose motto was that the way to a girl's heart was through jewellery: dead right, in the case of Violet.

Jack diddled around with the next part of the story. Should he keep the Hand hidden right up to the wedding itself? Should he conceal it in the long satin wedding-dress train and have it follow Violet up the aisle, only to pop forth and cause a sensation just before she said, *I do*? No, too many witnesses. They'd all chase it around the church like an escaped monkey, and the effect would be farcical rather than terrifying. Best to have it catch Violet alone; and, if possible, in a state of undress.

Several weeks before the wedding was to take place, a child at play in the park saw the housekeeper's crucifix glittering in the sun, picked it up, and took it home with her, thus nullifying its protective role. (In the film – the first film, not the remake – this scene was accompanied by an ominous, retro soundtrack. In the remake the child was replaced by a dog that carried the religious trinket to its owner, who, not being versed in any kind of useful lore, tossed it into a shrub.)

Then, on the night of the next full moon, up through the soil beside the park bench came William's hand, emerging like a sand crab or a mutated daffodil shoot. It was the worse for wear: brown and shrivelled, with long fingernails. It crept out of the park and down into a culvert, only to reappear with the callously discarded gold engagement band encircling its little finger.

It groped and scuttled its way to Violet's house and shinnied up the ivy and in through Violet's bedroom window, where it hid behind the dainty floral-patterned skirts of her dressing table and leered at her as she was taking off her clothes. Could it see? No, because it didn't have eyes. But it had a kind of visionless vision, since it was animated by the spirit of William. Or by part of that spirit: not the nicer part.

(The ancient Freudian critic at the special session of the Modern Language Association dedicated to *Dead Hand*, thirteen or was it fifteen years ago, said that the Hand meant the Return of the Repressed. The Jungian critic took issue with this interpretation, citing many instances of hacked-off hands in myth and magic: the Hand, she said, was an echo of the Hand of Glory cut from a hanged criminal's corpse and pickled, then set alight with embedded candles, long used in break-and-entering charms. It was known in French as main de gloire, thus giving its name to mandragore, or mandrake. The Freudian expert said this folkloric information was both obsolete and beside the point. Voices were raised. Jack, the honourary guest, excused himself and went for a smoke; that was when he was still smoking, and had not yet been ordered by his heart doctor to quit or die.)

While the Hand peeping-tommed from under the dressing table, Violet divested herself of all her clothing, then disported herself in the shower, leaving the door to her ensuite bathroom ajar to afford both the Hand and the reader a tantalizing view. Pink sumptuousness was described, curvaceous voluptuousness. Jack overwrote this part, he knows that now, but twenty-two-year-old guys go for broke on such details. (The director of the first film shot the shower scene as a homage to Alfred Hitchcock's *Psycho*, all the more appropriate as the first Violet was played by SueEllen Blake, a blond demigoddess who was a cross between Janet Leigh and Tippi Hedren, and whom Jack pursued relentlessly only to be disappointed: SueEllen was narcissistic enough to relish the preliminary gifts and acts of worship, but she didn't like sex per se and hated getting her makeup smeared.)

Irena in her student days had not been a wearer of makeup, probably because it cost money, but the effect had been a fresh delicacy, unadorned and honestly itself, like a shucked oyster. Also she left no beige and red smears on pillowcases. (Jack has come to appreciate this, in retrospect.)

The Hand, watching Violet soaping various parts of her body, could barely contain itself. But it did not choose this moment to tip its hand, so to speak. Instead it waited patiently as adjective after adjective was applied to Violet. Hand, reader, and Violet admired Violet's body as she patted it dry and teasingly rubbed aromatic lotion over its flawless, creamy surfaces. Then she slithered into a clinging, gold-sequined gown, outlined her lush mouth with ruby lipstick, clasped a glittering necklace around her sinuous, chokeable neck, draped a priceless white fur around her soft, inviting shoulders, and lilted out of the room with a jaw-dropping hip swivel. The Hand, of course, did not have a jaw that could be dropped, but it suffered from erotic frustration in its own way, signalled in both of the film versions by a fit of truly repulsive writhing.

Once Violet was out of the room, the Hand rummaged through her writing desk. It discovered her distinctive pink notepaper, embossed with her initials. Then, with her own silver fountain pen, it wrote a note, using the handwriting of the departed William, which needless to say it remembered.

I will love you forever, my darling Violet. Even after death. Yours everlastingly, William.

It placed this note on Violet's pillow along with a red rose it had plucked from the bouquet on her dressing table. The bouquet was fresh, since Alf of the Alfa Romeo sent her a dozen red roses every day.

Then the Hand scurried into Violet's closet and hid in a shoebox to await developments. The shoes in that box were the very same audacious red high heels Violet had been wearing while heartlessly spurning William, and the symbolism was not lost on the Hand. It ran its dried-up, long-nailed fingers over the red shoes in a manner both gloating and fetishistic. (This scene has come in for much analysis in the academic articles – largely French, but also Spanish – that have treated the film – the original, not the remake, which is dismissed with scorn by European cinéastes – as a late example of Puritanical American Neo-surrealism. Jack could give a fuck about that: he'd just wanted a dead hand getting it off with a pair of hot shoes. Though he's willing to admit it might amount to the same thing.)

The Hand waited for hours in the shoebox. It did not mind waiting: it had nothing else that it wanted to do. In the film (the original, not the remake), it occasionally drummed its fingers, indicating its impatience, but this was an afterthought, added at the request of the director – Stanislaus Ludz, an odd duck who thought of himself as a sort of Mozart of horror, and who later jumped off a tugboat – in the belief that watching a hand in a box doing nothing was not suspenseful.

In both of the films, the action cut back and forth between the Hand in the shoebox and Violet and Alf in a nightclub, dancing cheek to cheek and thigh to thigh, with Alf fingering Violet's jewel-bestrewn neck in a possessive way while whispering, 'Soon you'll be mine.' Jack hadn't written the nightclub scene in the book, but he would have if he'd thought of it; and he did think of it when he was writing the screenplay – both screenplays – so it was almost the same thing.

After enough of this dancing, fingering, and waiting in a box, Violet returned to her room, having swilled down several glasses of champagne with close-ups of her neck swallowing, and threw herself into bed without even a glance at the Hand's carefully composed love note and the rose on her pillow. She had two pillows, and the note and the rose were on the other one, which is why she neither saw the note nor got stuck with rose thorns.

What emotions was the Hand feeling, now that it had been overlooked once more? Sorrow or anger, or some of each? Hard to tell with a hand.

Stealthily it sidled out of the closet and made its way up via the carelessly flung bedspread to Violet in her lacework nightie as she lay in dishevelled slumber. Was it going to strangle her? Its gruesome fingers hesitated above her neck – screams from the film audiences here – but no, it still loved her. It began to stroke her hair, tenderly, longingly, lingeringly; then, unable to restrain itself, it stroked her cheek.

This wakened Violet, who, in the shadowy but moonlit room, found something like a huge five-legged spider on her pillow. More screams, this

219

time from Violet. The startled Hand made itself scarce, so by the time that Violet, gibbering with fright, managed to turn on the bedside lamp, it was cowering under the bed and thus nowhere in sight.

In tears, Violet phoned Alf and babbled incoherently, as a girl does under such circumstances, and Alf manfully soothed her by telling her she must have been having a nightmare. Comforted, she hung up and prepared to switch off the light; but then, what should catch her eye but the rose, and then the note, written in William's unmistakable and once beloved handwriting?

Wide eyes. Terrified gasp. This could not be happening! Not daring to remain in the room long enough to phone Alf again, Violet locked herself in the bathroom, where she spent a restless night huddled in the tub, covered inadequately with towels. (In the book she had some torturing memories of William, but it was decided not to show these in either of the films, so their place was taken by an episode of anguished finger-biting and stifled sobbing.)

In the morning, Violet cautiously emerged into a room flooded with cheerful sunlight. No pink note was to be seen, the Hand having done away with it. The rose was residing once more in its accustomed vase.

Deep breath. Sigh of relief. Only a nightmare, after all. Nonetheless Violet was spooked, and cast several nervous backward glances as she and her expensively sheath-skirted haunches prepared to go off for lunch with Alf.

Now the Hand busied itself once more. It riffled through Violet's diary and practised copying her writing. It stole several more sheets of her pink notepaper, and penned a torrid and obscene love letter to another man, proposing yet one more pre-marriage tryst at their usual meeting place, a seedy hooker-frequented motel on the outskirts of town right beside a wholesale carpet outlet. 'Darling, I know it's a risk, but I can't stay away,' it said. It made disparaging remarks about Alf and his inadequate lovemaking, with particular reference to the size of his dick. The note concluded by anticipating the delights in store once rich Alf had been married to Violet and then disposed of. A little antimony in his martini should do the trick, said the note, before ending with a paragraph of hot-blooded longing for the moment when the invented lover's electric eel would slide once more into Violet's moist and palpitating nest of seaweed.

(You couldn't use such euphemisms now, you'd have to name the names; but there was a limit in those days as to which unprintable words you could actually print. Jack regrets the lifting of those old taboos: they spurred inventive metaphors. With the young writers now it's F and C all day long, which he, personally, finds boring. Is he becoming a fogey? No: objectively speaking, it is boring.)

The pretend lover was called Roland. There

was a real Roland, who had been an earlier admirer of Violet's, though an unsuccessful one. Violet had preferred handsome William to him, and no wonder, because Roland was not only a yawn-making economist, but a mean-minded, shrivel-souled, corkscrew-hearted prick, sort of like Rod with his greenish-brown notebook. He was a dork, a dink, a dong . . .

This sounded too musical, so Jack scratched it out. Then he went into a caffeine-induced reverie: why should the male member be used as a term of abuse? No man hated his own dorkdinkdong, quite the opposite. But maybe it was an affront that any other man had one. That must be the truth. He should brush up this thesis and haul it out for display purposes at the next house party when the intellectual sparring got too irksome.

That way procrastination lay. Jack had pages to type before he slept. He had blood to spill.

'I brought you some soup,' said Irena, who'd come silently up the stairs to Jack's crow's-nest. She slid a plate and bowl onto the bridge table Jack was using as a writing desk. The soup was mushroom, and there were crackers.

'Thanks,' Jack said. This was more like it in the nurturing department. He thought about making a grab for Irena's be-aproned torso, overcoming her with impetuous and urgent élan vital, and pinning her to the floor, where she would swoon in surrender. But now was not the time: Roland needed to be massacred, Alf destroyed, Violet terrified out of her wits. First things first.

Over the next few days, Jack had to go back in the manuscript and insert Roland towards the beginning, now that he was needed for the plot. When asked for some scissors and Scotch tape, Irena briskly supplied them: anything that showed the novel project was moving forward was prompting new displays of helpfulness in her.

The Hand tucked its deceptive missive to Roland in among Violet's frothy underthings. Then it printed an anonymous message on another sheet of pink notepaper – *Alf, you're a fool. She's two-timing you, look in the frillies, second bureau drawer* – after which it scampered down the ivy-clad wall and across town to Alf's luxury penthouse pad, where it climbed the elevator shaft to the rooftop, holding the anonymous letter between pinky and ring finger. It slid the accusing note under the door, then capered back to Violet's house and concealed itself in a potted philodendron.

Violet returned from lunch and – a deft touch here, thought Jack – was trying on her wedding dress with the aid of a pudgy, sycophantic, comic-relief dressmaker when red-faced Alf stormed in, hurled wild accusations, and began flinging under-pants out of Violet's bureau drawers. Had he gone mad? No! For look – here was the torrid letter, on Violet's own notepaper, in Violet's own handwriting!

Weeping touchingly, Violet – towards whom the

film audiences were, by now, feeling sympathetic – protested that she had never, ever written such a thing, nor had she seen Roland for – well, for a very long time. Then she told the story of the night before, and the frightening billet-doux she herself had discovered on her pillow.

It was clear now that the two of them were the victims of a vile hoax, perpetrated no doubt by that scoundrel and jealous rat, Roland, who was attempting to break them up so he could have Violet for himself. Alf vowed he would get to the bottom of this: he would confront Roland and make him confess, and the sooner the better.

Violet pleaded with him not to do anything rash, which, however, only made Alf distrust her. Why was she trying to defend Roland from his righteous fury? If she was not telling the truth, he'd twist that beautiful neck of hers, he growled, and anyway, where was that note she'd claimed was on her pillow? Was she lying? He took tearful Violet by the throat and kissed her viciously, then threw her roughly onto the bed. By now, both reader and Violet were beginning to fear that Alf was unbalanced. The scarlet-winged Angel of Rape hovered in the air, but Alf satisfied himself with some cursing and with the flinging of his latest bouquet of roses onto the floor, where the vase shattered in a manner that gave both the Jungians and the Freudians much food for thought later.

No sooner had Alf stormed out than Violet found another note on the dressing table where no note had been just moments before: *You shall belong to no one but me. Death cannot part us. Watch your neck. Eternally yours, William.*

Violet's mouth opened and closed like that of a beached grouper. She was beyond screaming. Whoever was writing these notes was right in the house with her now! And she was all alone, the dressmaker having departed. It was too horrible!

The more horrible it became, the faster Jack wrote. He mainlined instant coffee, gobbled packaged peanuts, and snatched only a few hours of sleep per night. Irena, fascinated by his manic energy, brought him plates of noodle casserole in aid of his creative efforts. She even went so far as to do his laundry for him, tidy up his room, and change his sheets.

It was shortly after the change of sheets that Jack succeeded in wrestling her into bed. Or did she succeed in wrestling him into bed? He's never been sure. In any case his bed was where they'd ended up, and he didn't much care how they'd got there.

He'd looked forward to such an event for a long time, he'd fantasized about it, he'd strategized; but now that the opportunity had come he was rapid in the execution and inattentive in the aftermath: he'd neglected to murmur any terms of endearment, and he'd zonked off to sleep almost immediately. He admits that wasn't too suave. But there were reasons: he was young, he was over-tired, he had a lot on his mind. His energies were needed elsewhere, because he was almost up to the dénouement in *The Dead Hand Loves You*.

Alf was about to batter Roland to a pulp in an insane rage. Then, covered with blood, he would stagger off to his Alfa Romeo, where the Hand was lurking in the custom leather upholstery and would attempt to throttle him from behind. This would cause Alf to lose control of the car and crash it into a viaduct, incinerating him in the process. The Hand, though badly singed, would crawl out of the wreckage and limp over to Violet's house.

The unfortunate girl would just have been informed by the police about the murder of Roland and also the fatal accident; she'd be emotional rubble. The doctor would prescribe a sedative, and Violet would be drifting into an irresistible sleep when she would see, blistered, scarred, and charred to a crisp, the unstoppable Hand, dragging itself painfully but relentlessly towards her across the pillow . . .

'What are you writing about?' said Irena from Jack's own pillow, or one of them. He now had two, the second having been supplied by Irena herself. Her visits to his attic cubbyhole were becoming a habit. Sometimes she brought cocoa, and more and more frequently she stayed over-night, though her rump was not skinny, and Jack's old-fashioned double bed was a tight squeeze. Thus far she'd been content to cast herself in the role of handmaid to greatness – she'd even offered to retype the manuscript for him, being a fast and efficient typist, unlike Jack – but he'd fended her off. This was the first time she'd been inquisitive as to the nature of his project, though she'd assumed he was writing Literature; she had no idea that he was spinning a cheap and tawdry horror yarn about a dried-up hand.

'The materialism of our modern age, from an existential perspective,' said Jack. 'Inspired by *Steppenwolf*.' (*Steppenwolf!* How could he? Jack thinks now. Forgivable, however: *Steppenwolf* had not yet achieved the vulgar popularity that was just around the corner for it.) This answer wasn't exactly a lie, but, though truth of a kind, it was thinly stretched.

Irena was pleased. She kissed him lightly, put her economical black underwear back on, followed by her thick pullover and tweed skirt, and bustled downstairs to warm up some leftover meatballs for the collective mid-day meal.

In due course Jack finished the last chapter and slept for twelve hours straight, dreaming of nothing. Then he turned his attention to the peddling of his manuscript, because if he didn't show some alacrity in his efforts to make up the past and future rent owing he might still find himself ignominiously evicted. Though nobody could say he wasn't industrious. He'd gone all out on the typing part – Irena was his witness, he'd covered the pages – so maybe he'd get brownie points from his roommates for trying.

There were several publishing houses in New York that specialized in horror and terror, so Jack purchased some brown paper envelopes and mailed off the manuscript to three of them. Sooner than he'd expected – in reality, he hadn't expected anything – he received a terse reply. The book had been accepted. An advance was offered. It was a modest advance, but large enough to cover the rent owed, with enough left over to pay for the rest of his term.

There was even enough for a celebration party, which Jack threw, Irena assisting. Everyone congratulated him and wanted to know when the masterpiece was due to appear and who was publishing it. Jack dodged these questions, smoked some dope and drank too much Old Sailor Port and vodka punch, and retched up the cheeseballs baked by Irena in homage to his talent. He wasn't looking forward to the publication of his own book: too many cats would come swarming out of the bag, and his roommates were sure to recognize the funhouse mirror distortions of themselves he'd thoughtlessly inserted into his tale. Truth to tell, he hadn't believed it would ever see daylight.

Having recovered from the party, and with his obligations fulfilled and his degree just barely obtained, Jack was free to get on with the rest of his life, which turned out to involve advertising. He had a facility with adjectives and adverbs, he was told, which would come in handy once he'd learned the ropes. Though the four roommates had given up their house and found separate abodes, he was still seeing Irena, who'd decided to go to law school. Sex with her was an ongoing revelation to him. The first time had been rapturous for him, not to say jubilant, and repeated encounters were the same, despite Irena's traditional man-on-top parameters. She was a woman of few words, which he appreciated – more words for him – but he wouldn't have minded a phrase or two as to how he was doing, not having anything to compare his own performance with. Wasn't she supposed to do more moaning? He had to content himself with her blue-eyed gaze, which he found unreadable. Adoring? He certainly hoped so.

Although it was obvious from her dexterity that Irena herself had the wherewithal for comparisons, she had the tact not to mention it, another thing he appreciated. She wasn't his first love – that had been Linda, a pigtailed brunette in second grade – but she was his first sex. Like it or not, Irena had been a milestone. So whatever else, she exists in a mental grotto consecrated to her alone: Saint Irena of the Holy Orgasm. A plaster saint, as it's turned out, but still there in his head, posed in the act of removing her pragmatic black panties, her thighs incandescently white, her eyes downcast but sly, her half-open mouth smiling enigmatically. That image is quite different from the later image of the flinty, grasping harridan who cashes his cheques twice a year. He can't fit them together.

Over the next months, Irena bought him a set of mixing bowls and a kitchen garbage pail because she said he needed them – translation, *she* needed them in order to cook dinner for them over at his place – and she cleaned his bathroom, more than once. Not only was she moving in on him physically, she was beginning to dictate. She disapproved of his advertising job, and felt he should begin a second work of art, and by the way, wasn't the first work of art – which she was longing to read – due to be published soon? Meanwhile *The Dead Hand Loves You* lay doggo, and Jack hoped that the publisher had left the manuscript in a taxi.

But no such luck; for, like the severed hand of its title, *The Dead Hand Loves You* clawed its way to the surface and made its debut on the drugstore shelves of the nation. Jack had some furniture by then, including a beanbag chair and a good sound system, and he also had three suits, with ties to match. He regretted that he'd used his real name for the book instead of a nom de plume: would his new employers think he was a deranged pervert for writing this stuff? All he could do was keep his head down and hope no one noticed.

Again, no such luck. There was a chilly row with Irena when she discovered that his masterwork had in fact appeared and he hadn't told her. Then there were more stiff words when she read it and saw what kind of masterwork it was – a waste of his talent, a sellout, and a shameless act of slumming, so very much beneath him – and that the characters in it were thinly disguised portraits of his three former roommates, including herself.

'So this is what you really think of us all!' she said.

'But Violet is beautiful!' he protested. 'But the hero loves her!' It cut no ice. The love of a dried-up hand – however devoted – was not in any way flattering, according to Irena.

The final blow came after she'd been nosing through his mail when he was out – he never should have given her a key to his apartment – and realized that he was banking his royalty cheques rather than dividing them with his fellow shareholders. He was not honouring their contract! He was a crappy writer, a crappy lover, and a criminal cheat of a human being, she said. She would be contacting Jaffrey and Rod immediately, and she could imagine what they would have to say about this.

'But,' said Jack. 'I forgot about the contract thing. It isn't a real contract, it was only a joke, it was just a sort of . . .'

'It is a real contract,' said Irena icily. She knew quite a lot by then about real contracts. 'It proves intentionality.'

'Okay. I was going to do the split. I hadn't got around to it.'

'That's rubbish and you know it.'

'Since when can you read my mind? You think

you know everything about me. Just because I'm fucking you . . .'

'I will not have that language,' said Irena, who was a prude when it came to words, though in no other way.

'What do you want me to call it? You like it well enough when I do it. Okay, just because I'm sticking my carrot into your well-visited . . .'

Stomp, stomp, stomp. Across the floor, out the door. Slam. Was he happy or sad about that?

There followed a letter from the collective lawyer of the three irate shareholders. Demands. Threats. Then, on the part of Jack, capitulation. They had him dead to rights. As Irena claimed, there had indeed been intentionality.

Jack was upset about the departure of Irena – more upset than he could admit. He did make some attempts at fence-mending. What had he done? he asked her. Why was she writing him off?

No dice. She'd made an evaluation of him, she'd added him up and found him wanting, and no, she did not want to discuss it, and no, there wasn't anyone else, and no, she would not give them another chance. There was one thing Jack could do – should already have done, she said – but the fact that he had no idea of what it was merely underscored why she had left.

What did she want? he pleaded, though feebly. Why couldn't she tell him? She wouldn't say. It was baffling.

He drowned his sorrows, though like other drowned things they had a habit of floating to the surface when least expected.

On the sunny side, *The Dead Hand Loves You* was a hit in its own field, neglected though that field was by serious literati. As his editor put it, 'Yeah, it's a piece of shit, but it's good shit.' Even better, there was a film deal in the offing, and who more suitable than Jack to write the screenplay? And then to produce a sequel to *The Dead Hand Loves You*, or at any rate some other piece of good shit? Jack quit his advertising job and devoted himself to the life of the pen. Or rather, to the life of the Remington, soon to be replaced with an IBM Selectric, with the bouncing ball that let you change the typeface. Now that was cool!

His life as a scribe has had its ups and downs. Truth to tell, he's never lived up to the success of his first book, which is still the one he's known for and provides the bulk of his income; an income that, thanks to that youthful contract, is three times smaller than it ought to be. Which rankles. And as time passes and he finds it ever more difficult to churn out the verbiage, it's rankling more and more. *The Dead Hand* was his big thing; he won't, now, be able to repeat it. Worse, he's at the age at which younger, sicker, more violent writers are patronizing and dismissing him. *The Dead Hand*, yeah, it was, like, seminal, but tame by today's standards. Violet, for instance, did not get her intestines ripped out. There wasn't any torture, nobody's liver got fried in a pan, there wasn't any gang rape. So what's the fun of that?

They're likely to reserve their spike-haired, nose-ringed respect for the film, rather than the book – the original film, not the remake. The remake was more accomplished, yeah, like, if that's what you want. It had better technical values, it had – god knows – better special effects; but it wasn't fresh, it didn't have that raw, primitive energy. It was too manicured, it was too self-conscious, it lacked . . .

Here's our special guest for tonight: Jack Dace, the grand old man of horror. And what do you think about the film, Mr Dace? The second one, the dud, the failure. Oh. That was your screenplay? Wow, who knew? Nobody on this panel was even born then, right, guys? Haha, yes, Marsha, I know you aren't a guy, but you're an honorary guy. You've got more balls than half the guys in the audience! Am I right? Witless giggling.

Had he himself ever been that brash, that callow? Yes. He had.

Last week he received a proposal for a TV mini-series, linked to a video-game tie-in; both forms unhappily subject to the original four-party contract, according to his lawyer. There's also to be an entire symposium – in Austin, Texas, home of super-cool nerdery – devoted to Jack Dace and his work, his total oeuvre, and especially to *The Dead Hand Loves You*. This renewed activity and the accompanying social-media blitz will lead to more book sales, and more residuals, and more of everything that – fuckit! – has to be split four ways. This is his last gasp, it's his last hurrah, and he won't be able to enjoy it; he'll only be able to enjoy a quarter of it. The four-way splitting is supremely unfair and it's gone on long enough. Something has to give, someone has to go. Or several people.

How best to make it look natural?

He's kept track of all three of them, not that he had a choice. Their lawyers saw to that.

Rod was briefly married to Irena, but that's long over. He's retired from his position with an international brokerage firm and lives in Sarasota, Florida, where he's involved in the ballet and theatre communities as a volunteer financial adviser.

Jaffrey – who was also briefly married to Irena, but after Rod – is in Chicago, having tailored his philosophical debating talents to municipal politics. Fourteen years ago he was almost convicted on a charge of bribery, but he dodged the bullet and has carried on as a well-known backroom boy, spin-doctor, and candidate's consultant.

Irena is still in Toronto, where she heads up a company devoted to raising funds for worthy non-profits, such as kidneys. She's the widow of a man who did well in potash, and throws a lot of high-end dinner parties. She sends Jack a Christmas card every year, enclosing a form-letter account of her banal society doings.

Jack is not outwardly on bad terms with the threesome, having floated it about years ago that he accepts the situation for what it is. Still, he hasn't seen any of them for years. Make that decades. Why would he want to? He's had no desire to experience a burp from the past.

Not until now.

He decides to start with Rod, who lives the farthest away. Rather than emailing, he leaves a voice message: he'll be passing through Sarasota in connection with a film he's considering – he's looking for the right kind of setting – and how would Rod like to have lunch and catch up on old times? He's ready for a brush-off, but somewhat to his surprise Rod sends an acceptance.

They don't meet in a restaurant, or even at Rod's home. They meet in the discouraging cafeteria of the Buddhist palliative care centre where Rod is now a resident. White folks clad in saffron robes drift here and there, smiling benign smiles; bells ding; in the distance, chants are chanted.

Formerly stocky Rod has dwindled: he's yellowish grey and looks like an empty glove. 'Pancreatic cancer,' he tells Jack. 'It's a death sentence.' Jack says he had no idea, which is true. He also says – how does he come up with these platitudes? – that he hopes Rod is receiving the proper spiritual care. Rod says he isn't a Buddhist, but they do death well, and, having no family, he might as well be here as anywhere.

Jack says he is sorry. Rod says it could be worse and he can't complain. He's had a good run – partly thanks to Jack, he has the grace to add, since that *Dead Hand* money gave him the leg-up he needed at the beginning of his career.

They sit looking at their plates of vegetarian Buddhist-temple cuisine. There's not a lot more to say.

Jack is relieved he won't have to murder Rod after all. Did he really intend to go that far? Would he have been up to it? Most likely not. He never disliked Rod as such. That's a lie: he did dislike Rod, but not enough to kill him, then or now.

'You weren't really Roland,' he says. He owes at least this much of a lie to the suffering little bugger.

'I know that,' says Rod. He smiles, a watery smile. A middle-aged woman in an orange robe brings them green tea. 'We had fun, didn't we?' he says. 'In that old house. It was a more innocent age.'

'Yes,' says Jack. 'We did have fun.' From this distance it does resemble fun. *Fun* is not knowing how it will end.

'There's something I need to tell you,' Rod says finally. 'About that book of yours, and the contract.'

'Don't worry about it,' says Jack.

'No, listen,' says Rod. 'There's a side deal.'

'A side deal?' says Jack. 'How do you mean?'

'Between the three of us,' says Rod. 'If one of us dies, their share is split between the other two. It was Irena's idea.'

237

It would have been, thinks Jack. She's never missed a trick. 'I see,' he says.

'I know that's not fair,' says Rod. 'It should go to you. But Irena was angry because of the way you wrote about Violet, in the book. She thought it was a dig at her. After she'd been so, well, so kind to you.'

'It wasn't a dig,' says Jack, another semi-lie. 'What happens if all of you die?'

'Then our shares revert to you,' says Rod. 'Irena wanted everything to go to her kidney charity, but I drew the line.'

'Thanks,' says Jack. So, it's last man standing. At least he now has an overview of the state of affairs. 'And thanks for telling me.' He shakes Rod's wan hand.

'It's only money, Jack,' says Rod. 'Take it from me. At the end of the line, money means nothing. Let it go.'

Jaffrey is delighted to hear from Jack, or so he claims. What fine times those were, the days of their youth! What a blast! He seems to have forgotten that some of those days were spent in defrauding Jack, but since Jaffrey now devotes his entire life to defrauding people en masse, that long-ago, minor piece of sharp practice must have got lost in his inner shuffle. Not that Jaffrey hasn't feathered his nest plumply enough with Jack's earnings.

They're on a golf course, Jaffrey's suggestion. Play a round, have a couple of beers, what could be better? Jack hates golf, but is good at losing, and has a lot of practice at it: losing to film producers greases the wheels.

Smart Jaffrey: golf courses are the perfect cover. Private conversation is possible, but they're never out of view of others, so Jack can't simply brain the garrulous old fraud out of sight of witnesses. And Jaffrey *is* old, he's really old: his remaining hair is white, his spine is curved, his paunch is flabby. Jack himself is no printemps chicken, but at least he's kept in better shape than that.

Jaffrey garbles on about that slummy brick house where they'd had such carefree times: does Jack know there's a historical plaque on it? Commemorating Jack and *The Dead Hand*, of all things! How amazing that people now mistake that clumsy, cliché-ridden book of his for some kind of artistic accomplishment! Trust the French to do that, they think Jerry Lewis is a genius, but other people? Jaffrey has always found *The Dead Hand* side-splittingly funny, and he can only suppose Jack wrote it with that end in view. But great that it turned into such a gold mine, right? For all concerned. Chuckle, wink.

'Irena didn't find it funny,' Jack says. 'The book. She was pissed at me. She thought I'd led her on. She wanted me to be writing *War and Peace*, when all along it was about . . .'

'She knew what it was about,' Jaffrey says with that I've-scored-a-point philosophy-student grin of his. 'While you were writing it.'

'What?' says Jack. 'How do you mean? I never told . . .'

'Irena's the nosiest woman alive,' says Jaffrey. 'I should know, I was married to her. She's got a sixth sense. I only cheated on her seven or eight times, ten max, and she caught me out immediately every time. She's hell to play golf with too. You can't steal an inch.'

'She couldn't have known,' says Jack. 'I kept it under wraps.'

'You think she wasn't peeking at the manuscript every chance she could get?' says Jaffrey. 'You'd go to the can, she'd flip a few pages. She was riveted by it. She wanted to see if you were going to kill Violet. And she knew a pop-culture hit when she saw it.'

'But then she gave me shit,' says Jack. 'I don't get it.' He's feeling a little addled. Maybe it's the sun: he's not used to being out in it. 'She broke up with me because of that book. Betraying my true talent and yadda yadda.'

'That wasn't the reason,' says Jaffrey. 'She was in love with you. You didn't notice that? She wanted you to propose to her, she wanted to get married. She's very conventional, Irena. But you didn't come across. She felt very rejected.'

Jack is surprised. 'But she was in law school!' he says. Jaffrey laughs.

'That's no excuse,' he says.

'If that's what she wanted,' says Jack sulkily, 'why didn't she say so?'

'And have you turn her down?' says Jaffrey. 'You know her. She'd never put herself in such a vulnerable position.'

'But maybe I might have said yes,' says Jack. His life would have been very different if only he'd guessed, and then taken the chance. Better, or worse? He has no idea. Still, different. He might not feel so alone right now, just for instance.

He never did marry any of those other girls; none of the fangirls, none of the actresses he'd met through the films. He'd suspected all of them of loving his book and/or his money more than they loved him. But Irena, he now reflects, came before *The Dead Hand* hit the stands; before his success. Whatever else, he couldn't accuse her of ulterior motives.

'I think she's still carrying a torch for you,' says Jaffrey.

'She gave me holy hell for years,' says Jack. 'Over the royalties. If she hated the book that much, she should've refused any profit from it.'

'It was her way of keeping in touch with you,' says Jaffrey. 'Ever thought of that?' His divorce settlement with her – he tells Jack– was bizarre: Irena insisted that it had to include Jaffrey's share in *The Dead Hand Loves You*, the proceeds from which are paid over to her as soon as Jaffrey himself receives them. 'She thinks she inspired you,' he says. 'So she has a right.'

'Maybe she did inspire me,' says Jack. He'd been contemplating the various methods he might use to eliminate Jaffrey. Ice pick in the men's room, radioactive dust in the beer? It would have taken some planning, as Jaffrey must have made some powerful enemies during his backroom-boy decades and is surely alert to danger. But it seems Jack won't have to implement any of these schemes, since Jaffrey is out of the picture as far as *The Dead Hand* is concerned: he no longer benefits from it at all.

Jack sends Irena a note. Not an email, a note, with a stamp and everything: he wishes to create an aura of romance, all the better to lull her into a sense of security so he can lure her into an out-of-the-way place and shove her over a cliff, figuratively speaking. Why don't they meet for dinner? he suggests. He has some news about the future of their mutual book that he would like to share with her. She should choose the restaurant, cost no object. He'd really like to see her after all this time. She's always been very, very special to him, and she still is.

There's a hiatus; then he receives a reply: *Certainly, that would be appropriate. It will be so pleasant to recall the long and complex journey we have been on, both together and then on the parallel paths we have travelled along in our different but similar ways. There are invisible vibrations that have attached us to each other, as you yourself must realize. Cordially, your very old friend, Irena. P.S.: Our horoscopes have predicted this reunion.*

How to read this? Love, hate, indifference, camouflage? Or is Irena going batshit?

They meet at the upscale Canoe, far away from tuna-and-noodle casseroles. The venue is Irena's suggestion. They have one of the best tables, with a view out over the brightly lit city that gives Jack vertigo.

He turns away from the window, focuses instead on Irena. She's a bit wrinkled and quite a lot thinner, but all in all she's held up well. Her cheekbones stand out; she looks distinguished and expensive. Her astonishingly blue eyes are still unreadable. She's much better dressed than when they were roommates; but then, so is he.

The white wine comes, a cabernet sauvignon. They lift glasses. 'Here we are again,' says Irena with a trembly little smile. Is she nervous? Irena was never nervous before; or not that he could tell.

'It's wonderful to see you,' says Jack. Surprisingly, he means it.

'The foie gras is especially good here,' says Irena. 'I know you'll like it. That's why I chose this place for you: I always did know what you like.' She licks her lips.

'You were my inspiration,' Jack finds himself saying. Jack, you shameless cornball, he admonishes himself; but it seems he wants to give her pleasure. How did that happen? He needs to cut to the chase, toss her off a balcony, heave her down some stairs.

'I know,' says Irena, smiling wistfully. 'I was Violet, wasn't I? Only she was more beautiful, and I was never that selfish.'

'You were more beautiful to me,' Jack says.

Is that a tear, is she having an emotion? Now he's frightened. He always depended on Irena to keep herself under control, he now realizes. He won't be able to murder a sniffling Irena: to be murdered, she needs to be heartless.

'I bought those shoes, the red ones,' she says. 'Just like the ones in the book.'

'That's . . .' says Jack. 'That's wild.'

'I've always kept them. In their shoebox.'

'Oh,' says Jack. This is getting too strange. She's as nutty as some of his little Goth girls, she's fetishized him. Maybe he should forget about killing her. Make a run for it. Plead indigestion.

'It opened things up for me, that book,' she says. 'It gave me confidence.'

'Being stalked by a dead hand?' says Jack. He's losing focus. Had he really intended to steer Irena down a dark alley and hit her with a brick? That had only been a daydream, surely.

'I guess you must have hated me all those years, because of the money,' says Irena.

'No, not really,' says Jack untruthfully. He has indeed hated her. But he doesn't hate her now.

'It wasn't the money,' she says. 'I didn't want to hurt you, I just wanted to stay connected. I didn't want you to forget all about me, in your glamorous new life.'

'It's not so glamorous,' Jack says. 'I wouldn't have forgotten you. I could never forget you.' Is this bullshit, or does he really mean it? He's been in the bullshit world for so long it's hard to distinguish.

'I liked it that you didn't kill Violet,' she says. 'I mean, the Hand didn't. It was so touching, the way you ended it. It was beautiful. I cried.'

Jack had been intending to let the Hand strangle Violet: it seemed right, it seemed fitting. The Hand would cover her nose, her mouth; then it would close around her neck and squeeze with its dead shrivelled fingers, and her eyes would roll up like a saint's in ecstasy.

But at the last minute Violet had bravely overcome her terror and revulsion, and had taken the initiative. She'd extended her own hand, and reached out in love, and stroked the Hand, because she knew it was William really, or part of William. Then the Hand had vaporized in a silvery mist. Jack had stolen that from *Nosferatu*: the love of a pure woman had an uncanny power over the things of darkness. Maybe 1964 was the last moment when you could get away with that: try such a thing now and people would only laugh.

'I've always thought that ending was a message you were sending,' says Irena. 'To me.'

'A message?' says Jack. Is she wacko, or is she right? The Jungians and the Freudians would agree with her. Though if it was a message, fucked if he knows what it meant.

'You were afraid,' says Irena, as if in answer. 'You were afraid that if I really touched you, if I reached out and touched your heart – if you let me come too close to the truly fine, spiritual person you kept hidden inside – then you'd vanish. And that's why you couldn't, why you didn't . . . why it fell apart. But you can now.'

'I guess we'll find out,' says Jack. He grins what he hopes is a boyish grin. Does he have a fine spiritual person hidden inside? If he does, Irene is the only one who's ever believed in it.

'I guess we will,' says Irena. She smiles again and puts her hand on top of his; he can feel the bones inside her fingers. He covers their two joined hands with his second hand. He squeezes.

'I'm sending you a bouquet of roses tomorrow,' he says. 'Red ones.' He gazes into her eyes. 'Consider it a proposal.'

There. He's taken the plunge, but the plunge into what? Jack, be nimble, he tells himself. Avoid traps. She may be too much for you, not to mention crazy. Don't make a mistake. But how much time does he have left in his life to worry about mistakes?

STONE MATTRESS

At the outset Verna had not intended to kill anyone. What she had in mind was a vacation, pure and simple. Take a breather, do some inner accounting, shed worn skin. The Arctic suits her: there's something inherently calming in the vast cool sweeps of ice and rock and sea and sky, undisturbed by cities and highways and trees and the other distractions that clutter up the landscape to the south.

Among the clutter she includes other people, and by other people she means men. She's had enough of men for a while. She's made an inner memo to renounce flirtations and any consequences that might result from them. She doesn't need the cash, not any more. She's not extravagant or greedy, she tells herself: all she ever wanted was to be protected by layer upon layer of kind, soft, insulating money, so that nobody and nothing could get close enough to harm her. Surely she has at last achieved this modest goal.

But old habits die hard, and it's not long before she's casting an appraising eye over her fleece-clad fellow-travellers dithering with their wheely bags in the lobby of the first-night airport hotel. Passing over the women, she ear-tags the male members of the flock. Some have females attached to them, and she eliminates these on principle: why work harder than you need to? Prying a spouse loose can be arduous, as she discovered via her first husband: discarded wives stick like burrs.

It's the solitaries who interest her, the lurkers at the fringes. Some of these are too old for her purposes; she avoids eye contact with them. The ones who cherish the belief that there's life in the old dog yet: these are her game. Not that she'll do anything about it, she tells herself, but there's nothing wrong with a little warm-up practice, if only to demonstrate to herself that she can still knock one off if she wishes to.

For that evening's meet-and-greet she chooses her cream-coloured pullover, perching the Magnetic Northward nametag just slightly too low on her left breast. Thanks to Aquacise and core strength training, she's still in excellent shape for her age, or indeed for any age, at least when fully clothed and buttressed with carefully fitted underwiring. She wouldn't want to chance a deck chair in a bikini – superficial puckering has set in, despite her best efforts – which is one reason for selecting the Arctic over, say, the Caribbean. Her face is what it is, and certainly the best that money can buy at this stage: with a little bronzer and pale eyeshadow and mascara and glimmer powder and low lighting, she can finesse ten years.

'Though much is taken, much remains,' she murmurs to her image in the mirror. Her third husband had been a serial quotation freak with a special penchant for Tennyson. 'Come into the garden, Maud,' he'd been in the habit of saying just before bedtime. It had driven her mad at the time.

She adds a dab of cologne – an understated scent, floral, nostalgic – then she blots it off, leaving a mere whiff. It's a mistake to overdo it: though elderly noses aren't as keen as they may once have been, it's best to allow for allergies. A sneezing man is not an attentive man.

She makes her entrance slightly late, smiling a detached but cheerful smile – it doesn't do for an unaccompanied woman to appear too eager – accepts a glass of the passable white wine they're doling out, and drifts among the assembled nibblers and sippers. The men will be retired professionals: doctors, lawyers, engineers, stock-brokers, interested in Arctic exploration, polar bears, archeology, birds, Inuit crafts, perhaps even Vikings or plant life or geology. Magnetic Northward attracts serious punters, with an earnest bunch of experts laid on to herd them around and lecture to them. She's investigated the two other outfits that tour the region, but neither appeals. One features excessive hiking and attracts the under-fifties – not her target market – and the other goes in for singsongs and dressing up in silly outfits, so she's stuck with Magnetic Northward, which offers the comfort of familiarity. She travelled with this company once before, after the death of her third husband, five years ago, so she knows pretty much what to expect.

There's a lot of sportswear in the room, much beige among the men, many plaid shirts, vests with multiple pockets. She notes the nametags: a Fred, a Dan, a Rick, a Norm, a Bob. Another Bob, then another: there are a lot of Bobs on this trip. Several appear to be flying solo. Bob: a name once of heavy significance to her, though surely she's rid herself of that load of luggage by now. She selects one of the thinner but still substantial Bobs, glides close to him, raises her eyelids, and lowers them again. He peers down at her chest.

'Verna,' he says. 'That's a lovely name.'

'Old-fashioned,' she says. 'From the Latin word for "spring." When everything springs to life again.' That line, so filled with promises of phallic renewal, had been effective in helping to secure her second husband. To her third husband she'd said that her mother had been influenced by the eighteenth-century Scottish poet James Thomson and his vernal breezes, which was a preposterous but enjoyable lie: she had, in fact, been named after a lumpy, bun-faced dead aunt. As for her mother, she'd been a strict Presbyterian with a mouth like a vise grip, who despised poetry and was unlikely to have been influenced by anything softer than a granite wall.

During the preliminary stages of netting her

250

fourth husband, whom she'd flagged as a kink addict, Verna had gone even further. She'd told him she'd been named for 'The Rite of Spring,' a highly sexual ballet that ended with torture and human sacrifice. He'd laughed, but he'd also wriggled: a sure sign of the hook going in.

Now she says, 'And you're . . . Bob.' It's taken her years to perfect the small breathy intake, a certified knee-melter.

'Yes,' Bob says. 'Bob Goreham,' he adds, with a diffidence he surely intends to be charming. Verna smiles widely to disguise her shock. She finds herself flushing with a combination of rage and an almost reckless mirth. She looks him full in the face: yes, underneath the thinning hair and the wrinkles and the obviously whitened and possibly implanted teeth, it's the same Bob – the Bob of fifty-odd years before. Mr Heartthrob, Mr Senior Football Star, Mr Astounding Catch, from the rich, Cadillac-driving end of town where the mining-company big shots lived. Mr Shit, with his looming bully's posture and his lopsided joker's smile.

How amazing to everyone, back then – not only everyone in school but everyone, for in that armpit of a town they'd known to a millimetre who drank and who didn't and who was no better than she should be and how much change you kept in your back pocket – how amazing that golden-boy Bob had singled out insignificant Verna for the Snow Queen's Palace winter formal. Pretty Verna, three years younger, studious, grade-skipping, innocent

251

Verna, tolerated but not included, clawing her way towards a scholarship as her ticket out of town. Gullible Verna, who'd believed she was in love.

Or who *was* in love. When it came to love, wasn't believing the same as the real thing? Such beliefs drain your strength and cloud your vision. She's never allowed herself to be skewered in that tiger trap again.

What had they danced to that night? 'Rock Around the Clock.' 'Hearts Made of Stone.' 'The Great Pretender.' Bob had steered Verna around the edges of the gym, holding her squashed up against his carnation buttonhole, for the unskilled, awkward Verna of those days had never been to a dance before and was no match for Bob's strenuous and flamboyant moves. For meek Verna, life was church and studies and household chores and her weekend job clerking in the drugstore, with her grim-faced mother regulating every move. No dates; those wouldn't have been allowed, not that she'd been asked on any. But her mother had permitted her to go to the well-supervised high-school dance with Bob Goreham, for wasn't he a shining light from a respectable family? She'd even allowed herself a touch of smug gloating, silent though it had been. Holding her head up after the decampment of Verna's father had been a full-time job, and had given her a very stiff neck. From this distance Verna could understand it.

So out the door went Verna, starry-eyed with hero worship, wobbling on her first high heels. She was courteously inserted into Bob's shiny red convertible with the treacherous mickey of rye already lurking in the glove compartment, where she sat bolt upright, almost catatonic with shyness, smelling of Prell shampoo and Jergens lotion, wrapped in her mother's mothbally out-of-date rabbit stole and an ice-blue tulle-skirted dress that looked as cheap as it was.

Cheap. Cheap and disposable. Use and toss. That was what Bob had thought about her, from the very first.

Now Bob grins a little. He looks pleased with himself: maybe he thinks Verna is blushing with desire. But he doesn't recognize her! He really doesn't! How many fucking Vernas can he have met in his life?

Get a grip, she tells herself. She's not invulnerable after all, it appears. She's shaking with anger, or is it mortification? To cover herself she takes a gulp of her wine, and immediately chokes on it. Bob springs into action, giving her a few brisk but caressing thumps on the back.

'Excuse me,' she manages to gasp. The crisp, cold scent of carnations envelops her. She needs to get away from him; all of a sudden she feels quite sick. She hurries to the ladies' room, which is fortunately empty, and throws up her white wine and her cream-cheese-and-olive canapé into a cubicle toilet. She wonders if it's too late to cancel the trip. But why should she run from Bob again?

Back then she'd had no choice. By the end of

that week, the story was all over town. Bob had spread it himself, in a farcical version that was very different from what Verna herself remembered. Slutty, drunken, willing Verna, what a joke. She'd been followed home from school by groups of leering boys, hooting and calling out to her. *Easy out! Can I have a ride? Candy's dandy but liquor's quicker!* Those were some of the milder slogans. She'd been shunned by girls, fearful that the disgrace – the ludicrous, hilarious smuttiness of it all – would rub off on them.

Then there was her mother. It hadn't taken long for the scandal to hit church circles. What little her mother had to say through her clamp of a mouth was to the point: Verna had made her own bed, and now she would have to lie in it. No, she could not wallow in self-pity – she would just have to face the music, not that she would ever live it down, because one false step and you fell, that's how life was. When it was evident that the worst had happened, she bought Verna a bus ticket and shipped her off to a church-run Home for Unwed Mothers on the outskirts of Toronto.

There Verna spent the days peeling potatoes and scrubbing floors and scouring toilets along with her fellow delinquents. They wore grey maternity dresses and grey wool stockings and clunky brown shoes, all paid for by generous donations, they were informed. In addition to their scouring and peeling chores, they were treated to bouts of prayer and self-righteous hectoring. What had happened to them was justly deserved, the speeches went, because of their depraved behaviour, but it was never too late to redeem themselves through hard work and self-restraint. They were cautioned against alcohol, tobacco, and gum-chewing, and were told that they should consider it a miracle of God if any decent man ever wanted to marry them.

Verna's labour was long and difficult. The baby was taken away from her immediately so that she would not get attached to it. There was an infection, with complications and scarring, but it was all for the best, she overheard one brisk nurse telling another, because those sorts of girls made unfit mothers anyway. Once she could walk, Verna was given five dollars and a bus ticket and instructed to return to the guardianship of her mother, because she was still a minor.

But she could not face that – that or the town in general – so she headed for downtown Toronto. What was she thinking? No actual thoughts, only feelings: mournfulness, woe, and, finally, a spark of defiant anger. If she was as trashy and worthless as everyone seemed to think, she might as well act that way, and, in between rounds of waitressing and hotel-room cleaning, she did.

It was only by great good luck that she stumbled upon an older married man who took an interest in her. She traded three years of noontime sex with him for the price of her education. A fair exchange, to her mind – she bore him no ill will.

She learned a lot from him – how to walk in high heels being the least of it – and pulled herself up and out. Little by little she jettisoned the crushed image of Bob that she still carried like a dried flower – incredibly! – next to her heart.

She pats her face back into place and repairs her mascara, which has bled down her cheeks despite its waterproof claims. Courage, she tells herself. She will not be chased away, not this time. She'll tough it out; she's more than a match for five Bobs now. And she has the advantage, because Bob doesn't have a clue who she is. Does she really look that different? Yes, she does. She looks better. There's her silver-blond hair, and the various alterations, of course. But the real difference is in the attitude – the confident way she carries herself. It would be hard for Bob to see through that facade to the shy, mousy-haired, snivelling idiot she'd been at fourteen.

After adding a last film of powder, she rejoins the group and lines up at the buffet for roast beef and salmon. She won't eat much of it, but then she never does, not in public: a piggy, gobbling woman is not a creature of mysterious allure. She refrains from scanning the crowd to pinpoint Bob's position – he might wave to her, and she needs time to think – and selects a table at the far end of the room. But, presto, Bob is sliding in beside her without so much as a may-I-join-you. He assumes he's already pissed on this fire hydrant, she thinks. Spray-painted this wall. Cut the head off this trophy and got his picture taken with his foot on the body. As he did once before, not that he realizes it. She smiles.

He's solicitous. Is Verna all right? Oh, yes, she replies. It's just that something went down the wrong way. Bob launches straight into the preliminaries. What does Verna do? Retired, she says, though she had a rewarding career as a physiotherapist, specializing in the rehabilitation of heart and stroke victims. 'That must have been interesting,' Bob says. Oh, yes, Verna says. So fulfilling to help people.

It had been more than interesting. Wealthy men recovering from life-threatening episodes had recognized the worth of an attractive younger woman with deft hands, an encouraging manner, and an intuitive knowledge of when to say nothing. Or, as her third husband put it in his Keatsian mode, heard melodies are sweet, but those unheard are sweeter. There was something about the intimacy of the relationship – so physical – that led to other intimacies, though Verna had always stopped short of sex: it was a religious thing, she'd said. If no marriage proposal was forthcoming, she would extricate herself, citing her duty to patients who needed her more. That had forced the issue twice.

She'd chosen her acceptances with an eye to the medical condition involved, and once married she'd done her best to provide value for money.

Each husband had departed not only happy but grateful, if a little sooner than might have been expected. But each had died of natural causes – a lethal recurrence of the heart attack or stroke that had hit him in the first place. All she'd done was give them tacit permission to satisfy every forbidden desire: to eat artery-clogging foods, to drink as much as they liked, to return to their golf games too soon. She'd refrained from commenting on the fact that, strictly speaking, they were being too zealously medicated. She'd wondered about the dosages, she'd say later, but who was she to set her own opinion up against a doctor's?

And if a man happened to forget that he'd already taken his pills for that evening and found them neatly laid out in their usual place and took them again, wasn't that to be expected? Blood thinners could be so hazardous, in excess. You could bleed into your own brain.

Then there was sex: the terminator, the coup de grace. Verna herself had no interest in sex as such, but she knew what was likely to work. 'You only live once,' she'd been in the habit of saying, lifting a champagne glass during a candlelit supper and then setting out the Viagra, a revolutionary break-through but so troubling to the blood pressure. It was essential to call the paramedics in promptly, though not too promptly. 'He was like this when I woke up' was an acceptable thing to say. So was 'I heard a strange sound in the bathroom, and then when I went to look . . .'

258

She has no regrets. She did those men a favour: surely better a swift exit than a lingering decline.

With two of the husbands, there'd been difficulties with the grown-up children over the will. Verna had graciously said that she understood how they must feel. Then she'd paid them off, with more than was strictly fair considering the effort she'd put in. Her sense of justice has remained Presbyterian: she doesn't want much more than her due, but she doesn't want much less either. She likes balanced accounts.

Bob leans in towards her, sliding his arm along the back of her chair. Is her husband along for the cruise? he asks, closer to her ear than he should be, breathing in. No, she says, she is recently widowed – here she looks down at the table, hoping to convey muted grief – and this is a sort of healing voyage. Bob says he's very sorry to hear it, but what a coincidence, for his own wife passed away just six months ago. It had been a blow – they'd been really looking forward to the golden years together. She'd been his college sweetheart – it was love at first sight. Does Verna believe in love at first sight? Yes, Verna says, she does.

Bob confides further: they'd waited until after his law degree to get married and then they'd had three kids, and now there are five grandkids; he's so proud of them all. If he shows me any baby pictures, Verna thinks, I'll hit him.

'It does leave an empty space, doesn't it?' Bob

says. 'A sort of blank.' Verna admits that it does. Would Verna care to join Bob in a bottle of wine?

You crap artist, Verna thinks. So you went on to get married and have children and a normal life, just as if nothing ever happened. Whereas for me . . . She feels queasy.

'I'd love to,' she says. 'But let's wait until we're on the ship. That would be more leisurely.' She gives him the eyelids again. 'Now I'm off to my beauty sleep.' She smiles, rises from the table.

'Oh, surely you don't need that,' Bob says gallantly. The asshole actually pulls out her chair for her. He hadn't shown such fine manners back then. Nasty, brutish, and short, as her third husband had said, quoting Hobbes on the subject of natural man. Nowadays a girl would know to call the police. Nowadays Bob would go to jail no matter what lies he might tell, because Verna was underage. But there had been no true words for the act then: rape was what occurred when some maniac jumped on you out of a bush, not when your formal-dance date drove you to a side road in the mangy twice-cut forest surrounding a tin-pot mining town and told you to drink up like a good girl and then took you apart, layer by torn layer. To make it worse, Bob's best friend, Ken, had turned up in his own car to help out. The two of them had been laughing. They'd kept her panty-girdle as a souvenir.

Afterwards, Bob had pushed her out of the car halfway back, surly because she was crying. 'Shut up or walk home,' he'd said. She has a picture of herself limping along the icy roadside with her bare feet stuck in her dyed-to-match ice-blue heels, dizzy and raw and shivering and – a further ridiculous humiliation – hiccupping. What had concerned her most at that moment was her nylons – where were her nylons? She'd bought them with her own drugstore money. She must have been in shock.

Did she remember correctly? Had Bob stuck her panty girdle upside down on his head and danced about in the snow with the garter tabs flopping around like jester's bells?

Panty girdle, she thinks. How prehistoric. It, and all the long-gone archeology that went with it. Now a girl would be on the pill or have an abortion without a backward glance. How Paleolithic to still feel wounded by any of it.

It was Ken – not Bob – who'd come back for her, told her brusquely to get in, driven her home. He, at least, had had the grace to be shamefaced. 'Don't say anything,' he'd muttered. And she hadn't, but her silence had done her no good.

Why should she be the only one to have suffered for that night? She'd been stupid, granted, but Bob had been vicious. And he'd gone scot-free, without consequences or remorse, whereas her entire life had been distorted. The Verna of the day before had died, and a different Verna had solidified in her place: stunted, twisted, mangled. It was Bob who'd taught her that only the strong can win, that weakness should be mercilessly exploited. It

261

was Bob who'd turned her into – why not say the word? – a murderer.

The next morning, during the chartered flight north to where the ship is floating on the Beaufort Sea, she considers her choices. She could play Bob like a fish right up to the final moment, then leave him cold with his pants around his ankles: a satisfaction, but a minor one. She could avoid him throughout the trip and leave the equation where it's been for the past fifty-some years: unresolved. Or she could kill him. She contemplates this third option with theoretical calm. Just say, for instance, if she were to murder Bob, how might she do it during the cruise without getting caught? Her meds-and-sex formula would be far too slow and might not work anyway, since Bob did not appear to suffer from any ailments. Pushing him off the ship is not a viable option. Bob is too big, the railings are too high, and she knows from her previous trip that there will always be people on deck, enjoying the breathtaking views and taking pictures. A corpse in a cabin would attract police and set off a search for DNA and fabric hairs and so forth, as on television. No, she would have to arrange the death during one of the onshore visits. But how? Where? She consults the itinerary and the map of the proposed route. An Inuit settlement will not do: dogs will bark, children will follow. As for the other stops, the land they'll be visiting is bare of concealing features. Staff with guns will accompany them to protect against polar bears. Maybe an accident with one of the guns? For that she'd need split-second timing.

Whatever the method, she'd have to do it early in the voyage, before he had time to make any new friends – people who might notice he was missing. Also, the possibility that Bob will suddenly recognize her is ever present. And if that happens it will be game over. Meanwhile, it would be best not to be seen with him too much. Enough to keep his interest up, but not enough to start rumours of, for instance, a budding romance. On a cruise, word of mouth spreads like the flu.

Once on board the ship – it's the *Resolute II*, familiar to Verna from her last voyage – the passengers line up to deposit their passports at reception. Then they assemble in the forward lounge for a talk on procedure given by three of the discouragingly capable staff members. Every time they go ashore, the first one says with a severe Viking frown, they must turn their tags on the tag board from green to red. When they come back to the ship, they must turn their tags back to green. They must always wear life jackets for the Zodiac trips to shore; the life jackets are the new, thin kind that inflate once in water. They must deposit their life jackets on the shore when landing, in the white canvas bags provided, and put them back on when departing. If there are any tags unturned or any life jackets left in the bags, the staff will know that

263

someone is still ashore. They do not want to be left behind, do they? And now a few housekeeping details. They will find laundry bags in their cabins. Bar bills will be charged to their accounts, and tips will be settled at the end. The ship runs on an open-door policy, to facilitate the work of the cleaning staff, but of course they can lock their rooms if they wish. There is a lost-and-found at reception. All clear? Good.

The second speaker is the archeologist, who, to Verna, looks about twelve. They will be visiting sites of many kinds, she says, including Independence 1, Dorset, and Thule, but they must never, never take anything. No artifacts, and especially no bones. Those bones might be human, and they must be very careful not to disturb them. But even animal bones are an important source of scarce calcium for ravens and lemmings and foxes and, well, the entire food chain, because the Arctic recycles everything. All clear? Good.

Now, says the third speaker, a fashionably bald individual who looks like a personal trainer, a word about the guns. Guns are essential, because polar bears are fearless. But the staff will always fire into the air first, to scare the bear away. Shooting a bear is a last resort, but bears can be dangerous, and the safety of passengers is the first priority. There is no need to fear the guns: the bullets will be taken out during the Zodiac trips to and from shore, and it will not be possible for anyone to get shot. All clear? Good.

Clearly a gun accident won't do, Verna thinks. No passenger is going to get near those guns.

After lunch, there's a lecture on walruses. There are rumours of rogue walruses that prey on seals, puncturing them with their tusks, then sucking out the fat with their powerful mouths. The women on either side of Verna are knitting. One of them says, 'Liposuction.' The other laughs.

Once the talks are over, Verna goes out on deck. The sky is clear, with a flight of lenticular clouds hovering in it like spaceships; the air is warm; the sea is aqua. There's a classic iceberg on the port side, with a centre so blue it looks dyed, and ahead of them is a mirage – a fata morgana, towering like an ice castle on the horizon, completely real except for the faint shimmering at its edges. Sailors have been lured to their deaths by those; they've drawn mountains on maps where no mountains were.

'Beautiful, isn't it?' Bob says, materializing at her side. 'How about that bottle of wine tonight?'

'Stunning,' Verna says, smiling. 'Perhaps not tonight – I promised some of the girls.' True enough – she's made a date with the knitting women.

'Maybe tomorrow?' Bob grins and shares the fact that he has a single cabin: 'Number 222, like the painkiller,' he quips, and it's comfortably amidship. 'Hardly any rock and roll at all,' he adds. Verna says that she, too, has a single: worth the extra expense, because that way you can really relax. She draws out 'relax' until it sounds like a voluptuous writhe on satin sheets.

Glancing at the tag board while strolling around the ship after dinner, Verna notes Bob's tag – close enough to her own. Then she buys a pair of cheap gloves in the gift shop. She's read a lot of crime novels.

The next day starts with a talk on geology by an energetic young scientist who has been arousing some interest among the passengers, especially the female ones. By great good fortune, he tells them, and because of a change in itinerary owing to ice pack, they'll be making an unanticipated stop, where they'll be able to view a wonder of the geological world, a sight permitted to very few. They'll be privileged to see the world's earliest fossilized stromatolites, clocking in at an astonishing 1.9 billion years old – before fish, before dinosaurs, before mammals – the very first preserved form of life on this planet. What is a stromatolite? he asks rhetorically, his eyes gleaming. The word comes from the Greek *stroma,* a mattress, coupled with the root word for *stone*. Stone mattress: a fossilized cushion, formed by layer upon layer of blue-green algae building up into a mound or dome. It was this very same blue-green algae that created the oxygen they are now breathing. Isn't that astonishing?

A wizened, elf-like man at Verna's lunchtime table grumbles that he hopes they'll be seeing something more exciting than rocks. He's one of the other Bobs: Verna's been taking an inventory.

An extra Bob may come in handy. 'I'm looking forward to them,' she says. 'The stone mattresses.' She gives the word *mattress* the tiniest hint of suggestiveness, and gets an approving twinkle out of Bob the Second. Really, they're never too old to flirt.

Out on deck after coffee, she surveys the approaching land through her binoculars. It's autumn here: the leaves on the miniature trees that snake along the ground like vines are red and orange and yellow and purple, with rock surging out of them in waves and folds. There's a ridge, a higher ridge, then a higher one. It's on the second ridge that the best stromatolites are to be found, the geologist has told them.

Will someone who has slipped behind the third ridge be visible from the second one? Verna doesn't think so.

Now they're all stuffed into their waterproof pants and their rubber boots; now they're being zipped and buckled into their life jackets like outsized kindergarten kids; now they're turning their tags from green to red; now they're edging down the gangway and being whisked into the black inflatable Zodiacs. Bob has made it into Verna's Zodiac. He lifts his camera, snaps her picture.

Verna's heart is beating more rapidly. If he recognizes me spontaneously, I won't kill him, she thinks. If I tell him who I am and he recognizes me and then apologizes, I still won't kill him.

That's two more escape chances than he gave her. It will mean forgoing the advantage of surprise, a move that could be hazardous – Bob is much bigger than she is – but she wishes to be more than fair.

They've landed and have shed their life jackets and rubber footwear and are lacing up their hiking boots. Verna strolls closer to Bob, notes that he hasn't bothered with the rubber boots. He's wearing a red baseball cap; as she watches, he turns it backward.

Now they're all scattering. Some stay by the shore; some move up to the first ridge. The geologist is standing there with his hammer, a twittering cluster already gathered around him. He's in full lecture mode: they will please not take any of the stromatolites, but the ship has a sampling permit, so if anyone finds a particularly choice fragment, especially a cross-section, check with him first and they can put it on the rock table he'll set up on board, where everyone can see it. Here are some examples, for those who may not want to tackle the second ridge . . .

Heads go down; cameras come out. Perfect, Verna thinks. The more distraction the better. She feels without looking that Bob is close by. Now they're at the second ridge, which some are climbing more easily than others. Here are the best stromatolites, a whole field of them. There are unbroken ones, like bubbles or boils, small ones, ones as big as half a soccer ball. Some have lost their tops, like eggs in the process of hatching. Still others have been ground down, so that all that's left of them is a series of raised concentric oblongs, like a cinnamon bun or the growth rings on a tree.

And here's one shattered into four, like a Dutch cheese sliced into wedges. Verna picks up one of the quarters, examines the layers, each year black, grey, black, grey, black, and at the bottom the featureless core. The piece is heavy, and sharp at the edges. Verna lifts it into her backpack.

Here comes Bob as if on cue, lumbering slowly as a zombie up the hill towards her. He's taken off his outer jacket, tucked it under his backpack straps. He's out of breath. She has a moment of compunction: he's over the hill; frailty is gaining on him. Shouldn't she let bygones be bygones? Boys will be boys. Aren't they all just hormone puppets at that age? Why should any human being be judged by something that was done in another time, so long ago it might be centuries?

A raven flies overhead, circles around. Can it tell? Is it waiting? She looks down through its eyes, sees an old woman – because, face it, she is an old woman now – on the verge of murdering an even older man because of an anger already fading into the distance of used-up time. It's paltry. It's vicious. It's normal. It's what happens in life.

'Great day,' Bob says. 'It's good to have a chance to stretch your legs.'

269

'Isn't it?' Verna says. She moves towards the far side of the second ridge. 'Maybe there's something better over there. But weren't we told not to go that far? Out of sight?'

Bob gives a rules-are-for-peasants laugh. 'We're paying for this,' he says. He actually takes the lead, not up the third ridge but around behind it. Out of sight is where he wants to be.

The gun-bearer on the second ridge is yelling at some people straying off to the left. He has his back turned. A few more steps and Verna glances over her shoulder: she can't see anyone, which means that no one can see her. They squelch over a patch of boggy ground. She takes her thin gloves out of her pocket, slips them on. Now they're at the far side of the third ridge, at the sloping base.

'Come over here,' Bob says, patting the rock. His backpack is beside him. 'I brought us a few drinks.' All around him is a tattered gauze of black lichen.

'Terrific,' Verna says. She sits down, unzips her backpack. 'Look,' she says. 'I found a perfect specimen.' She turns, positioning the stromatolite between them, supporting it with both hands. She takes a breath. 'I think we've known each other before,' she says. 'I'm Verna Pritchard. From high school.'

Bob doesn't miss a beat. 'I thought there was something familiar about you,' he says. He's actually smirking.

She remembers that smirk. She has a vivid

picture of Bob capering triumphantly in the snow, sniggering like a ten-year-old. Herself wrecked and crumpled.

She knows better than to swing widely. She brings the stromatolite up hard, a short sharp jab right underneath Bob's lower jaw. There's a crunch, the only sound. His head snaps back. Now he's sprawled on the rock. She holds the stromatolite over his forehead, lets it drop. Again. Once again. There. That seems to have done it.

Bob looks ridiculous, with his eyes open and fixed and his forehead mashed in and blood running down both sides of his face. 'You're a mess,' she says. He looks laughable, so she laughs. As she suspected, the front teeth are implants.

She takes a moment to steady her breathing. Then she retrieves the stromatolite, being careful not to let any of the blood touch her or even her gloves, and slides it into a pool of bog water. Bob's baseball cap has fallen off; she stuffs it into her pack, along with his jacket. She empties out his backpack: nothing in there but the camera, a pair of woollen mitts, a scarf, and six miniature bottles of Scotch. How pathetically hopeful of him. She rolls the pack up, stuffs it inside her own, adds the camera, which she'll toss into the sea later. Then she dries the stromatolite off on the scarf, checking to make sure there's no visible blood, and stows it in her pack. She leaves Bob to the ravens and the lemmings and the rest of the food chain.

Then she hikes back around the base of the third ridge, adjusting her jacket. Anyone looking will assume she's just been having a pee. People do sneak off like that, on shore visits. But no one is looking.

She finds the young geologist – he's still on the second ridge, along with his coterie of admirers – and produces the stromatolite.

'May I take it back to the ship?' she asks sweetly. 'For the rock table?'

'Fantastic sample!' he says.

Travellers are making their way shoreward, back to the Zodiacs. When she reaches the bags with the life jackets, Verna fumbles with her shoelaces until all eyes are elsewhere and she can cram an extra life jacket into her backpack. The pack is a lot bulkier than it was when she left the ship, but it would be odd if anyone noticed that.

Once up the gangway, she diddles around with her pack until everyone else has moved past the tag board, then flips Bob's tag from red to green. And her own tag too, of course.

On the way to her cabin she waits till the corridor is clear, then slips through Bob's unlocked door. The room key is on the dresser; she leaves it there. She hangs up the life jacket and Bob's waterproof and baseball cap, runs some water in the sink, messes up a towel. Then she goes to her own cabin along the still-empty corridor, takes off her gloves, washes them, and hangs them up to dry. She's broken a nail, worse luck, but she can repair that.

She checks her face: a touch of sunburn, but nothing serious. For dinner, she dresses in pink and makes an effort to flirt with Bob the Second, who gamely returns her serves but is surely too decrepit to be a serious prospect. Just as well – her adrenaline level is plummeting. If there are northern lights, they've been told, there will be an announcement, but Verna doesn't intend to get up for them.

So far she's in the clear. All she has to do now is maintain the mirage of Bob, faithfully turning his tag from green to red, from red to green. He'll move objects around in his cabin, wear different items from his beige-and-plaid wardrobe, sleep in his bed, take showers, leaving the towels on the floor. He will receive a first-name-only invitation to have dinner at a staff table, which will then quietly appear under the door of one of the other Bobs, and no one will spot the substitution. He will brush his teeth. He will adjust his alarm clock. He will send in laundry, without, however, filling out the slip: that would be too risky. The cleaning staff won't care – a lot of older people forget to fill out their laundry slips.

The stromatolite will sit on the geological samples table and will be picked up and examined and discussed, acquiring many fingerprints. At the end of the trip it will be jettisoned. The *Resolute II* will travel for fourteen days; it will stop for shore visits eighteen times. It will sail past ice caps and sheer cliffs, and mountains of gold and copper and ebony black and silver grey; it will glide through pack ice; it will anchor off long, implacable beaches and explore fjords gouged by glaciers over millions of years. In the midst of such rigorous and demanding splendour, who will remember Bob?

There will be a moment of truth at the end of the voyage, when Bob will not appear to pay his bill and pick up his passport; nor will he pack his bags. There will be a flurry of concern, followed by a staff meeting – behind closed doors, so as not to alarm the passengers. Ultimately, there will be a news item: Bob, tragically, must have fallen off the ship on the last night of the voyage while leaning over to get a better camera angle on the northern lights. No other explanation is possible.

Meanwhile, the passengers will have scattered to the winds, Verna among them. If, that is, she pulls it off. Will she or won't she? She ought to care more about that – she ought to find it an exciting challenge – but right now she just feels tired and somewhat empty.

Though at peace, though safe. Calm of mind all passion spent, as her third husband used to say so annoyingly after his Viagra sessions. Those Victorians always coupled sex with death. Who was that poet anyway? Keats? Tennyson? Her memory isn't what it was. But the details will come back to her later.

TORCHING THE DUSTIES

The little people are climbing up the night-stand. Today they're wearing green: the women in pannier overskirts, broad-brimmed velvet hats, and square-cut bodices shimmering with beads, the men in satin knick-erbockers and buckled shoes, with bunches of ribbons fluttering from their shoulders and outsized bird plumes decorating their tri-corns. They have no respect for historical accuracy, these people. It's as if some bored theatrical costume designer got drunk behind the scenes and raided the storage boxes: an early Tudor neckline here, a gondolier's jacket there, a Harlequin outfit over there. Wilma has to admire the splapdash abandon.

Up they come, hand over hand. Once level with her eyes, they link arms and dance, gracefully enough considering the obstacles in their way: the night light, the jeweller's loupe sent by her daughter Alyson – a kind gesture but not very helpful – the e-reader that magnifies type. *Gone with the Wind* is the book she's struggling with at the moment. She's lucky if she can grope her way through a single page in fifteen minutes, though happily she can remember the main parts from the first time she read it. Maybe that's where the green fabrics on the tiny folk have come from: those famous velvet curtains that headstrong Scarlett sewed into a gown to disguise herself as respectable.

The little people twirl about, the skirts of the women billowing. They're in a good mood today: they nod at one another, they smile, they open and close their mouths as if they're speaking.

Wilma's fully aware that these apparitions aren't real. They're only symptoms: Charles Bonnet's syndrome, common enough at her age, especially in those with eye problems. She's fortunate, because her manifestations – her Chuckies, as Dr Prasad calls them – are mostly benign. Only rarely do these people scowl, or swell out of proportion, or dissolve into fragments. Even when they're angry or sullen, their fits of ill temper surely can't have anything to do with her, since the little folk never acknowledge her; which is also – says the doctor – par for the course.

She likes the miniature Chuckies, much of the time; she wishes they would talk to her. Be careful what you wish for, said Tobias when she shared this thought with him. Number one, once they start talking they might never shut up, and number two, who knows what they'd say? He then launched into an account of one of his past affairs; long past, needless to say. The woman was ravishing, with the breasts of an Indian goddess and the marble thighs of a Greek statue – Tobias is given to archaic, overblown comparisons – but every time she opened her mouth such banalities would emerge that he would almost burst with repressed irritation. It was a protracted and stressful campaign to get her into bed: chocolates were involved, in a heart-shaped golden box, the very best quality, no expense spared. Also champagne; but this had not made her more willing, only more fatuous.

According to Tobias, it was more difficult to seduce a stupid woman than an intelligent one because stupid women could not understand innuendo or even connect cause with effect. The fact that a pricey dinner ought to be followed, as the night the day, by the compliant opening of their peerless legs was lost on them. Wilma has not considered it tactful to suggest to him that the blank stares and cluelessness might well have been acting on the part of these beauties, who would not be averse to a free meal if all it cost them was a widening of their huge, dumb, heavily fringed eyes. She remembers confidences exchanged in ladies' powder rooms, back when they were called 'powder rooms'; she remembers conspiratorial tittering, she remembers helpful how-to hints exchanged concerning the gullibility of men, in between the lipsticking of mouths and the pencilling of eyebrows. But why upset suave Tobias by revealing all this? It's too late for such inside information to be of practical use to him, and it would only tarnish his rose-tinted memories.

'I should have known you back then,' Tobias says

to Wilma during his chocolates-and-champagne recitals. 'What sparks we would have struck!' Wilma parses this in silence: is he saying that she's intelligent, and therefore a quick lay? Or would have been then. Does he realize that a more easily offended woman might take this as an insult?

No, he does not realize. It's meant to be a gallantry. He can't help it, poor man, being partly Hungarian in origin, he claims; so Wilma lets him prattle on, divine breasts here, marble thighs there, and doesn't comment crisply on his redundancies – as she might once have done – when he relates the same seduction over and over. We have to be kind to one another in here, she tells herself. We're all we have left.

The bottom line is that Tobias can still see. She can't afford to be annoyed by the irritating physical attractions of stale-dated stunners as long as Tobias can look out the window and tell her what's going on down there in the grounds outside the imposing front door of Ambrosia Manor. She likes to be kept in the loop, insofar as there is one.

She squints at her big-numbers clock, then moves it to the side of her head where she can get a better view. It's later than she thought, as always. She fumbles around on the night table until she locates her bridge and slips it into her mouth.

The little people, waltzing now, don't even break stride: her fake teeth are of no interest to them. Or to anyone, come to think of it, except Wilma herself and possibly Dr Stitt, wherever he may be now. It was Dr Stitt who'd convinced her to have several of her about-to-splinter molars Roto-Rootered out and then to get the implants installed – fourteen or fifteen years ago, that must have been – so she'd have something to attach a bridge to, supposing she needed it in the future. Which he predicted she would, because her teeth, being pre-fluoridation, would shortly be crumbling away like wet plaster.

'You'll thank me later,' he'd said.

'If I live that long,' she'd replied with a laugh. She'd still been at the age when she'd liked to make death into a conversational flippancy, thus showing what a lively, game old bird she was.

'You'll live forever,' he'd said. Which had sounded more like a warning than a reassurance. Though maybe he was only anticipating future business from her.

But now it is later, and she does thank Dr Stitt, silently, every morning. It would be dire to be toothless.

Smooth white smile inserted, she slides out of bed, feels with her toes for her terrycloth slippers, and shuffles her way to the bathroom. The bathroom is still manageable: she knows where everything is in there, and it isn't as if she can't see at all. From the corners of her eyes she can still get a working impression, though the central void in her field of vision is expanding, as she's been told it would. Too much golf without sunglasses, and then there was the sailing – you get a double dose of the rays from the reflection off the water – but who knew anything then? The sun was supposed to be good for you. A healthy tan. They'd covered themselves in baby oil, fried themselves like pancakes. The dark, slick, fricasseed finish looked so good on the legs against white shorts.

Macular degeneration. *Macular* sounds so immoral, the opposite of *immaculate*. 'I'm a degenerate,' she used to quip right after she'd received the diagnosis. So many brave jokes, once.

Putting her clothes on is still possible as long as there aren't any buttons: two years ago, or is it longer, she weeded the buttons out of her wardrobe. There's now Velcro throughout, and zippers too, which are fine as long as they're end-stop zippers: slotting the little thingy into the other little thingy is no longer possible.

She smooths her hair, feels for stray wisps. Ambrosia Manor has its own salon complete with hairdresser, thank providence, and she relies on Sasha there to keep her trimmed. The most worrisome item during her morning preparation is her face. She can scarcely make it out in the mirror: it's like one of those face-shaped blanks that once appeared on Internet accounts when you hadn't added your picture. So no hope for the eyebrow pencil or the mascara, and hardly any for the lipstick, though on optimistic days she pretends to herself she can draw that on sightlessly. Should she chance it today? Maybe she'll look like a clown. But if so, who would care?

She would. And Tobias might. And the staff, though in a different way. If you look demented they're more likely to treat you as if you really are. So better to avoid the lipstick.

She finds the cologne bottle where it always resides – the cleaners have strict instructions not to move anything – and dabs herself behind the ears. Attar of Roses, with an undertone of something else, a citrus. She breathes in deeply: thank heavens she can still smell, unlike some of the others. It's when you can't smell any more that your appetite goes and you dwindle to nothing.

As she turns away she does manage to catch a glimpse of herself, or of someone: a woman disconcertingly like her own mother as she was in old age, white hair, crumpled tissue-paper skin and all; though, as the eyes are sideways, more mischievous. Possibly more malevolent as well, like an elf gone to the bad. That sideways glance lacks the candour of a full frontal gaze, a thing she will never see again.

Here comes Tobias, punctual as ever. They always have breakfast together.

He knocks first, like the courtly gentleman he purports to be. The time you should wait before entering a lady's chamber, according to Tobias, is the time it would take the other man to dive under the bed. Appearances should be preserved when it comes to wives, several of whom have been undergone by Tobias. They were cheaters

281

every one, though he doesn't hold it against them any more because it would be hard to respect a woman who wasn't desired by other men. He never let the wives know he knew, and he always enticed them back and made sure they were worshipping him again before giving them a sudden boot out the door, with no explanation, because why lower himself by accusing them? A firmly closed door was more dignified. That was the way to deal with wives.

In the case of mistresses, however, spontaneous emotion is likely to take over. A suspicious lover infuriated by jealousy and his own wounded honour is tempted to barge right in without knocking, and then there will be bloodshed, right there on the spot, with a knife or bare hands, or else in the form of duels, later.

'Did you ever kill anyone?' Wilma asked once, during this recitation.

'My lips are sealed,' Tobias replied solemnly. 'But a wine bottle – a *full* wine bottle – can crush in a skull, at the temple. And I was a crack shot.'

Wilma kept her mouth still: she can't see Tobias, but he can see her, and a smirk would hurt him. She finds these kinds of details rococo, like the vanished gold chocolate boxes, and suspects Tobias of making them up, not out of whole cloth but from creaky, ornate operettas and once-fashionable continental novels and the reminiscences of dandyish uncles. He must think that naive, bland, North American Wilma finds him decadent and glamorous, quite the roué; he must think she swallows this stuff whole. But maybe he believes it himself.

'Come in,' she says now. A blob appears in the doorway. She regards it sideways, sniffs the air. It's Tobias for sure, it's his aftershave: Brut, if she's not mistaken. Has her sense of smell become sharper as her eyesight has faded? Probably not, though it's comforting to think so. 'How lovely to see you, Tobias,' she says.

'Dear lady, you are radiant,' says Tobias. He advances, plants a kiss of greeting upon her cheek with his thin, dry lips. A few bristles: he hasn't shaved yet, just splashed on the Brut. Like herself, he must be worried about how he smells: that acid, stale odour of aging bodies so noticeable when all the Ambrosiads are assembled in the dining room, their base note of slow decay and involuntary leakage papered over with applied layers of scent – delicate florals on the women, bracing spices on the men, the blooming rose or brusque pirate image inside each of them still fondly cherished.

'I hope you slept well,' says Wilma.

'I had such a dream!' says Tobias. 'Purple. Maroon. It was very sexual, with music.'

His dreams are frequently very sexual, with music. 'It ended well, I hope?' she says. She's overusing the word *hope* today.

'Not very well,' says Tobias. 'I committed a murder. It woke me up. What shall we have today? The oat creations, or the bran ones?' He never pronounces the actual names of the dry breakfast cereals in Wilma's repertoire: he finds them banal. Soon he will make a remark about the absence of good croissants in this place, or indeed of any croissants whatsoever.

'You choose,' she says. 'I'll have a mixture.' Bran for the bowels, oats for the cholesterol, though the experts keep changing their minds about that. She hears him rummaging: he's familiar with her small kitchenette, he knows where the packages are kept. Here at the Manor, lunch and dinner are served in the dining room, but they have their breakfasts in their own apartments; those of them in the Early Assisted Living wing, that is. In the Advanced Living wing, things are different. She hasn't wished to imagine exactly how different.

There's a clanking of plates, a rattle of cutlery: Tobias is setting out their breakfast on the small table over by the window. He's a dark shape silhouetted against the bright glaring square of daylight.

'I'll get the milk,' says Wilma. She can do that much, at least: open the mini-fridge door, locate the cool plasti-coated cardboard oblong, carry it to the table without spilling.

'It's done,' says Tobias. Now he's grinding the coffee, a miniature buzz-saw whirr. He doesn't tell the story today about how much better it would be to grind the coffee in a hand grinder, a red one with a brass handle, as was the custom in his youth, or possibly in the youth of his mother. In somebody's youth. Wilma is familiar with this red,

284

brass-handled coffee grinder. It's as if she once owned it herself, though she never did. Yet she feels its loss; it's become part of her inventory, it's joined the other objects that she has in fact lost.

'We should have eggs,' says Tobias. Sometimes they do, though the last occasion was a minor disaster. Tobias boiled the eggs but not enough, so Wilma made a shambles of hers, and it squirted all over her front. Taking the top off the shell is a precise operation: she can no longer aim the spoon with accuracy. Next time she'll suggest an omelette, though that may be beyond the culinary skills of Tobias. Maybe if she directs him, step by step? No, too hazardous: she wouldn't want him to get burned. Something in the microwave, perhaps; some baked French toast affair. A cheese strata; she used to make those, when she had a family. But how to find a recipe? And then follow it. Maybe there are audio recipes?

They sit at the table, munching their cereals, which are brittle and cindery and take a lot of chewing. The sound inside her head, thinks Wilma, is of crisp snow underfoot, or of Styrofoam packing peanuts. Maybe she should switch to a softer cereal option, like instant porridge. But Tobias might disdain her for even mentioning such a thing: he scorns anything instant. Bananas: she'll try for bananas. They grow on trees, or plants, or bushes. He can't possibly object to bananas.

'Why do they make them into circles?' Tobias says, not for the first time. 'These oat things.'

'It's the shape of an O,' Wilma says. 'O for oat. It's a sort of pun.' Tobias shakes his blobby head against the light.

'A croissant would be preferable,' he says. 'These also are made in a shape, a crescent, from when the Moors almost captured Vienna. I do not see why . . .' But he breaks off. 'Something is happening at the gate.'

Wilma has binoculars, sent to her by her Alyson for viewing birds, though the birds she had managed to view were mainly starlings and the binoculars aren't of use to her any more. Her other daughter sends mostly slippers; Wilma has a glut of slippers. Her son sends postcards. He doesn't seem to grasp the fact that she can no longer read his handwriting.

She keeps the binoculars on the windowsill, and Tobias wields them to survey the grounds: the curved driveway; the lawn with its clipped shrubs – she remembers those from when she first came here, three years ago – the fountain with a replica of a famous Belgian statue, a naked angel-faced boy urinating into a stone basin; the high brick wall; the imposing gateway with its overhead arch and its two ostentatious, depressed-looking stone lions. The Manor was once a mansion in the countryside, back when people built mansions, back when there was a countryside. Hence the lions, most likely.

Sometimes there's nothing to be seen by Tobias except the usual comings and goings. Every day there will be visitors – 'civilians,' Tobias calls them – marching briskly from the guest car park towards the main door, bearing a potted begonia or geranium, hauling a young, reluctant grandchild, summoning up false cheer, hoping to get this rich-old-relative thing over with as fast as possible. There will be staff, both medical and cooking/cleaning, who drive in through the gate and then around to the staff parking and the side doors. There will be snazzily painted delivery vans bringing groceries and washed linens, and sometimes flower arrangements ordered up by guilty family members. The less dapper vehicles, such as the garbage collection trucks, have an ignominious back-entrance gate of their own.

Every once in a while there's a drama. An inhabitant of the Advanced Living wing will escape despite all precautions, and will be seen wandering aimlessly, in pyjamas or partly clothed, peeing here and there – an activity welcome in a cherubic fountain ornament but not acceptable in a decrepit human being – and there will be a mild-mannered but efficient chase to surround the errant one and lead him back inside. Or her: sometimes it's a her, though the men seem to take more initiative in escaping.

Or an ambulance will arrive and a brace of paramedics will hurry in, carrying their equipment – 'like the war,' Tobias once remarked, though he must have been referring to films because he hasn't been in any wars that Wilma is aware of – and then after a while they will exit at a more leisurely pace, wheeling a shape on a gurney. You can't tell from here, says Tobias as he peers through the binoculars, whether the body is alive or dead. 'Maybe you can't even tell from down there,' he's been known to add as a sepulchral joke.

'What is it?' Wilma asks now. 'Is it an ambulance?' There haven't been sirens: she's sure of that, she still hears quite well. It's at times like this that her disability is most discouraging to her. She'd rather see for herself; she doesn't trust Tobias to interpret; she suspects him of holding things back. Protecting her, he'd call it. But she doesn't want to be protected in that way.

Perhaps in response to her frustration, a phalanx of little men forms up on the windowsill. No women this time, it's more like a march-past. The society of the tiny folk is socially conservative: they don't let women into their marches. Their clothing is still green, but a darker green, not so festive. Those in the front rows have practical metal helmets. In the ranks behind them the costumes are more ceremonial, with gold-hemmed capes and green fur hats. Will there be miniature horses later on in the parade? It's been known to happen.

Tobias doesn't answer at once. Then he says, 'Not an ambulance. Some sort of picketing. It looks organized.'

'Maybe there's a strike,' says Wilma. But who

among the workers at Ambrosia Manor would be striking? The cleaners would have the most reason, they're underpaid; but they're also the least likely, being illegal at worst, and at best in strong need of the money.

'No,' says Tobias slowly. 'I don't think it's a strike. Three of our security are talking with them. There's a cop, as well. Two cops.'

It startles Wilma whenever Tobias uses slang words like *cop*. They don't go with his standard verbal ensemble, which is much more pressed and deliberate. But he might permit himself to say 'cop' because it's archaic. He once said, 'Okey-dokey' and at another time, 'Scram.' Maybe he gets these words out of books: dusty second-hand murder mysteries and the like. Though who is Wilma to make fun of him? Now that she can no longer fool around on the Internet, Wilma has lost track of how people talk. Real people, younger people. Not that she'd fooled around on the Internet very much. She was never interactive, she was just a lurker, and she was only beginning to get the hang of it before her eyes started to go.

She'd once said to her husband – when he was still alive, not during that year-long dream-nightmare period of mourning when she'd continued to talk to him after his death – that she'd have *lurker* written on her tombstone. Because hadn't she spent most of her life just watching? It feels like that now, though it didn't at the time, because she'd been so busy with this and that. Her degree had been in History – a safe-enough thing to study while waiting to get married – but a fat lot of good all that History is doing her at the moment, because she can't remember much of it. Three political leaders who died having sex, that's about it. Genghis Khan, Clemenceau, and what's-his-name. It will come to her later.

'What are they doing?' she asks. The marchers on the windowsill have been heading to the right, but suddenly they wheel around and quickstep left. They've added lances with glittering points, and some of them have drums. She tries not to be too distracted by them, though it's such a pleasure to be able to see anything in such intricate and concrete detail. But Tobias doesn't like it if he senses that her attention is not fully focused on him. She wrenches herself back to the solid, invisible present. 'Are they coming in here?'

'They're standing around,' says Tobias. 'Loitering,' he adds disapprovingly. 'Young people.' He's of the opinion that all young people are lazy free-loaders and should get jobs. The fact that there are few jobs available for them doesn't register with him. If there are no jobs, he says, they should create some.

'How many are there?' asks Wilma. If only a dozen or so it's nothing serious.

'I'd say about fifty,' says Tobias. 'They've got signs. Not the cops, the other ones. Now they're trying to block the Linens for Life van. Look, they're standing in front of it.'

He's forgotten she can't look. 'What's on the signs?' she asks. Blocking the Linens for Life van is not compassionate: today is the day the beds are changed, for those who don't need extra linen services and a rubber sheet. The Advanced Life wing is on a more frequent schedule; twice a day, she's heard. Ambrosia Manor isn't cheap, and the relatives would not take kindly to ulcerating rashes on their loved ones. They want their money's worth, or so they'll claim. What they most likely want in truth is a rapid and blame-free finish for the old fossils. Then they can tidy up and collect the remnants of the net worth – the legacy, the leftovers, the remains – and tell themselves they deserve it.

'Some of the signs have pictures of babies,' says Tobias. 'Chubby, smiling babies. Some say *Time to Go.*'

'Time to go?' says Wilma. 'Babies? What does that mean? This isn't a maternity hospital.' About the opposite, she thinks caustically: it's an exit from life, not an entrance. But Tobias doesn't answer.

'The cops are letting the van through,' he says.

Good, thinks Wilma. Change of sheets for all. We won't get so smelly.

Tobias leaves for his morning nap – he'll come by again at noon to lead her to the dining room for lunch – and, after a few false starts and a cheese-board knocked to the floor, Wilma locates the radio

291

she keeps on her kitchenette counter and switches it on. It's specially made for those of diminished vision – the on-off and the tuning dial are the only buttons, and the whole radio is sheathed in grip-friendly, waterproof lime-green plastic. Another gift from Alyson on the West Coast, who worries that she's not doing enough for Wilma. She would surely visit more frequently if it weren't for the teenaged twins with unspecified issues and the demands of her own career in a large international accounting firm. Wilma must call her later today to assure her that she herself is still alive, at which time the twins will be forced to say hello to her. How tedious they must find these calls, and why not? She finds them tedious herself.

Perhaps the strike, or whatever it is, will be on the local news. She can listen while washing the breakfast dishes, which she does fairly well if she goes slowly. In case of broken glass she'll have to connect with Services on the intercom and then wait for Katia, her personal on-call cleaner, to arrive and sweep up the damage, tut-tutting and lamenting in her Slavic accent all the while. Splinters of glass can be treacherously sharp, and it would be unwise of Wilma to risk a cut, especially since she's temporarily forgotten which bathroom drawer she keeps the Band-Aids in.

Blood puddles on the floor would give the wrong signal to the management. They don't really believe she's able to function on her own; they're just waiting for an excuse to slot her into Advanced

Living and grab the rest of her furniture and her good china and silver, which they'll sell to support their profit margin. That's the deal, she signed it; it was the price of entry, the price of comfort, the price of safety. The price of not being a burden. She's kept two of her nice antiques, the little escritoire and the dressing table – the last relics of her former household. The rest went to her three children, who had no use for such things really – not their taste – and no doubt stuck them all in the cellar, but who were reverentially grateful.

Upbeat radio music, jovial chit-chat between the male host and the female one, more music, the weather. Heat wave in the north, flooding out west, more tornadoes. A hurricane heading for New Orleans, another one pummelling the eastern seaboard, the usual thing for June. But in India it's the opposite story: the monsoons have failed and there are worries about a coming famine. Australia is still gripped by drought, with, however, a deluge in the Cairns area, where crocodiles are invading the streets. Forest fires in Arizona, and in Poland, and also in Greece. But right here all is well: it's a good moment for the beach, grab some rays, don't forget the sunblock, though watch out for storm cells popping up later. Have a good day!

Here's the main news. First, a regime topple in Uzbekistan; second, a mass shooting in a shopping mall in Denver, the doubtless hallucinating assailant then killed by a sniper. But third – Wilma listens harder – on the outskirts of Chicago, an old-age home has been set on fire by a mob wearing baby masks; and a second one near Savannah, Georgia, and a third one in Akron, Ohio. One of the homes was state-run, but the other two were private institutions with their own security, and the inhabitants of them, some of whom were fried to a crisp, were not poor.

It was not a coincidence, says the commentator. It was coordinated arson: a group naming itself Artern has claimed responsibility on a website whose account-holders the authorities are attempting to track down. The families of the elderly dead people are naturally – says the newscaster – in shock. An interview with a weeping, incoherent relative commences. Wilma switches it off. There was no mention of the gathering outside Ambrosia Manor, but it's probably too small and non-violent to have registered.

Artern. That's what it sounded like: they didn't spell it. She'll ask Tobias to watch the television news – an activity he claims to dislike, though he's always doing it – and tell her more. She ignores the festival of little people that's going on in the vicinity of the microwave, a pink and orange theme with multiple frills and grotesquely high beflowered wigs, and goes to lie down for her morning nap. She used to hate naps, and she still does: she doesn't want to miss anything. But she can't get through the day without them.

* * *

Tobias leads her down the hallway towards the dining room. Theirs is the second sitting: Tobias considers it gauche to lunch before one. He's walking more quickly than usual and she asks him to slow down. 'Of course, dear lady,' he says, squeezing her elbow, which he's using to propel her. Once he'd slipped his arm around her waist – she still does have a waist, more or less, unlike some of the others – but that had unbalanced him, and the two of them had almost toppled over. He's not a tall man, and he's had a hip replacement. He needs to watch his equilibrium.

Wilma doesn't know what he looks like, not any more. She's probably embellished him; made him younger, less withered, more alert. More hair on top.

'I have so much to tell you,' he says, too close to her ear. She wants to tell him not to shout, it's not as if she's deaf. 'I have learned they are not strikers, these people. They are not retreating, they have increased in number.' This turn of events has energized him; he's almost humming.

In the dining room he pulls out her chair, guides her into it, pushes the chair back in just as her bottom is descending. It's an almost-lost art, she thinks, this graceful ladies' chair push, like shoeing horses or fletching arrows. Then he sits down opposite her, an obscure shape against the eggshell wallpaper. She turns her head sideways, gets a vague impression of his face, with its dark, intense eyes. She remembers them as intense.

'What's on the menu?' she says. They're given a printed menu for each meal, on a single sheet of paper with an embossed, fraudulent crest. Smooth, creamy paper, like the theatre programs of a former era, before they became flimsy and cluttered up with advertisements.

'Mushroom soup,' he says. Usually he dwells on the daily offerings, disparaging them gently while reminiscing about gourmet banquets from his past and reflecting that no one knows how to cook properly any more, especially not veal, but today he skips all that. 'I have been delving into it,' he says. 'In the Activity Centre. I have been trolling.'

He means he's been using the computer and searching the Internet for clues. They aren't allowed personal computers in Ambrosia, the official explanation being that the system isn't up to speed. Wilma suspects the real reason is that they're afraid the women will fall victim to online scammers and start up unsuitable romances and then piddle away their money, and the men will be sucked into the Internet porn and then get overheated and have heart attacks, thus causing Ambrosia Manor to be sued by indignant relatives who will claim the staff ought to have monitored the old boys more carefully.

So no individual computers; but they can use those in the Activity Centre, where controls can be put on access, as for prepubescent children. Though management tries to steer the inhabitants away from the addictive screens: they'd rather have the customers fumbling around in mounds of wet clay or gluing geometric shapes of cardboard into patterns; or playing bridge, which is supposed to delay the onset of dementia. Though, as Tobias says, with bridge players how can you tell? Wilma, who once played a lot of bridge, declines to comment.

Shoshanna, the occupational therapist, does the rounds at dinnertime, pestering the clientele about everyone's need to express themselves through Art. When urged to participate in the finger-painting or pasta-necklace-making or whatever other bright idea Shoshanna has cooked up to give them all a reason for staying on the planet for another sunrise, Wilma pleads her limited sight. Shoshanna once upped the ante with some yarn about blind potters, several of whom had achieved international recognition for their beautiful hand-thrown ceramics, and wouldn't Wilma like to expand her horizons by giving it a try? But Wilma froze her out. 'Old dog.' She smiled with her hard, false teeth. 'No new tricks.'

As for the Internet porn, some of the crafty lechers have cellphones and treat themselves to the full freakshow that way. This is according to Tobias, who gossips with anyone in sight when he isn't gossiping with Wilma. He claims he himself doesn't bother with the tawdry and inelegant cellphone porn, because the women on view are too tiny. There's a limit, he says, as to how much you can shrink the female body without turning it into an ant with mammary glands. Wilma doesn't entirely believe this tale of abstinence, though maybe he's not lying: he just might find his own invented sagas more erotic than anything a mere phone can come up with, and they have the added virtue of starring him.

'What else did you learn?' Wilma asks. All around them is the clanking of spoons on china, the murmur of thinning voices, an insect vibration.

'They say it's their turn,' says Tobias. 'That's why they put *Our Turn* on the signs.'

'Oh,' says Wilma. Light dawns: *Artern. Our Turn.* She'd misheard. 'Their turn at what?'

'At life, they say. I heard one of them on the television news; naturally they're being interviewed all over the place. They say we've had our turn, those our age; they say we messed it up. Killing the planet with our own greed and so forth.'

'They have a point there,' says Wilma. 'We did mess it up. Not on purpose, though.'

'They're only socialists,' says Tobias. He has a dim opinion of socialists; everyone he doesn't like is a socialist in some disguise or other. 'Just lazy socialists, always trying to grab what others worked for.'

Wilma has never been sure how Tobias made his money, enough money to be able to afford not only all the ex-wives, but his quite large suite in Ambrosia Manor. She suspects he was involved in some dubious business deals in countries in which all business deals are dubious, but he's cagey about his earlier financial life. All he'll say is that he owned several companies in international trade and made sound investments, though he doesn't call himself rich. But then rich people never call themselves rich: they call themselves comfortable.

Wilma herself was comfortable, back when her husband was alive. She's probably still comfortable. She no longer pays much attention to her savings: a private management company takes care of that. Alyson keeps an eye on them, as much as she can from the West Coast. Ambrosia Manor hasn't kicked Wilma out onto the street, so the bills must be getting paid.

'What do they want from us?' she asks, trying not to sound peevish. 'Those people with the signs. For heaven's sakes. It's not as if we can *do* anything.'

'They say they want us to make room. They want us to move over. Some of the signs say that: *Move Over.*'

'That means *die*, I suppose,' says Wilma. 'Are there any rolls today?' Sometimes there are the most delicious Parker House rolls, fresh from the oven. As a way of helping their clients feel at home, the Ambrosia Manor dieticians make a conscious effort to re-create what they imagine were the menus of seventy or eighty years ago. Macaroni and cheese, soufflés, custards, rice pudding, Jell-O dolloped with whipped cream. These menus have the added virtue of being soft, and thus no threat to wobbly teeth.

'No,' says Tobias. 'No rolls. Now they are bringing the chicken pot pies.'

'Do you think they're dangerous?' says Wilma.

299

'Not here,' says Tobias. 'But in other countries they are burning things down. This group. They say they are international. They say millions are rising up.'

'Oh, they're always burning things down in other countries,' Wilma says lightly. *If I live that long,* she hears herself saying to her former dentist. It's the same throwaway tone: *None of this can possibly ever happen to me.*

Idiot, she tells herself. Wishful thinking. But she simply can't bring herself to feel threatened, or not by the foolishness outside the gates.

In the afternoon Tobias invites himself for tea. His own room is on the other side of the building. It has a view out over the back grounds with their gravelled walks, their frequent park benches for the easily winded, their tasteful gazebos for shelter from the sun, and their croquet lawn for leisurely games. Tobias can see all of this, which he has described to Wilma in gloating detail, but he can't see the front gate. Also he has no binoculars. He's here in her apartment for the vista.

'There are more of them now,' he says. 'Maybe a hundred. Some are wearing masks.'

'Masks?' Wilma asks, intrigued. 'You mean, like Halloween?' She pictures goblins and Draculas, fairy princesses, witches and Elvis Presleys. 'I thought masks are illegal. At public gatherings.'

'Not quite like Halloween,' says Tobias. 'Masks of babies.'

'Are they pink?' says Wilma. She feels a slight tremor of fear. Baby masks on a mob: it's disconcerting. A horde of life-sized, potentially violent babies. Out of control.

There are twenty or thirty small people holding hands, circling what is most likely the sugar bowl: Tobias likes sugar in his tea. The women are wearing skirts that appear to be made out of overlapping rose petals, the men shimmer in iridescent peacock-feather blue. How exquisite they are, how embroidered! It's hard to believe they aren't real; they're so physical, so finely detailed.

'Some of them,' says Tobias. 'Some are yellow. Some brown.'

'They must be trying for an inter-racial theme,' says Wilma. Stealthily she inches her hand across the table towards the dancers: if only she could catch one, hold it between thumb and forefinger like a beetle. Maybe then they'd acknowledge her, if only by kicking and biting. 'Do they have baby outfits on, as well?' Diapers maybe, or onesies with slogans on them, or bibs with incongruously vicious images such as pirates and zombies. Those had been all the rage, once.

'No, just the faces,' says Tobias. The tiny dancers won't give Wilma the satisfaction of allowing her fingers to pass through them, thus demonstrating their non-reality once and for all. Instead they curve their dance line to evade her, so perhaps they're aware of her after all. Perhaps they're teasing, the little rascals.

301

Don't be silly, she tells herself. It's a syndrome. Charles Bonnard. It's well documented, other people have it. No, Bonnet: Bonnard was a painter, she's almost sure of that. Or is it Bonnivert?

'Now they're blocking another van,' says Tobias. 'The chicken delivery.' The chickens come from a local organic and free-range farm, as do the eggs. Barney and Dave's Lucky Cluckies. They always come on Thursdays. No chickens and no eggs: that might get serious in the long run, thinks Wilma. There will be querulousness inside the walls. Voices will be raised. *This is not what I paid for.*

'Are there any cops?' she says.

'I don't see any,' says Tobias.

'We need to ask at the front desk,' says Wilma. 'We need to complain! They ought to be cleared away, or something – those people.'

'I already asked,' says Tobias. 'They don't know any more about it than we do.'

The evening's dinner is more vivacious than usual: more chattering, more clattering, more sudden bursts of reedy laughter. The dining room appears to be short-staffed, which on a normal evening might result in increased peevishness, but as things are there's an atmosphere of subdued carnival. A tray is dropped, a glass shatters, a cheer goes up. The clients are warned to be aware of the spilled ice cubes, which are barely visible and slippery. We wouldn't want any broken hips, now, would we? says the voice of Shoshanna, who is wielding the microphone.

Tobias orders a bottle of wine for the table. 'Let's live it up,' he says. 'Here's looking at you!' Glasses clink. He and Wilma are not a twosome tonight, they're at a table for four. Tobias proposed it, and Wilma surprised herself by agreeing: if there's no safety in numbers, at least there's the illusion of safety. If they stick together they can keep the unknown at bay.

The other two at the table are Jo-Anne and Noreen. Too bad there can't be another man, thinks Wilma, but in this age group the women outnumber the men four to one. According to Tobias, women hang around longer because they're less capable of indignation and better at being humiliated, for what is old age but one long string of indignities? What person of integrity would put up with it? Sometimes, when the bland food gets too much for him or when his arthritis is acting up, he threatens to blow his head off, if he could only lay his hands on the necessary weapon, or slit his wrists in the bath with a razor blade, like an honourable Roman. When Wilma protests, he calms her: that's just the morbid Hungarian in him, all Hungarian men talk like that. If you're a Hungarian man you can't let a day pass without a suicide threat, though – he'll joke – not nearly enough of them follow through.

Why not the Hungarian women? Wilma has asked him several times. Why is that they too are

303

not razoring their wrists in the tub? She enjoys re-asking questions because the answers are sometimes the same, sometimes not. Tobias has had at least three birthplaces and has attended four universities, all at once. His passports are numerous.

'The Hungarian women aren't up to it,' he said once. 'They never know when it's game over, in love, life, or death. They flirt with the undertaker, they flirt with the guy shovelling the dirt onto their coffin. They never give up.'

Neither Jo-Anne nor Noreen is Hungarian, but they too are displaying impressive flirting skills. If they had feather fans they'd be hitting Tobias with them, if bouquets they'd be tossing him a rosebud, if they had ankles they'd be flashing them. As it is they're simpering. Wilma longs to tell them to act their age, but what would it be like if they did?

She knows Jo-Anne from the swimming pool. She tries to do a few laps twice a week, manageable as long as someone helps her in and out and guides her to the change room. And she must have met Noreen before at some group function like a concert: she recognizes that pigeon-shaped laugh, a tremulous coo. She has no idea what either of them looks like, though she notes via her side vision that they're both wearing magenta.

Tobias is far from unhappy to have a whole new female audience. Already he's told Noreen that she's radiant tonight, and has hinted to Jo-Anne that she wouldn't be safe in the dark with him if he were still the man he once was. 'If youth only knew, if age only could,' he says. Is that the sound of hand-kissing? Gigglings come from the two of them, or what would formerly have been gigglings. Closer to squawkings, or cluckings, or wheezings: sudden gusts of air through autumn leaves. The vocal cords shorten, Wilma thinks sadly. The lungs shrink. Everything gets drier.

How does she feel about the flirtation that's going on over the clam chowder? Is she jealous, does she want Tobias all to herself? Not all of him, no; she wouldn't go so far. She has no desire to roll around in the metaphorical hay with him, because she has no desire. Or not much. But she does want his attention. Or rather she wants him to want her attention, though he seems to be doing well enough with the two inferior substitutes on hand. The three of them are bantering away like something in a Regency Romance, and she has to listen because there's nothing to distract her: the little people haven't shown up.

She tries to summon them. *Come out*, she commands silently, fixing what would once have been her gaze in the direction of the artificial flower arrangement in the centre of the table – top quality, says Tobias, you can hardly tell the difference. It's yellow, which is about all she can say for it.

Nothing happens. No manikins appear. She can control neither their appearances nor their disappearances; which seems unfair, since they're products of nobody's brain but hers.

⋆   ⋆   ⋆

The clam chowder is succeeded by a ground beef casserole with mushrooms, followed in turn by rice pudding with raisins. Wilma concentrates on eating: she must locate the plate out of the corners of her eyes, she must direct the fork as if it's a steam shovel: she must approach, swivel, acquire payload, lift. This takes effort. At long last the cookie plate descends, shortbread and bars as usual. There's a brief glimpse of seven or eight ladies in off-white frilly petticoats, a can-can flash of their silk-stockinged legs, but they morph back into shortbread cookies almost immediately.

'What's happening outside?' she says into a gap left in the web of compliments that's been spinning itself among the others. 'At the main gate?'

'Oh,' says Noreen gaily, 'we were trying to forget all that!'

'Yes,' says Jo-Anne. 'It's too depressing. We're living for the moment, aren't we, Tobias?'

'Wine, women, and song!' Noreen announces. 'Bring on the belly dancers!' Both of them cackle.

Surprisingly, Tobias does not laugh. Instead he takes Wilma's hand; she feels his dry, warm, boney fingers enclosing hers. 'More are gathering. The situation is more grave than we at first apprehended, dear lady,' he says. 'It would be unwise to underestimate it.'

'Oh, we weren't *underestimating* it,' says Jo-Anne, striving to keep her conversational soap bubbles in the air. 'We were just *ignoring* it!'

'Ignorance is bliss!' chirps Noreen; but they're

no longer cutting any ice with Tobias. He's dumped his *Scarlet Pimpernel* foppish-aristocrat frippery and has swung into his Man of Action mode.

'We must expect the worst,' he says. 'They will not catch us napping. Now, dear lady, I will escort you home.'

She breathes out with relief: he's come back to her. He'll take her as far as the door of her apartment; he does this every evening, faithful as clockwork. What has she been afraid of? That he'd leave her to fumble her way ignominiously, deserted in full view of all, and scamper off into the shrubbery with Noreen and Jo-Anne to commit threefold sexual acts with them in a gazebo? No chance of that: the security men would scoop them up in no time flat and frog-march them into the Advanced Living wing. They patrol the grounds at night, with flashlights and beagles.

'Are we ready?' Tobias asks her. Wilma's heart warms to him. *We.* So much for Jo-Anne and Noreen, who are, once again, merely *they.* She leans on him as he takes her elbow, and together they make what she's free to picture as a dignified exit.

'But what is the worst?' she says to him in the elevator. 'And how can we prepare for it? You don't think they'll burn us down! Not here! The police would stop them.'

'We cannot count on the police,' says Tobias. 'Not any more.'

Wilma is about to protest – *But they have to*

protect us, it's their job! – but she stops herself. If the police were all that concerned, they would have acted by now. They're holding back.

'These people will be cautious, at first,' says Tobias. 'They will proceed by small steps. We still have a little time. You must not worry, you must sleep well, to build up your strength. I have my preparations to make. I will not fail.'

It's strange how reassuring she finds this snippet of melodrama: Tobias taking charge, having a deep plan, outfoxing Fate. He's only a feeble old man with arthritis, she tells herself. But she's reassured and soothed all the same.

Outside her apartment they exchange their standard peck on the cheek, and Wilma listens while he limps away down the hall. Is this regret she's feeling? Is this a fluttering of ancient warmth? Does she really want him to enfold her in his stringy arms, make his way in towards her skin through the Velcro and zippers, attempt some ghostly, creaky, arthropod-like reprise of an act he must have committed effortlessly hundreds, indeed thousands of times in the past? No. It would be too painful for her, the silent comparisons that would be going on: the luscious, chocolate-sampling mistresses, the divine breasts, the marble thighs. Then only her.

You believed you could transcend the body as you aged, she tells herself. You believed you could rise above it, to a serene, non-physical realm. But it's only through ecstasy you can do that, and ecstasy is achieved through the body itself. Without the bone and sinew of wings, no flight. Without that ecstasy you can only be dragged further down by the body, into its machinery. Its rusting, creaking, vengeful, brute machinery.

When Tobias is out of earshot she closes the door and embarks on her bedtime routine. Shoes replaced by slippers: best to take that slowly. Then the clothes must come off, one Velcro tab after another, and must be arranged on hangers, more or less, and placed in the closet. Underwear into the laundry hamper, and none too soon: Katia will deal with that tomorrow. Peeing accomplished with not too much effort, toilet flushed. Vitamin supplements and other pills washed down with ample water, because having them dissolve in the esophagus is unpleasant. Death by choking avoided.

She also avoids falling down in the shower. She takes hold of the grips and doesn't overuse the slippery shower gel. Drying is best done sitting down: many have come to grief attempting to dry their own feet while standing up. She makes a mental note to call Services for an appointment at the salon to get her toenails trimmed, which is another thing she can no longer do herself.

Her nightgown, clean and folded, has been placed ready on her bed by silent hands at work behind the scenes during the dinner hour, and the bed itself has been turned down. There's always a chocolate on the pillow. She gropes for it and finds it, and peels off the foil paper, and eats the chocolate greedily. It's the details that differentiate Ambrosia Manor from its rivals, said the brochure. Cherish yourself. You deserve it.

Next morning Tobias is late for breakfast. She senses this lateness, then confirms it with the talking clock in the kitchen, another gift from Alyson: you hit the button – if you can find the button – and it tells you the time in the voice of a condescending grade two arithmetic teacher. 'It is eight thirty-two. Eight thirty-two.' Then it's eight thirty-three, then eight thirty-four, and with every minute Wilma can feel her blood pressure shooting up. Maybe something has happened to him? A stroke, a heart attack? Such things occur in Ambrosia Manor every week: a high net worth is no defence against them.

Finally, here he is. 'There is news,' he tells her, almost before he's inside the door. 'I have been to the Dawn Yoga Class.'

Wilma laughs. She can't help herself. It's the idea of Tobias doing yoga, or even being in the same room with yoga. What had he chosen to wear for this event? Tobias and sweatpants don't compute. 'I understand your mirth, dear lady,' says Tobias. 'This yoga business is not what I would choose, given other pathways. But I have made a sacrifice of myself in the interests of obtaining information. In any case there was no class, because there was no instructor. So the ladies and I – we could chat.'

310

Wilma sobers up. 'Why wasn't there any instructor?' she asks.

'They have blockaded the gate,' Tobias announces. 'They refuse to let anyone in.'

'What's happened to the police? And the Manor security?' *Blockaded*: this is not frivolous. Blockades require heavy lifting.

'They are nowhere in sight,' says Tobias.

'Come in and sit down,' says Wilma. 'Let's have some coffee.'

'You are right,' says Tobias. 'We must think.'

They sit at the little table and drink their coffee and eat their oat cereal; there's no more bran, and – Wilma realizes – scant hope of getting any. I must appreciate this cereal, she thinks as it crunches inside her head. I must savour this moment. The little people are agitated today, they're whirling around in a fast waltz, they sparkle all over with silver and gold sequins, they're putting on a grand show for her; but she can't attend to them right now because there are more serious matters to be considered.

'Are they letting anyone out?' she asks Tobias. 'Through the blockade.' What was that book she read about the French Revolution? Versailles blockaded, with the royal family stewing and fretting inside.

'Only the staff,' says Tobias. 'They are more or less ordering them to go. Not the inhabitants. We have to stay. So they appear to have decreed.'

Wilma thinks about this. So the staff are allowed

to leave, but once out, they won't be readmitted. 'And no delivery vans,' she says, a statement rather than a question. 'Such as chickens.'

'Naturally not,' says Tobias.

'They want to starve us to death,' she says. 'In that case.'

'It would appear so,' says Tobias.

'We could disguise ourselves,' says Wilma. 'To get out. As, well, as cleaners. Muslim cleaners, with our heads covered up. Or something.'

'I doubt very much that we would pass unchallenged, dear lady,' Tobias says. 'It is a question of the generations. Time leaves its markings.'

'There can be some quite old cleaners,' Wilma says hopefully.

'It is a matter of degree,' says Tobias. He sighs, or is it a wheeze? 'But do not despair. I am not without resources.'

Wilma wants to say that she is not despairing, but she refrains because it could get too complicated. She can't pinpoint exactly what it is that she's feeling. Not despair, not at all. And not hope. She only wants to see what will happen next. It certainly won't be the daily routine.

Before doing anything else, Tobias insists that they fill up Wilma's bathtub, as a provision for the future. His own bathtub is already filled. Sooner or later the electricity will be cut, he says, and then the water will cease to flow; it is only a matter of time.

Then he makes an inventory of the supplies in Wilma's kitchen and mini-fridge. There isn't much because she keeps no lunch or dinner staples on hand. Why would she, why would any of them? They never cook those meals.

'I've got some yogourt raisins,' says Wilma. 'I think. And a jar of olives.'

Tobias makes a scoffing sound. 'We cannot live on these things,' he says, shaking a cardboard box of something or other as if scolding it. Yesterday, he tells her, he took the precaution of visiting the snack shop on the ground floor and making a discreet purchase of energy bars, caramel popcorn, and salted nuts.

'How clever of you!' Wilma exclaims.

Yes, Tobias admits. It was clever. But these emergency rations will not hold them for long.

'I must go down and explore the kitchen,' he says. 'Before any of the others might have that idea. They are likely to raid the stores, and trample one another. I have seen such a thing.' Wilma wants to come with him – she might act as a buffer against trampling, for who would consider her a threat? And if they have indeed beat out the raiding hordes, she could carry some of the supplies back up to her apartment in her purse. But she does not suggest this, because she would of course get in the way: he'll have enough to do without shepherding her hither and thither.

Tobias seems to know of her wish to be of use. He has considerately thought of a role for her: she

313

is to remain in her apartment and listen to the news. Intelligence gathering, he calls it.

Once he's gone, Wilma turns on her kitchenette radio and prepares to gather intelligence. A news report adds little to what they already know: Our Turn is a movement, it's international, it appears aimed at clearing away what one of the demonstrators refers to as 'the parasitic dead wood at the top' and another one terms 'the dustballs under the bed.'

The authorities are acting sporadically, if at all. They do have more important things to attend to: more floods, more runaway forest fires, more tornadoes, all of which are keeping them on the hop. Sound bites from various head honchos are played. Those in the targeted retirement institutions should not succumb to panic, and they should not attempt to wander out onto the streets where their safety cannot be guaranteed. Several who rashly decided to brave the mobs did not survive the attempt, one of these having been manually torn apart. The blockaded ones should stay where they are, as everything would soon be under control. Helicopters may be deployed. The relatives of those under siege should not attempt any interventions on their own, as the situation is unstable. Everyone should obey the police, or the troops, or the special forces. The ones with megaphones. Above all, they must remember that help is on the way.

Wilma doubts this, but she stays tuned for the panel discussion that follows. The host first suggests that each one of the panellists state his or her age and position, which is done: academic, thirty-five, social anthropologist; energy-sector engineer, forty-two; financial expert, fifty-six. Then they quibble to and fro about whether this thing that's going on is an outbreak of thuggery, an assault on the whole notion of elders and civility and families, or is on the other hand understandable, considering the challenges and provocations and, to speak quite frankly, the shambles, both economic and environmental, that those under, say, twenty-five have been saddled with.

There is rage out there, and yes, it's sad that some of the most vulnerable in society are being scapegoated, but this turn of affairs is not without precedent in history, and in many societies – says the anthropologist – the elderly used to bow out gracefully to make room for young mouths by walking into the snow or being carried up mountainsides and left there. But that was when there were fewer material resources, says the economist: older demographics are actually big job creators. Yes, but they are eating up the health-care dollars, most of which are spent on those in the last stages of . . . yes, that is all very well, but innocent lives are being lost, if I may interrupt, that depends on what you call innocent, some of these people . . . surely you are not defending, of course not, but you have to admit . . .

The host announces that they will now take calls from their listeners.

'Don't trust anyone under sixty,' says the first caller. They all laugh.

The second caller says he does not understand how they can be making light of this. The people of a certain age have worked hard all their lives, they've been taxpayers for decades and most likely still are, and where is the government in all of this, and don't they realize the young never vote? Revenge will be taken at the polls on the elected representatives if they don't snap to it and get this thing cleaned up right now. More jails, that's what is needed.

The third caller begins by saying that he does vote, but it's never done him any good. Then he says, 'Torch the dusties.'

'I didn't catch that,' says the host. The third caller begins screaming, 'You heard me! Torch the dusties! You heard me!' and is cut off. Upbeat radio music.

Wilma switches off: that's enough intelligence for today.

As she's rummaging around for a teabag – risky, making tea, she might scald herself, but she'll be very careful – her big-numbers phone rings. It's the old kind of phone, with a receiver; she can't manage a cellphone any more. She locates the phone in her peripheral vision, ignores the ten or twelve little people who are skating on the kitchen counter in long fur-bordered velvet cloaks and silver muffs, and picks it up.

'Oh, thank god,' says Alyson. 'I've seen what's

going on, they showed your building on TV with all those people outside and the overturned laundry van, I've been so worried! I'm getting on a plane right now, and . . .'

'No,' says Wilma. 'It's fine. I'm fine. It's under control. Stay where you . . .' Then the line goes dead.

So now they're cutting the wires. Any minute now the electricity will go off. But Ambrosia Manor has a generator, so that will hold things in place for a while.

As she's drinking her tea the door opens, but it's not Tobias: no scent of Brut. There's a rush of footsteps, a smell of salt and damp cloth, a gust of weeping. Wilma is enfolded in a strong, dishevelling embrace. 'They say I must leave you! They say I must! We are told to leave the building, all workers, all healthcares, all of us, or they will . . .'

'Katia, Katia,' says Wilma. 'Calm down.' She disengages the arms, one at a time.

'But you are like a mother to me!' Wilma knows a little too much about Katia's tyrannical mother to find this complimentary, but it's kindly meant.

'I'll be fine,' she says.

'But who will make your bed, and bring your fresh towels, and clean up the things you have broken, and place upon your pillow the chocolate, in the night . . .' More sobbing.

'I can manage,' Wilma says. 'Now, be a good girl and don't cause trouble. They're sending the army.

317

The army will help.' It's a lie, but Katia needs to leave. Why should she be trapped inside what's looking more and more like a besieged fortress?

Wilma asks Katia to bring her purse, then gives her all the petty cash left inside it. Someone might as well get the use out of it; she herself won't be going on a shopping spree any time soon. She tells Katia to add the stash of wrapped floral-scented soaps from the bathroom, leaving two of them for Wilma just in case.

'Why is there water in the bath?' Katia asks. At least she's stopped weeping. 'It is cold water! I will make it hot!'

'It's all right,' says Wilma. 'Leave it there. Now, hurry along. What if they barricade the doors? You don't want to be late.'

When Katia has gone, Wilma shuffles into the living area, knocking something off a bookshelf in the process – the pencil jar, there's a sound of wooden sticks – and collapses into the armchair. She intends to take stock of her situation, review her life or something of the sort, but first she'll try to wend her way through another sentence or two of *Gone with the Wind* on the big-print e-reader. She gets the thing turned on and finds her place, a wonder in itself. Is it time for her to learn Braille? Yes, but that's unlikely now.

Oh, Ashley, Ashley, she thought, and her heart beat faster . . . Idiot, thinks Wilma. Destruction is at hand and you're mooning over that wimp? Atlanta will burn. Tara will be gutted. Everything will be swept away.

Before she knows it, she's nodded off.

She's wakened by Tobias, gently shaking her arm. Was she snoring, was her mouth open, is her bridge in place? 'What time is it?' she says.

'It is time for lunch,' says Tobias.

'Did you find any food?' Wilma asks, sitting up straight.

'I have acquired some dried noodles,' says Tobias. 'And a can of baked beans. But the kitchen was occupied.'

'Oh,' says Wilma. 'Some of them stayed? The cooking staff?' That would be consoling news: she notes that she's hungry.

'No, they are all gone,' says Tobias. 'It is Noreen and Jo-Anne, and some of the others. They have made a soup. Shall we descend?'

The dining room is in full swing, judging from the noise: everyone's getting into the spirit of things, whatever that spirit may be. Hysteria, would be Wilma's best guess. They must be carrying the soup in from the kitchen, acting as waiters. There's a crash; much laughter.

Noreen's voice looms up, right behind her ear. 'Isn't this something?' she says. 'Everyone's just rolling up their sleeves and pitching in! It's like summer camp! I suppose they thought we couldn't cope!'

'What do you think of our soup?' Jo-Anne, this time. The question is not addressed to Wilma but to Tobias. 'We made it in a cauldron!'

'Delicious, dear lady,' Tobias says politely.

'We raided the freezer! We put in everything!' says Jo-Anne. 'Everything but the kitchen sink! Eye of newt! Toe of frog! Finger of birth-strangled babe!' She giggles.

Wilma is attempting to identify the ingredients. A piece of sausage, a fava bean, a mushroom?

'The state of that kitchen is disgraceful,' says Noreen. 'I don't know what we were paying them for, the so-called staff! Certainly not for cleaning! I saw a rat.'

'Shhh,' says Jo-Anne. 'What they don't know won't hurt them!' They both laugh gleefully.

'I am not alarmed by a simple rat,' says Tobias. 'I have seen worse.'

'But it's awful, about the Advanced Living wing,' says Noreen. 'We went to see if we could bring them some soup, but the connecting doors are locked.'

'We couldn't open them,' says Jo-Anne. 'And the staff are all gone. That means . . .'

'It's terrible, it's terrible,' says Noreen.

'There is nothing to be done,' says Tobias. 'The people in this room could not care for those other people, in any case. It is beyond our powers.'

'But they must be so confused in there,' says Noreen in a small voice.

'Well,' says Jo-Anne. 'Once we've had lunch, I

think all of us should just stiffen our will power and form up into a double line and march right out of here! Then we can tell the authorities, and they'll come in and get the doors open and move those poor people into a proper location. This whole thing is beyond disgraceful! As for those stupid baby face masks they've got on . . .'

'They will not let you through,' says Tobias.

'But we'll all go together! The press will be there. They wouldn't dare stop us, not with the whole world watching!'

'I would not count on that,' says Tobias. 'The whole world has an appetite for ringside seats at such events. Witch-burnings and public hangings were always well attended.'

'Now you're frightening me,' says Jo-Anne. She doesn't sound very frightened.

'I'm going to have a nap first,' says Noreen. 'Gather my strength. Before we march out. At least we don't have to do the dishes in that filthy kitchen, since we won't be here much longer.'

Tobias has done a circuit of the grounds: the back gate is besieged as well, he says, as of course it would be. He spends the rest of the afternoon in Wilma's apartment, availing himself of her binoculars. More people are gathering outside the lion gate; they're brandishing their usual signs, he says, plus some new ones: TIMES UP. TORCH THE DUSTIES. HURRY UP PLEASE ITS TIME.

Nobody ventures inside the perimeter wall, or

nobody Tobias has spotted. The day is overcast, which makes for lower visibility. It's going to be an unusually chilly evening for this time of year, or that's what the TV was saying before it went silent. His cellphone is now inoperative, he tells Wilma: the young people out there, although lazy and communistic, are adept at manipulating digital technology. They tunnel secretly here and there inside the Internet, like termites. They must have got hold of a list of Ambrosia's inhabitants and accessed their accounts, and switched them all off.

'They have oil drums,' he says. 'With fires inside. They're cooking hot dogs. And drinking beer, I suspect.' Wilma would like a hot dog herself. She can picture walking out there and asking politely whether they might be inclined to share. But she can also picture the answer.

Around five o'clock a scanty clutch of Ambrosia Manor inhabitants musters outside the front door. Only about fifteen, says Tobias. They're arranging themselves in a double line, as if for a procession: twos, and the odd three. The crowd outside stills: they're watching. Someone among the Ambrosiads has found a megaphone: Jo-Anne, says Tobias. Orders are given, indecipherable through the window glass. The line moves forward, haltingly.

'Have they reached the gate?' asks Wilma. How she wishes she could see this! It's like a football game, back when she was an undergraduate! The tension, the opposing teams, the megaphones. She was always in the audience, never in the game, because girls did not play football: their role was to gasp. And to be fuzzy about the rules, as she is now.

The suspense is making her heart beat faster. If Jo-Anne's group can make it through, the rest of them can get organized and try the same thing.

'Yes,' says Tobias. 'But something has happened. There has been an incident.'

'What do you mean?' says Wilma.

'It's not good. Now they're coming back.'

'Are they running?' says Wilma.

'As much as possible,' says Tobias. 'We will wait until dark. Then we must leave quickly.'

'But we can't leave!' Wilma almost wails. 'They won't let us!'

'We can leave the building,' says Tobias, 'and wait in the grounds. Until they go away. Then we will be unimpeded.'

'But they aren't going away!' says Wilma.

'They will go away when it's over,' says Tobias. 'Now we will eat something. I will open this can of baked beans. Humanity's failure to invent a can opener that actually functions has never ceased to dismay me. The design of the can opener has not been improved since the war.'

What do you mean by *over*? Wilma wants to ask; but doesn't.

Wilma prepares herself for the proposed excursion. Tobias has told her they may be outside for some hours, or possibly days; it all depends. She puts on a cardigan, and takes a shawl and a packet of biscuits; also her jeweller's loupe and the e-reader, which is light enough to be portable. She worries about trifles; she knows they're trifles, but still, where is she going to put her teeth tonight? Her expensive teeth. And what about clean underwear? They can't carry much with them, says Tobias.

Now they will venture forth, like mice in moonlight. It is the right time, says Tobias. He leads her by the hand, down the back stairs, then through the corridor to the kitchen, then through the storage area and past the trash bins. He names each stage of their journey so she will know where they are; he pauses at each threshold. 'Do not worry,' he says. 'There is no one here. They have all departed.'

'But I heard something,' she whispers, and she did: a scuttling, a rustling. A squeaking, as of tiny, shrill voices: are the little people talking to her at last? Her heartbeat is annoyingly rapid. Is that a smell, a fetid animal smell like overheated scalps, like unwashed armpits?

'It's rats,' he says. 'There are always rats in places like this, in hiding. They know when it is safe for them to come out. They are smarter than us, I think. Take my arm, there is a step down.'

Now they've gone through the back entrance; they're outside. There are distant voices, there is chanting – it must be coming from the crowd at the front gate. What is it they're saying? *Time to*

Go. Fast Not Slow. Burn Baby Burn. It's Our Turn.
An ominous rhythm.

But it's coming from afar; here at the back of the building it's quiet. The air is fresh, the night is cool. Wilma worries that they'll be seen, mistaken for intruders or for escapees from Advanced Living, though surely there's no one around. No men with beagles. Tobias uses his flashlight to guide his own steps and by extension hers, switching it on and then off again.

'Are there fireflies?' Wilma whispers. She hopes so, for if not, what are those sparkles of light at the edges of her vision, pulsing like signals? Is it some new neural anomaly, her brain short-circuiting like a toaster dropped into the bath?

'Many fireflies,' Tobias whispers back.

'Where are we going?'

'You'll see,' he says, 'when we get there.'

Wilma has an unworthy and then a frightening thought. What if Tobias has made the whole thing up? What if there are no crowds of baby-faced protesters at the gates? What if it's a mass hallucination, like statues that weep blood or Virgin Marys in the clouds? Or worse: what if it's all been an elaborate ruse designed to lure her out here where Tobias can strangle her to death? What if he's a thrill killer?

But the radio broadcasts? Easily faked. But Noreen and Jo-Anne, their soup kitchen? Paid actors. And the chanting she can hear right now? A recording. Or a group of student recruits – they'd be happy to chant for minimum wage. Nothing like that would be impossible for a well-organized lunatic with money.

Too many murder mysteries, Wilma, she tells herself. If he wanted to kill you he could have done it earlier. And even if she's right, she can't go back: she wouldn't have the least idea of where *back* is.

'Here we are,' says Tobias. 'Grandstand seats. We'll be quite comfortable here.'

They're in one of the gazebos, the one to the extreme left. It's on the far side of the ornamental pond, and commands, according to Tobias, a partial view of Ambrosia Manor's main entrance. He's brought the binoculars.

'Have some peanuts,' he says. There's a crackle – the package – and he transfers a clutch of ovoids into the cusp of her hand. How reassuring they are! Her panic ebbs. He stashed a blanket in the gazebo earlier in the day, and two thermoses of coffee. He produces them now, and they settle down to their unusual picnic. And, just as in earlier, dimly remembered picnics she'd been on with young men – campfire events, with hot dogs and beer – an arm solidifies out of the darkness and slides itself confidently but shyly around her shoulders. Is it really there, that arm, or is she imagining it?

'You are safe with me, dear lady,' says Tobias. Everything's relative, thinks Wilma.

'What are they doing now?' she asks with a little shiver.

'Milling around,' says Tobias. 'Milling around is first. Then people get carried away.' He draws the blanket around her solicitously. There's a line of little people, men and women both, in dull red velvet costumes, richly textured and patterned in gold; they must be on the railing of the gazebo, which she can't see. They're involved in a stately promenade, arm in arm, couple by couple; they walk forward, stop, turn, bow and curtsey, then walk forward again, golden toes pointed. The women have flowery butterfly-wing crowns; the men have mitres, like bishops. There must be music playing for them, at a range beyond the human.

'There,' says Tobias. 'The first flames. They have torches. No doubt they have explosives as well.'

'But the others . . .' says Wilma.

'There is nothing I can do for the others,' says Tobias.

'But Noreen. But Jo-Anne. They're still inside. They'll be . . .' She's clutching – she notices – her own hands. They feel like somebody else's.

'It was always that way,' he says mournfully. Or is it coldly? She can't tell.

The rumbling from the crowd is swelling. 'They've come inside the walls now,' says Tobias. 'They're piling objects against the door of the building. The side door too, I suppose. To prevent exit, or entrance as well. And the back door; they will be thorough. They are rolling the oil drums inside the gate, and they have driven a car up onto the front steps, to block any attempt.'

'I don't like this,' says Wilma.

There's a sudden bang. If only it were fireworks.

'It's burning,' says Tobias. 'The Manor.' There's a thin, shrill screaming. Wilma puts her hands over her ears, but she can still hear. It goes on and on, loud at first, then dwindling.

When will the fire trucks come! There are no sirens.

'I can't bear this,' she says. Tobias pats her knee.

'Perhaps they will jump out of the windows,' he says.

'No,' says Wilma. 'They won't.' She wouldn't, if it was her. She would just give up. Anyway the smoke will get them first.

The flames have taken over now. They're so bright. Even gazing directly, she can see them. Blended with them, flickering and soaring, are the little people, their red garments glowing from within, scarlet, orange, yellow, gold. They're swirling upward, they're so joyful! They meet and embrace, they part; it's an airy dance.

Look. Look! They're singing!